"Joseph Cummins has written a groundbreaking first novel that tackles nothing less daunting than the fragile psyche of early childhood. Midwestern suburbia has never looked more terrifying than through the eyes of this young boy, Robbie, who tries to make order of the incomprehensible chaos raging around him. Mr. Cummins brings childhood closer than any other writer in years, with fresh and beautiful descriptions of what it actually feels like to be in the helpless body of a small child. Darkness looms on every page—forces greater than this little boy are out to get him, and he feels powerless to stop them. And as in James' classic, *The Turn of the Screw*, the reader never knows where the true enemy lurks. A real tour de force."

—Kaylie Jones, author of *A Soldier's Daughter Never Cries*

THE SNOW TRAIN

A NOVEL

by Joseph Cummins

Akashic Books
New York, NY

This is a work of fiction. All names, characters, places, and incidents are the product of the author's imagination. Any resemblance to real events or persons, living or dead, is entirely coincidental.

Published by Akashic Books
© 2001 Joseph Cummins

ISBN: 1-888451-23-8
Library of Congress Control Number: 2001089854
First printing
Printed in Canada

Akashic Books
PO Box 1456
New York, NY 10009
Akashic7 aol.com
www.akashicbooks.com

To Irene Kenney Cummins

Acknowledgments

I'd like to thank Johnny Temple, publisher of Akashic Books, for taking a chance on *The Snow Train*. I would also like to thank Henry Flesh and Mark and Elly Sullivan, who have been unflagging in their support and strong encouragement.

Special thanks to my editor Wendy Lochner for her precise and sensitive work; to Sarah Rutledge for her unerring copyedits; to Jennifer Harris for her singular cover art; to Vince Scilla and Joan Szatkowski for their own cover approaches; and to Tracy Adams for her strong design contributions.

Others who have been important to me during the writing of *The Snow Train* include Noreen Conklin; Rosemary Duffy; Mariah Fredericks; Karen Houppert; Kaylie Jones; Sally Lord; David Rosen; Jeff Wine; Ed Wyatt; and my father, sister, and brother.

Finally, this book is for Dede Kinerk and Carson Irene Cummins.

Part One: 1952

Rosemary

I.

"Look at the baby demon," Rosemary said.

She was holding me under the arms. I could barely stand. I looked into the mirror. The baby demon stared back at me with his big round head and his flat eyes, his bad light-colored eyes. It looked like he had red jam all around his mouth and cheeks. His ears had little scabs on them and his forehead had cuts and scratches.

"Mommy," I said.

"Don't even *think* about crying," said Rosemary. She gave me a little spank on my pajamas. "Mommy can't hear you. Mommy's in her room. I'm in charge now."

We were standing on the old green couch, looking into the mirror behind it. Rosemary was hurting me under the arms, pinching me. I struggled and she let go and I fell over onto the cushion.

Rosemary sat down next to me and stuck her legs out over the edge of the couch and kicked them up and down.

Book, I said, but it wouldn't come out.

"When you were first born I said, 'Put him in the garbage can!' but they didn't listen to me. Now look at you."

"Book," I said.

"No book now."

She got off the couch and pulled me down to the floor with her. The dark furniture crowded around us.

"Let me see," she said.

"No."

"Just let me see a little bit."

She pulled up my pajama leg. The rash prickled as the air came on it.

Rosemary stared.

"You've been scratching."

She took her finger and lightly touched a red sore, a bad red sore. It was hard at the center.

"If I was a nurse, I could make it all better."

She pressed the sore gently.

"I can hear you scratching all night. I can't stand that sound. I wish we didn't have to sleep in the same room."

I heard steps. Mommy was there with her skirts all around me.

"What are you two doing?"

"I think he scratched," said Rosemary. Her hands left me and she stood up. "I heard him when he was taking his nap."

"Rosie, he's not a plaything. He's a little boy."

I thought I was going to cry. Mommy picked me up and I buried my head in her neck. We rocked and bumped to her room. She put me down on the big bed and unbuttoned my pajamas.

"Shhhh," she said.

There was much more light in her room and I watched it. It grew out of the window and I saw that it came from the sky. Gretl jumped up on the bed to see me.

"Shoo," Mommy said. She was frowning.

My clothes were all off and I was a naked little boy now.

"Baby demon," I said.

"Babdeem to you, too," Mommy said. "What are we going to do with you? Wait here."

She went away. I lay there in the center of the big bed. I was sailing through the world. The sky outside the window rushed through me. We were flying.

Mommy came back and bent down. She had my big jar of cream. Her face was so close. I put my arms up. My legs kicked.

"Oh, it's bad today." She made her sound: "Tcch, tchhh, tcchh."

I closed my eyes. Mommy put the cream all along my arms and slid her hands up and down my chest. My skin shivered. She turned me over and rubbed me on the backs of my legs and behind my knees and on my bum. She took my feet in her hands and rubbed them.

All over. All over me. My skin rose up and drank. I sighed and squirmed.

Her face hovered close to my face. She put little dabs on my forehead and my cheeks and my ears. I could feel her breath on my eyelids, puffing on me.

"Gently," she whispered. "Very gently."

She moved away from me and I shivered all over. I heard the birdies crying outside the window. She came back with my blanket and puppy and wrapped me up and then lay down next to me. I didn't move. I was falling and we were sailing. In the dark I could feel her sing and I arched up to her:

Little bird, have you heard?
There's a happy sky, happy sky
Somewhe-eere...

2.

I sat up in my playpen in the dark living room. Rosemary was reading to me from the book. The book's stiff wings spread open.

"There are devils and demons," she read. "The devils are the big ones and the demons are the little ones. You're the baby demon."

Rosemary moved her finger along the rough lines of the book. I put my hands on the bars of my playpen and stared at her.

"When you were just eight months old a devil came out while you were sitting in your highchair and scratched you around the mouth while Mommy was feeding you creamed spinach. That was the mark of the demon. You were marked forevermore!"

Rosemary smacked the book with her hand.

"I tried to save you. I went to the Devil and I said, 'Do you need *this* baby demon? Why not pick somebody else? There are plenty of baby boys around here.' I shook my fist at him."

Rosemary shook her fist. Her eyes opened wide.

But then she looked sad.

"Alas, it was too late. The deed was done! And that's the end of the story."

She put the book down. It fell over and lay on one wing.

"More?" I said.

"More what?"

She started crawling across the rug, first her elbow, then her knee.

"Here I come."

The tingling laughter rose up in me. Rosemary weaved her head back and forth as she crawled.

"I'm coming to get you."

"No."

Rosemary buried her face deep in the thick rug. Her dark eyes shined up at me. Her pigtails had white bows on them.

"You'll never get away," she whispered. *"Never!"*

She sprang at the playpen and rattled the bars. The wood shook and clattered.

"You're mine!" she cried. She tried to force her head through the bars. "I'm coming to eat you," she moaned. "I'm going to come right in there and eat you for dinner!"

I couldn't breathe. I rolled over and hugged my puppy and kicked my legs up.

"You'll never get away. *Never!"*

I crawled back into the corner. The ceiling spun as the playpen shook. The top of Rosemary's head tried to squeeze through the bars. It wasn't Rosemary anymore. It was a little animal coming to get me. I laughed and laughed.

Rosemary stopped and sat back. Her face was all red.

"It's too dark in here. You're not even taking your nap."

She got up and opened the heavy curtains. Light slapped off the coffee table. Sounds pushed against the big window glass. A car went by. The tall black wet tree had leaves that were tiny and green. The sky was pale blue.

Rosemary stood by the playpen.

"Get up," she said.

The Snow Train

I hung onto the bars with my head up. The big window rose over us.

"That's the outside," said Rosemary. "There are outside people and inside people. Right now, you're an inside person, but when you're bigger, you'll go away into the outside every day, just like Daddy does. I'll stay home inside, here."

My mouth opened wide. I watched ladies walking by on the street.

"You walk through that glass and the outside is where you live. Sort of like the animals do, except you go to a big place and they pay you money to talk on the telephone and write on papers."

Rosemary and I stared outside. I saw that a baby was lost on the sidewalk and his Mommy came to get him. He was crawling by himself.

Rosemary knelt down right next to me.

"You only come home at night. That's when *I* have the dinner ready."

Her face was warm next to mine.

"We'll live together like Great Aunt Peggy and Uncle Bob," she whispered. "I'll make dinner for you."

I looked at my rash. In the sunlight it sparkled at me. It was red all over me.

The rash moved in the sunlight. It crawled on me.

"Look?" I said.

"I read it in the book," Rosemary said, "in case you have any doubt. It said we were going to live together. You'll be the daddy and I'll be the mommy. You go to work and I'll stay home and drink coffee and write poems all day."

We heard Gretl crying from somewhere. I turned to the left and to the right. I couldn't see her.

Owwoooo, Owwooooo, she cried. *Ooooooowwwww.*

Where was she? Her cry floated up on the ceiling. I stared at my rash.

"She is crying, 'Who am I? Who am I?'" Rosemary said. "That's what cats cry when they're alone."

"Look me?" I said. I offered her my arm.

"No, thank you," said Rosemary. "I've had quite enough for one day."

3.

I opened my eyes. The moonlight was melting all over me. It was as thick as my blankets. I squinted and tossed. I tried to throw it off.

I held up my arms. The rash flamed. It was like ants. The ants were covering me up. They were biting and tearing. They swarmed over my hands. My hands tore at each other. My fingers scratched my fingers.

Rosemary was asleep on her stomach in her bed in the bright moonlight. Her head stuck straight up out of the covers, her eyes were shut, her fists were clenched on the pillow.

The moonlight disappeared, the bedroom tumbled into black. I scratched hard. I kicked the crib. I rolled over and over and scraped my skin against the sheets.

It bit me. The rash nipped and bit me. I turned and pulled my legs up and scratched all over them. I pulled my fingers up and down my arms. I stopped and the burning came in. My fingers were wet.

The burning dug and ate at me. I tossed and rolled. The whole bedroom hurt and twisted in on me. The walls were mean, I wanted to scrape against them.

Rosemary's mouth was open. The moonlight appeared on her dark eyebrows and her mean chin.

I began to cry. It wouldn't leave me alone, wouldn't leave me alone, wouldn't leave me alone! The hard scabs came off on my fingernails in shreds. I cried and kicked up.

I scratched and scratched and scratched. The walls of the bedroom shook, the house shook and fell down.

Where was Mommy? I cried and no one came, I bounced and scratched, and Rosemary's eyes were squeezed shut.

The moon came softly this time. It went away. It was there, it blew its breath, it went away.

I stopped and lay. My hands were frozen up and my legs were curled up. I couldn't unbend my knees. I was like a little frog on its back.

The moon blew over me.

Rosemary's black eyes opened. They looked at me. They closed up.

I curled inside myself.

4.

Rosemary wore little boy pants instead of her dress. They were stiff jeans with the bottoms rolled up. Her feet stuck out from them. She was a cowgirl. She had a rope and a big hat and she danced in the grass at the back of the house.

"Yippee!" she yelled. Her pigtails flew up.

I lay on the blanket in the sunlight. Gretl sneaked through the grass. Her fur ruffled. The trees waved. The bushes rose up in the breeze. My hat flapped on my head.

The blanket rippled in the wind. Its corners flipped up and snapped. The people cried "Oh!" and put their hands down on it. The sun sparkled off their plates and glasses. The people laughed, the sun shined down on the back of the wind, it heated up the wind, the wind crashed off the house and came back at us.

My hat blew off my head.

"Oh-oh," I said.

The woman with the red hair picked me up and smiled with her wide red mouth and floated me high above her head.

"Whee!" she said. The trees reeled in the sky.

I laughed and kicked. My stomach turned over. She put me down and I walked over the blanket, stomping through the glasses and bowls and jars.

"Dance baby dance," I said.

All the people pulled things out of my way and laughed. Mommy grabbed my sleeve.

"Whoa, Buster Brown!"

"Dance baby dance," I said.

I danced, I jumped up and down, I twirled, go baby go.

Mommy clapped her hands.

"It's his new trick. He's a dancing fool!"

They were all clapping their hands. I danced. I stumbled. My face flushed up. Dance baby dance. The ground came up uneven and I staggered and I fell. I sat up and everyone clapped again. I looked over at Rosemary. Her rope was down and she had stopped jumping. She was holding onto Daddy and crying.

"He ruins everything!" she said. "It's *my* birthday!"

The people were all quiet. Their clothes fluttered. Rosemary stared at me. Her eyes were black and hard. I felt a quivering in my chest and my heart popped out.

The house sat looking at us. It had little red bricks and it loomed up. Inside, it was so dark. I stared at it. I saw the baby demon in his playpen with his big round head and his bad red skin.

The wind crashed off the house. The grass bent flat.

I was very proud of me. I knew me. I was me. I needed to go off somewhere and scratch. Gretl and I could go. We could crawl away...

"Let's all dance together," said Daddy in his quiet voice. "We can all do that, can't we?"

Mommy watched.

"Rosie, he's just a baby," she said. "We've been through this before. He doesn't know any better."

"Hah!" said Rosemary. "He knows better. He does it on purpose."

We stared at each other.

5.

Strong silver rain came down against the big window. The tall tree blew and tossed. The living room was very dark.

My blanket lay in wrinkles at the foot of my playpen. I put my blocks in a jumble on it. They cheered and laughed. They were babies younger than me. They liked the blanket wrinkles.

There was a big flash. I threw my head up. The tall tree shook. It tumbled its leaves at me. The rain hit the window over and over.

I stood up. I picked up my puppy. He had a blue ribbon around his neck. One of his eyes had fallen out. I shook him hard and then threw him down.

"Wosie?" I said.

Where was she?

I walked back and forth. The coffee table was shining in the dark. Mommy's rocking chair was rocking by itself. I grabbed the playpen bars and pulled myself up. I came up to the top, but then I fell back again. I pulled up again hard and got my legs over. I hung at the top. The playpen teetered. I was high above the room. Then I fell with a crash. The floor banged my knee hard.

The playpen was on top of me. I lay there curled up. I was crying. I pushed up on the playpen with my arms. I crawled out from under it.

The Snow Train

"Wosie?" I cried.

I stood up and kicked at the playpen.

"Stop!" I said. I held out my arms. I nearly fell over but I stayed standing.

My puppy stared at me. The old green couch grumbled, but I started walking. I was me.

I walked into the other room and under the big table. I walked into chair legs. I kept walking and pushed them into a tangle. I bumped my head. I crawled out and got up. There was a silver flash and then a bang. The lights winked. The room was suddenly brown. Then it was light.

"Kids?" Mommy called. "Children?"

"Judas Priest!" I heard Rosemary say.

"Mommy?" I said.

Mommy didn't answer. The rumbling was all around. "Wosie!" I cried.

The lights winked again.

I went fast down the hallway.

The bathroom door was closed partway. I looked inside. Rosemary was on the potty. She had her skirt up around her waist and she was looking at herself. Her face was red. She tickled herself. She had her eyes closed. Then she tinkled. She sighed.

"Oh, Arbo," she said. "Where can you be?"

"Wosie?" I said.

Her eyes popped open and her eyebrows flew up.

"Go away!" she yelled.

I ran down the hall. The hall stretched a long way. The walls were tall and high and white. The wood shone dark under my feet. There were little round rugs on it. I jumped from rug to rug.

"Mommy!" I called.

I took off my top and threw it down. I started laughing. I pushed down my diapers and left them on the floor.

"Potty!" I said.

At the end of the hallway I stopped and looked into Mommy and Daddy's room. Mommy was sitting at her desk in front of the window with her face in her hands looking at a piece of paper in her *tackety-tack* machine.

I stared at her. She got up. I held out my arms.

"Mommy, *tackety-tack*," I said, but she didn't look at me. She walked up and down in front of the bed. Her skirt was very big. It blew out like the curtains blowing out of the window. She walked right past me. The breeze of her skirt blew on my face. She was talking to herself.

"Look, see the pretty children go," she said. "Through gardens white with deadly snow."

She went back to her desk and started tapping fast at the *tackety-tack* machine. I heard the toilet flush and I ran across the hall into our room. Rosemary's toy trunk was open. All her animals were there. I pulled out her tiger and took him into the closet with me.

The rain drummed and banged against the windows. I sat there with the tiger in my lap. I chewed his ear. I hugged him. Rosemary's dresses jumped and shook above my head. I thought of the bad Mommy with her skirt flashing in her room.

I looked at my rash. It was red and sore. It was a thousand little red bumps. They were moving all over me in the dark light.

The window blinked. The light cracked through the room. Rosemary came in and sat down on the floor in front of the bed with her dolls and her dishes. A bright smile filled her face.

"Oh, Arbo," she cried. "You're here!"

Mommy walked into the room and stood over Rosemary.

The Snow Train

"What is his diaper doing in the middle of the hallway?"
Rosemary didn't look at her.

"He must've left it there," she said.

"Where is he?"

"I don't know."

"You don't what?"

"He's in his playpen."

Mommy grabbed Rosemary and yanked her up by her arm.

"Hey!" said Rosemary.

Mommy pulled her out of the room. Rosemary's legs scrambled and kicked in the air.

The window shook and the cracking noise came again.

"Arbo," I said.

The room turned black. The rumbling came up from under the floor. I crawled farther back into the closet, behind some old pillows. There was a blanket there and I went under it. I put my arms around the tiger and squeezed him hard.

The rain rumbled down for a long time. I was floating in the sky. The clouds came and spun me in the dark sky. Mommy called my name but she was too far away. Everything stretched out. I was flying with the tiger, it sailed me through the sky. Then I was falling. My stomach sank deep inside me.

I cried out, kicked up, I couldn't breathe. I pushed the blanket off. It was cold. The air on my skin felt heavy and wet.

There were voices. "Look! Look!"

Arms reached down for me and pulled me. I went up into the air. Daddy held me high and hugged me against his hard chest.

"He's shivering!" Mommy said. "Sweetie!"

She put her face up close to mine over Daddy's shoulder. Her face was as big the moon.

"He's fine," Daddy said. "He's fine, Jeannie."

The room was full of people. Daddy held me and Mommy put a blanket around me. I looked down to see Rosemary standing there jumping up and down.

"Robbie! Robbie!"

"Wosie!"

We went out into the hallway and bumped down it to the living room. All the lamps were on. There were people in the kitchen and dining room. They smiled at me as I went by. I felt their pats on me.

Rosemary followed us. She was crying.

Mommy took me from Daddy and we sat down on the old green couch. She stood me up on her lap.

"Are you a mess?" she said. "Aren't you a mess?"

Daddy stood at the door. The people were leaving. He stood up very stiff and straight and shook hands. His shirt was very white and his hair was very dark. He came back in and sat down on the coffee table across from me and Mommy. Rosemary laid her head on his knee and closed her eyes.

"Christ," he said.

"Rosie, come here," Mommy said.

Rosemary raised her head and looked at her.

"Jeannie," Daddy said.

"Here," Mommy said to Daddy.

She held me up to him and he took me. Rosemary tried to run away, but Mommy grabbed her.

"No!" cried Rosemary.

I couldn't get turned around. I was standing on Daddy's lap. I struggled.

"Mommy, please!" Rosemary yelled.

The Snow Train

I heard spanks. Rosemary was crying. Daddy picked me up and took me back down the hall and into our room. He put me in my crib. I was very afraid. My stomach hurt.

He left the room and came back holding Rosemary under his arm. She didn't look like Rosemary. Her face was very red and her pigtails were sticking out crooked and her dress was all mussed up. She was shrieking, "Daddy, Daddy, Daddy!"

I started to cry. I threw my hands in the air. Daddy was holding Rosemary on her bed and she was kicking.

"She spanked me! She spanked me!"

Mommy came rushing in and Rosemary shrieked louder. Mommy took some diapers out of the dresser and then picked me up. We went into the kitchen and she put me down on a towel on the table.

It was cold. I kicked up. Rosemary's red face froze in my head. Mommy pinned up my diapers. The roaring started inside me. It spun through me. Everywhere it spun was bad.

6.

Bright light shined in my eyes from the window by Mommy's desk. I put up my head. Thin voices came from outside.

I got down from the bed and ran over to the window. I stood on my tiptoes and looked out.

"Robbie," Mommy said.

Rosie was outside in the backyard running with a blonde girl. They leapt and ran. Daddy was raking leaves and they fell into a big pile of them. He shook his rake at them. They got up and ran again. Their mouths opened up and thin voices came out.

Everything was red and gold. The sky was bright blue. I looked at the blonde girl. She laughed and hopped. She was very small. She was like a little animal. She chased Rosemary around. She made her run. She wouldn't let her alone.

"Sweetie, stop."

Mommy was kneeling right next to me. She grabbed my hands. My rash burned. The ants crept up me. I struggled.

"Darling, stop it! You'll tear yourself right up."

She picked me up and carried me back to the bed and we got on it. Mommy's papers were all around us. She pushed my sleeves up and took my cream from the jar. She rubbed it on me.

"Out," I said.

"No."

"Mommy!"

"No!" She tapped my arm. "Don't start. Rosie needs time with her friend."

"Don't," I said.

"I'm not doing anything to you." She put my cream away. "There."

"Wosie," I said.

"Christ," Mommy said.

She put her pencil behind her ear and picked up her paper. Her head was down. Her pencil stuck out of her hair. I crawled over the papers. They crackled. I stopped by Mommy and reached up for her ear.

"Sweetie, please."

I put my hands to my eyes. My face turned hot.

"Oh, hell," Mommy said.

She picked me up and put me in her lap. She leaned back against the pillows. I hid my face in her warm neck. She leaned over and put her face down and pushed my head with it. Her cheek came next to mine. Her eye fluttered on my cheek.

"Are you my big handsome boy?"

Her green eyes were very big. Her hair was so dark and her skin was so white.

I shivered. I ducked my head. I bumped against her.

"I'll bet you are."

She put her lips down and kissed my forehead. I hunched up and giggled. Mommy's face followed me. I ducked into her neck. She put her face down. She blew in my ear. I laughed.

"That's my happy boy," she said. I looked up at her. Her eyes were bright.

"Mommy, look," I said. I had my overalls on. I showed her my buttons. They were silver.

"That's very good," she said. She rubbed her nose against mine. "Why not let Mommy write her poem? Please? Help old Mommy out?"

"No!" I said.

Mommy reached for her paper. She put her arms down around me and held the paper out in front of her.

I hit the paper.

"Hey!" she said.

I slapped again, but she held the paper up high. I stretched out my hand. I couldn't reach it. The window light shined right through it.

"Arbo," I said.

"Arbo?" Mommy said. She put the paper down. "Is Arbo here?"

"He ran," I said.

Arbo was outside. Or was he in the bathroom? He ran. He was a little boy. He pushed her. The blonde girl hurt.

Outside, the thin voices came. I turned around to get off the bed.

"Whoa," said Mommy. She lifted up my foot and pulled papers out from under it. "He tramples upon her work."

"Mommy!"

She took me under the arms and lifted me high in the air. She wiggled me there. I kicked. "Mommy!"

"Are you Arbo? Who's this Arbo I keep hearing about?"

She swooped me down. Her face was right in front of me. I floated in the air.

"Identify yourself," she said. "Are you the sprite? The infant king?"

Her breath blew on my face. We were very still. I stared at her eyes. They were green and shiny.

"Up," I said. I spread my arms. "Up!"

I was flying. She pulled me back down. She hugged me to her hard.

31

"Oof!" she said.

"Up!"

She squeezed me very tight. Her arms were around my head. Tingles went up and down me. Her heart was pounding inside my ear. I spread my arms and kicked my feet.

"Up!"

"Gotcha, gotcha, gotcha!" she said. "Pay attention to your mom."

She rolled over and let go of me and I sat up and breathed the cool light air. She lay there and looked up at the ceiling. She was long and white. Her shirt was purple and her pants were black. Her toes were bumpy. She lay still. Her eyes closed. Her chest went up and down. Outside the thin voices came again. I got down off the bed and went over to the window.

I stood on tiptoe. The blonde girl's hair flew. The light shined. Arbo chased them in the red leaves.

7.

Rosemary and I sat on the living room floor in our 'jams with our backs against the old green couch. We had a blanket over us. We were both holding the book. I pulled it. She pulled it back.

"Keep it in the middle," she said. "Be careful with it. Do you know where this book came from? All the way from Africa. Daddy got it there. A native carved it from a piece of driftwood. It's supposed to be the Bible, but it contains all the stories in the world, from having sailed the seven seas."

It was dark in the living room, but yellow light came from the kitchen. I could hear plates clink. Mommy was mad at Gretl.

"Scat. Get away!"

Gretl came running out into the living room with her tail straight out behind her. Her colors were all crazy, she was black and white and orange. Her eyes twisted up and spun in her head. She went behind the couch.

The snow came down faster and faster. The big window was white. I couldn't see the houses across the street. The tall black tree was very blurry.

Rosemary was looking, too.

"It's so exciting," she said. "Have you ever seen so much snow? Aren't you glad we're cozy?" She stared out the window. "It's like ghosts! Ghosts flying through the air. Some of them are probably knocking on the window right now. Do you hear that whistling? It's the wind." She put her hands to her face. "Oooohh!"

A little shiver ran inside me.

I tugged the book. Rosemary tugged it back. She cleared her throat.

"Today I am going to tell the story of this family." She put her finger on the book and began to read: "The story of this family is the story of a happy group of people. A sister and little brother, a Mommy and Daddy. They stay together and live happily ever after."

I grabbed the book and pulled it onto my lap.

"Arbo came," I said. I ran my finger up and down the book. "Find Arbo. Bad boy."

"That's just perfect," said Rosemary.

"Boy! Boy! Boy!" I said. I slapped the book.

"It's obvious you don't know how to play with it," Rosemary said.

She pulled the book back onto her lap.

"I'll tell you the story of Arbo, since you're so curious. Arbo lives in a land where there aren't any parents. It's a sad place. I hate even talking about it. It's full of rocks.

"You can see Arbo, if you want to. He's been visiting this house since before anyone here was born. All you have to do is be very quiet. A tunnel lets him out behind this couch. He darts. He races. You have to have good eyes."

"Kids, let's go." Daddy was standing by the table in the dining room. He clapped his hands and whistled. "Chop-chop."

I got up and ran to him and he reached down and stretched me up high in the air and put me in my chair. Mommy and Rosemary came and sat down. Daddy put the pancake on my plate.

I pushed it with my spoon and ate it. It was soft and sweet. It sponged in my mouth.

There was no juice. I banged my cup.

"What do you say?" said Rosemary.

Mommy poured me juice.

"Mommy, what does he say?"

I drank my juice and gulped. I held out my cup and Mommy put in more. I looked out the window. The snow floated up like white blankets. It grew bigger and bigger. It blew over me.

The shiver moved inside of me again. My head felt very light.

"I'm here, Mommy," I said.

"We know where you are," Rosemary said.

"Look at all that snow," Mommy said to me. "Do you remember snow?"

"Sure, he remembers it," Daddy said.

"He remembers it, but not all the time," said Rosemary.

I was full, I pushed the plate away. "Down."

"Not yet," Mommy said.

"Potty," I said.

"Did you hear that?" Mommy said.

"Robbie go potty," I said.

"Very good," Mommy said.

Daddy got up and swooped me up from my chair. We went into the bathroom. He put my seat on the potty and I sat down on it. He sat down on the bathtub.

The bathroom was cold. I couldn't go.

"I'm done," I said.

"You can do it," Daddy said. "Try real hard."

I pushed and pushed. Nothing came out. "Down."

"Not yet."

The Snow Train

"Daddy."

"Try a little bit, Rob. You're a big boy. Push."

I was pushing. I pushed and pushed. We heard the phone ringing. Daddy stood up and listened.

"Tom!" Mommy called.

"Stay put," Daddy said. He walked out. I was by myself. I looked at the empty air in the hallway. Gretl walked by with her tail up. I heard Daddy talking. Rosemary came and looked in at me.

"Stop it," I said.

"Poophead. Can't you take a poop?"

"Stop it!"

Rosemary laughed and ran down the hallway. I got down off the seat but my 'jams caught my legs and I fell over. I pushed them off and then I got up and ran after her. The hallway jiggled up and down. She ran into the bedroom and fell on her bed. I jumped on it and crawled on top of her. She started shrieking.

"You've got poop on you! You're poopy!"

"Poopy you!" I said.

"Get off me!"

I got down to get my train from my toys. I started pulling it around the floor by its string.

"Choo-choo!" I said. "Puffa-puffa!"

The little train followed me. I was a good boy. I wouldn't go out even if they asked me. I was a good boy.

"No, Mommy," I said. "I'm here."

Rosemary sat on her bed and watched me.

I pulled the train along the floor and dragged it up the side of the dresser. Rosemary stood up and began walking around the room. All of a sudden, she crouched down and jumped forward. She did it again.

"Jump!" she said. "Like a frog. Can you do this?" She bent her knees and then jumped straight up. Her pigtails bounced. "You jump and then hang in the air as long as you can. Sometimes I think I can actually fly. Try it."

I jumped up, but I couldn't get into the air.

"No," said Rosemary. "You have to really crouch down and then jump way up. Put your bum down and then jump."

I jumped. My feet went out from under me and I landed hard. I was going to cry, but Rosemary started laughing. She stood over me.

"This is so much fun," she said. "I feel like we're a real brother and sister. Like we're sweethearts." She stared down at me. Her hands were on her hips. "It's true what Mommy says. You're getting to be more fun."

She reached down and grabbed me under the arms.

"I can carry you."

"No."

She picked me up and held me around my stomach. She gripped me tight and started walking. My feet kicked out. Her breath was in my ear.

"I'm big and strong for a girl."

She hugged me and walked all over the room. My feet tangled with her feet and we fell down with a bang. She landed on top of me. The air came out of me. I lay on the floor and I was choking.

Rosemary rolled off me. My mouth was open.

Mommy! I said. Nothing came out.

"Don't," she whispered. She rubbed my head. "You don't have to cry. It's all right."

My breath came back and I started to cry.

Rosemary threw her arms around me. "Don't cry. Please! I'll

do anything. I promise. I'll make you a snowman."

"Mommy!" I yelled.

Rosemary got up and stomped her foot.

"You're a big baby. Why is it always Mommy, Mommy, Mommy with you? What about me? I'm your sister."

"Wosie," I said. I crawled behind her on the floor and hugged her. She looked down at me.

"I love you," she said. "Do you love me? Say, 'I love you.'"

"I love you," I said.

We ran over and got on her bed and looked out the window.

"Look at it," Rosemary said. The snow was thick and white in the air. She pointed. "There's Arbo."

I looked. I darted my head. The snow covered the backyard. There was nothing there.

"How did he get out there?" said Rosemary. "Oh, Robbie, we have to go find him. We have to let him in." She clasped her hands to her chest. "Oh, he's cold out there! He just has his 'jams on."

Her voice filled me. I got down off the bed and put my bum down to the floor and jumped up high.

"Shhhh," she whispered. "We have to let him in without them knowing."

I thought of Arbo. He looked like a little boy. He had a hat on with his 'jams. He was cold. We had to let him in.

"Run!" I said. I ran to the door, but Rosemary caught me before I got out and made me go behind her. Arbo was in my mind. There were rocks in the snow. He couldn't get inside. He raced back and forth.

We went into the kitchen and down the stairs to the back door. The door was by the coats and boots and Gretl's box.

Rosemary reached up and pulled at the doorknob. The cold wind blew snow into my face. My bare feet froze.

Rosemary's face was red. She put her hands to her mouth.

"Arbo," she cried. "Arbo, you have to come in. You can't stay out there!"

I heard footsteps behind us.

"Here he comes," Rosemary said.

"Judas Priest," Daddy said. "Rosie!"

Daddy started to shut the door and Arbo raced inside quick. He was out of breath. He was white all over. Then he was gone.

The wind stopped. I was wet. There was water on the floor. Daddy picked me up and we went back to the bedroom. I stood on Rosemary's bed while he put my clothes on.

My teeth were shaking.

"Stick your arms straight up," Daddy said.

He pulled my shirt down my arms and over my head.

"No pants, Daddy," I said. I started to get off the bed.

"Whoops," Daddy said. His arm was behind my knees and I fell back on the pillow. "Some boy fell down."

He ticked me under the arms. I laughed and my legs kicked up.

"Gotcha!" he said. He pushed my pants on my legs. I rolled over and knelt up. He tucked in my shirt. "All set."

Rosemary went to the closet and came out with a pink frilly dress on a hanger.

"This is so beautiful," she said. She took it off the hanger and laid it on the bed. "I have pink ribbons."

She pulled her drawer open and looked inside.

"Rosie, that's for dress-up," Daddy said. "You know that."

"I can wear it with my white shoes."

"You can't play in the snow in that, sweetie."

"Yes, I can."

Daddy picked up the dress.

"Daddy!"

Daddy put it down and Rosemary sat next to it on the bed and patted it. "This is my favorite dress."

I saw Arbo. He had gotten inside the dresser drawer she opened. Just his head was sticking out. He was wearing a little round hat. He had a bad boy's face, but he was smiling. His mouth was open. His eyes were bright.

He ducked away.

I put my hands on my face. I started to laugh. How did he get in there?

"C'mon, princess," Daddy said. "Let's hang it back up."

Rosemary put the dress on the hanger and took it back into the closet. She was sucking on her mouth. Her eyes were big and dark. I stared at the drawer, but Arbo didn't come up again.

When Rosemary came back, Daddy pulled off her 'jams and she didn't say anything at all. She just had her underpants on. Her stomach stuck out and her head looked too big. Her arms were very skinny.

Daddy sat down on the bed and picked her up and hugged her.

"B-rr-rr," he said. "You're like ice."

He lay back on the bed with his arms around Rosemary. She lay with her head on his chest. Her pigtail fell down her cheek.

I crawled up on Daddy's chest next to her. She stared at me.

I whispered in her ear. I put both hands around it: "Arbo."

Rosemary didn't say anything. I tried to snuggle next to her.

Her skin was very cold. It was very white. Her eyebrows were black. Her black eye stared. Her back was moving up and down. There was a little black bump on it. It looked like a bug. I touched it, and she jumped.

"Wosie sad?" I said.

"Sometimes even a brave little girl just needs a hug," Daddy said.

"You never come home," said Rosemary. "We wait and we wait."

"I come home every night, honey. I've just had a tough week this week."

"Me too," I said.

"And Robbie, too," said Daddy. "We've all had tough weeks."

"Hah!" said Rosemary. "He doesn't have tough weeks." She raised her head and looked at me. "He just sits around."

Mommy came in wiping her hands on a towel.

I got down off Daddy and jumped to the floor.

"Snowing!" I yelled.

I ran out of the room as fast as I could. I heard Mommy laughing.

I ran all the way into the living room. I was laughing as hard as I could. Arbo was in front of me and he jumped out the window. I stood on tiptoe to see him diving into the snow. I waited for him to come out but he didn't.

Mommy came into the living room. She was holding Arbo. He was all white and he was laughing. He had a white face and a white hat and his eyes were white. He was just a baby. I began to cry. Arbo stared at me. He rubbed his eyes with his fists. He looked at me. He looked sad. He wasn't laughing anymore.

Mommy asked me what the matter was. She was holding a little coat in her hands and snowpants and boots.

I opened my mouth and stared up at her.

"Mommy?" I said.

:ie, what is it?" She knelt down next to me. "I've got v stuff. See? Let's go out and play."

"I aon't," I said.

I stopped. My mouth dropped open. I stared at her.

"Where's your train? Didn't I see it in your room?"

"The baby," I said.

"You can take it outside with you. You can drag it up and down! Come on."

She sat down next to me and put my snow clothes on. She held out a boot and put my foot in it. "Push."

My foot tried to go inside, but it couldn't. Mommy turned it with her hand. I looked around the living room.

"Sweetie, pay attention."

My foot plopped in. Where was Arbo? Where did he go? I tried to get down from the couch.

"Other one," Mommy said.

I twisted and turned my head. Where did he go? Arbo was the baby. Mommy took my foot and put it into the boot. She put my other clothes on. She zipped me up. My coat trapped my chin.

She put a round hat like Arbo's on my head.

"The baby," I said.

Rosemary came out from the kitchen. She had on a white hat that tied under her chin. Her hair was squished down under the hat and it came sticking straight out in front over her forehead. Her face was red and fat.

I ran up to her and grabbed her.

"Out," I said. "Out!" I pulled her sleeve. "Let's go!"

Arbo lived in the rocks that went under the snow. He was our baby. I tugged her.

"What in the world is the matter with him?" Mommy said.

42

Rosemary bumped me with her chest. "He looks like a little stuffed dog."

We went into the hallway by the door and stood there while Daddy and Mommy put their coats on. Daddy opened the door and Rosemary laughed and ran outside. I held onto Mommy's hand and went down the steps one by one. It was hard going down them. My boots sank in. It was very cold. I was very careful.

"One at a time," Mommy said.

When I got to the bottom I stood and looked. The sky was dark. The air was filled with scraping sounds. There was a car stuck in the middle of the street, hissing. Snow flew up from its wheels. Men were around it with shovels. They yelled. Daddy ran over but before he got there the car leapt forward and all the men jumped away from it.

Rosemary fell over into a pile of snow. She lay on her back and kicked her arms and legs.

"I'm an angel," she said.

The cold ate inside my head and blew out of my mouth. Mommy knelt down next to me. My ears hurt. I didn't know what to do.

The wind blew at my face. The baby was gone.

"Here," Mommy said.

She was holding a handful of snow to me. I looked at it. Then I hit it. It puffed up in her face. She laughed.

"Look," she said. "Try this."

She fell back in the snow and waved her arms and legs like Rosemary. Suddenly her shadow was in the snow. Her shadow was white. It spread wider and wider.

I put one foot into the snow. It sank in.

"Mommy!"

The Snow Train

l right," said Mommy. "Fall down. Go ahead."

t down in the snow. At first it didn't feel like anything, but then it was cold. I fell down. It hit my face. I moved and squirmed my arms.

I rolled over next to Mommy. I kicked my arms and legs.

Daddy came over and pulled Mommy up from the snow and gave her a big kiss. Mommy laughed. Daddy pulled her right up against him.

"Mush," said Rosemary.

Daddy kissed her and bent her back. Mommy's hat came off and snow fell from her black hair. She hit his face with her mitten and he let go.

"Such exuberance!" she said.

Rosemary flopped into the snow next to me and put her arms around me. She pressed her mouth against my lips. Her face was bright cold. It burned me. I struggled in the snow.

I pushed her away and got up.

"Smack! Smack!" said Rosemary.

I took a big step and then another. I fell down and got up. I looked up and stopped. A boy was standing a few feet away. He was much bigger than me. He was looking at us. He had on big round glasses and a hat with furry earflaps. Rosemary came up next to me.

"Hello," she said.

"Hi," the boy said. "Do you want to get into a snowball fight? Or we could build a snowman."

"Aren't you Goodie's brother?"

"She's not here," said the boy.

"I can tell *that*." Rosemary put her hands on her hips. "Why do you want to play with girls?"

"I have to go," said the boy. He turned around and walked away. He lifted his feet in and out of the snow and walked very slowly.

"Leave us alone!" cried Rosemary. The boy kept walking.

Rosemary laughed and jumped in the air. The dark light reeled through the big black tree. I stared up. Arbo jumped from the branches. He jumped like a squirrel. He was all white!

"Look!" called Daddy.

Mommy laughed and clapped her mittens. "It's the triplets."

A big long sled was coming down the street. A man was pulling it by a rope and running as hard as he could. Snow flew up from its curved front. In it were three little girls who were exactly the same size. They all had red hats. Their mommy was in the back of the sled and she had on a white hat. The little girls were yelling, "Choo-choo, Daddy! Choo-choo!"

"How darling," Mommy said. She waved at the woman in the sled. The woman waved back and then all the children waved. Other people came out to the street and waved at them, and the children in their red hats waved back.

I watched them with my mouth open.

"Look, see the pretty children go," Mommy said with a smile. The words puffed out of her in little clouds. Her cheeks were red. Rosemary jumped up and down.

"Look, see the pretty children go," she cried.

Mommy smiled. I threw myself on her leg. I pushed it. I tried to push it over. I was pushing hard. The shivering was all over me and it was making me tingle with cold. My mouth felt hot. I leaned down and picked up some snow and put it in. My mouth was stuffed full. My teeth hurt. I spat out the snow.

The Snow Train

Arbo came up. He was waving at me. He had on a red hat. He turned and ran after the sled. I chased him. I fell down in the snow and then got up and ran, and then I fell down again.

He was my baby, I had to hug him.

"Look at him," Rosemary said.

"Robbie!" Daddy called.

I ran into the street. It was very big and wide. The cars along the curb had heaps of snow on them. People were standing with shovels. They stared at me.

The children in the sled looked back. They waved.

"Choo-choo!" I cried. "Choo-choo!"

The houses stretched far away. I could see the tops of trees where the dark sky came down on them.

Everything was whizzing. The wind blew in my face.

Suddenly I went flying into the air. I hung there. A man was holding me up. He had a big blue hat with a long beak. His face had whiskers.

"Just where do you think you're going, sport?"

Arbo was in the sleigh with the little girls. He waved at me.

Daddy came and took me away from the man and brought me back to Mommy and Rosemary. He put me on the ground and I stood up and started walking. Rosemary picked up some snow and came up to me. There was a wide smile on her face. Her eyes were shining. She threw the snow at me. It fell apart into a white mist in the air. The white mist floated down and prickled me. It sparkled. I threw up. It came out of me and flew onto my jacket and the snow.

My mouth burned. The throw-up dripped out of my nose. I knelt down in the snow. I threw up some more. I shook.

Mommy knelt in front of me. She took off her mitten and pressed her hand against my face. "Tom!" she cried. Rosemary came up. I saw her black boots. Her face was all red. Her hat pressed down on her head and made it round as an apple. Her chin stuck out. Her eyes were bright and black.

"You need to go inside," she said.

There was yellow light. I kicked and squinted. A little girl stood by my crib in a pink dress. She glowed. She spun around. Then she knelt down.

"Shhh," she said. Her face looked through the crib bars. "I came in to see you."

I tasted my mouth. It was very dry. I tried to roll over but the blankets caught me. I was very hot.

"Look at my dress," the little girl said. She twirled around in the air with her arms out. "See how it floats out? Like a dancer's?"

The girl stopped her dance and ran and jumped on the bed and pressed her nose right up against the window.

"This is such a day!" she said. "I'll never forget this day. I'm kissing the window as a thank-you present. Smack! Thank you, window. You were the first thing I saw when I woke up this morning."

The little girl laughed and jumped once into the air. The bed bounced her up. Her pink dress flopped. She landed on her knees and bounced up and fell over and kicked her feet in the air. She had on shiny white shoes and pink socks.

She got up and came over and knelt down next to my crib. Shadows floated over her face.

"You look like a little Eskimo baby all wrapped up like that," she said. "How does it feel to be sick, sick, sick? I'm never sick."

She went away. Arbo sat next to me and held onto the crib

bars. I reached for him. He stuck his feet through the bars and kicked them up and down. He was wearing 'jams. He looked at me. His face was dark and light. He was bigger than me. We tried to say the names of things but they came out wrong. He cried. His eyes rose up. He was all white. He had a little round hat on. His diapers stuck out of his 'jams. He came down next to me. I hugged him. I took care of him. I got very hot. I was wet all over.

"See, Mommy?" said Rosemary.

I was all wrapped up in my blankets. Mommy had me on her lap. We were on Rosemary's bed. Rosemary was next to us. Her skirt fluffed on the bedspread. Her white hand spread on my head.

"He's so sweaty."

"He'll be fine, sweetie," said Mommy. "Actually, I think it's breaking a little."

Their voices were whispers. My head felt very light and cool. My mouth fell open. I blew a bubble. I watched it blow. Mommy wiped me off.

There was a baby in the window. I watched him. His eyes were bright. He had a big head. He lived in an egg made out of blankets.

"We had fun today, though, didn't we?" Mommy said.

"It was the best day," Rosemary said. "And we were good, weren't we?"

Mommy laughed. "You were very good."

The baby looked in the window. There was a mommy with short dark hair. Her skin was very white. She bobbed down to talk to the little girl.

The mommy laughed. She hugged the little girl. Then she started whispering. She rocked the baby back and forth. Her warm whisper blew in his ear.

The baby in the window stared at the mommy with his head turned up. His mouth opened. The mommy's whispers made him sleepy. The little girl put her arms around the mommy. She pressed her head against her. She hugged the mommy tight.

"When you're big will you still love me?" said Mommy.

Rosemary closed her eyes. "Oh, yes, Mommy."

The baby blew a bubble from his mouth. He held his hand up and curled his finger. His leg kicked in the blanket. The heat flamed in him.

I was falling and Mommy laid me down in the crib and tucked my blanket around me. She gave me my puppy and kissed me. She stood up. She took the little girl's hand and walked away with her into the yellow light. I was floating and burning. The snow came down all white and falling. Arbo was there, running. He was pulling the snow train on a string. *Choo-choo!* He had 'jams on and his diaper stuck out of them. All the pretty children waved their hands. They wore red hats.

Arbo waved bye-bye.

In the black the wind blew and the tall tree walked. It carried Rosemary in its branches and it bent over her bed to grab her and shake her and take her away.

I cried out.

"Shhhh," Daddy said.

8.

The tiny green leaves on the tall black tree fluttered in the warm breeze.

We were outside on the porch. Mommy put me on the stool and tucked a sheet tight around my neck. The comb and scissors clicked at me. Black and silver clicking, pointed mouths like bird beaks. Birds clicked against each other, their bird beaks pecked.

"Hey," said Mommy. She pushed my chin.

I opened my eyes. The green trees were all around me, the warm air was like my bath. The comb teeth scraped and tickled my neck.

"All done."

I sat on the steps and leaned against the railing. My head felt very light and cool. The sunlight was soft on me.

Gretl ran on the grass in short darts. Her patches of color rippled. She crept and pounced. She arched and pawed. Her tail swished and her eyes rolled.

Rosemary climbed up on the stool and Mommy wrapped the sheet around her and took the rubber bands out of her pigtails. She fluffed out her hair.

A tear rolled down Rosemary's cheek.

Mommy pulled some of Rosemary's hair up into a little bunch and cut the top off it. She did another bunch, and then another. Her hands flew.

"Don't give me little baby bangs," Rosemary said.

I got up and went down the steps onto the grass. I walked in a slow circle. The breeze shined my face and hummed my ears. I thought I was going to disappear.

I didn't know whether I was a boy or a baby. I looked up at the blue sky. High up, white clouds raced by. Everything seemed so far away.

I put out my arms and spun around and around and around, faster and faster and faster.

"You're not doing it even!" Rosemary cried.

The ground grew very heavy and the sky grew very light. My head jangled up and I fell down hard and lay there. After a while, I opened my eyes. Mommy was standing with her hands on her hips. Rosemary's head hung down. The sheet wrapped her up tight. Her cheeks had big red spots on them.

"How can you do this?" she said. "You don't love either one of us. You just do what you want to do!"

She turned her head away. Mommy came up with the scissors and comb and kept on cutting. I flopped over on my stomach. I thought of the chocolate eggs and bunnies that Daddy hid. They were supposed to be a secret, but I could see them from where I was lying. They stuck up out of secret places in the bushes. I knew where they were waiting.

Rosemary came running down the steps. Her forehead was as big as an elephant's. Her eyes bulged. She threw herself down on the grass and started ripping it up. Her face was shiny. Her hair was in little chops and feathers.

Rosemary's dark eye came up, and it was wet.

"I'm running away," she whispered. "The minute she goes inside."

The Snow Train

Mommy was shaking the sheet off the porch.

"Me, too," I said.

"No, you're not."

Mommy went inside and the door slammed. Rosemary started to get up. I ran over and wiggled under the bushes in front of the porch. The branches prickled me and the thick black dirt came on my pants, but I didn't care. The air inside the bushes was cold and sweet. I saw a glittery thing and it was an egg in silver foil. There was another one right next to it in the dirt. A tall bunny with pink and silver ears was in a bush. I grabbed it.

I backed out of the bushes. Rosemary was standing there.

"There," I said. I dumped the eggs and bunny on the grass.

"They're for the Easter hunt," Rosemary whispered. She knelt on one knee and scooped them up into her arms. She looked at me. "If you come with you can't suddenly turn around and want to come back. Okay?"

"Okay."

She put a finger to her mouth. "Follow me. Keep close to the house."

We hugged the side of the house as we ran up the driveway. Then we darted through the backyard. As we got to the fence and went under the torn part into the alley, *tackety-tacks* tapped out of Mommy's window. We ran away until we couldn't hear them and then we walked slow down the alleyway.

"This is a secret street," Rosemary said. "It's like the street behind the street."

The alley went between the garages. They were like little white houses with their paint all scraped and torn. They had garbage cans next to them that were tumbling over. The gravel was like a grey rash on the dirt. There were hard flat puddles in it that caught the sky. I ran ahead of Rosemary and saw the tops of the garages in the puddles. Inside the breeze there was a cold wind that was just starting. It pushed me harder and harder. It made me be a little boy.

Words came out of me, I couldn't stop them.

"A real rabbit," I said.

"What are you talking about?"

I tried to tell her. I threw my arms up.

"The bunnies bounced," I said.

I tried to bounce but I stumbled and fell. I pushed myself up and was running again. I had sharp elbows. I wanted to throw myself at something. I lowered my shoulders, ready. I looked around. I leaned forward.

Rosemary caught up with me. Her white socks had dirt on them, and her blue shoes were scuffed, but her legs were white like chalk. Her cheeks were red and she was breathing fast.

She looked down at a puddle and stopped. She stared at herself in the water. She dropped the candy. The breeze fluttered her choppy hair.

"I look like a dandelion," she said.

She puffed her cheeks out. She took her hands and scratched her hair with them. She threw her head back. She moaned. She put her fists in her hair and rubbed hard. She pounded and roughed up her hair. It stuck straight out!

"I'm ugly, ugly, *ugly*."

It was very quiet. Rosemary bit her lip. She picked up the bunnies and eggs and walked on. I followed her. Her white legs moved slowly in and out of the puddles. The alley gravel crunched.

A bad spotted white dog ran up and smashed against the fence in his backyard, barking and rattling.

The Snow Train

"Aaaahhh!" Rosemary screamed.

She jumped and grabbed me and I nearly fell into a puddle. She hung onto me. We ran as hard as we could. The dog threw himself at the fence with his paws out, barking and barking.

We ran and ran until we couldn't see him anymore. Even then Rosemary held onto me.

"They should lock that dog up." She kept looking behind us. "Dumb dog!"

The garages stopped and the alley ran into a little green hill with trees and bushes on it. We climbed up it on a dirt path and sat down behind some trees. The ground had a cold mud smell. All around us I could hear birds. I looked straight up. The black trees wobbled in the blue sky. The clouds came racing past.

Rosemary gave me an egg and took one for herself. She started picking off the foil. We heard voices.

"Shhh!" she said. She pushed her chin forward and peered through the branches of a prickly green bush. I put my head next to hers and looked. We saw Goodie and her brother walking up the alley. Goodie had thick glasses and yellow hair. Her brother had thick glasses and black hair. His head was big, like a rock. They had sticks in their hands and they were poking them in the ground and in puddles. Sometimes Goodie's brother picked up stones and threw them at the garages.

They walked up to where the alley ended, just down the hill from us. They stood there looking around. Rosemary grabbed my hand and squeezed it hard.

"When you lift your foot up your shadow is stuck on it," Goodie said. "You can't shake it off."

She lifted her foot and shook it.

"She's a moron," Rosemary whispered.

Her brother poked his stick at a puddle and splashed water at her.

"Hey!" said Goodie.

Her brother turned around and walked back up the alley without saying anything. After a second, Goodie followed him.

Rosemary stared after them for a long time. The breeze blew her cropped hair. Her eyes got smaller and smaller as Goodie and her brother got farther and farther away.

When they were gone, Rosemary finished unwrapping her egg.

"I don't always like to play with her," she said. "I get tired of her."

She took a bite out of the egg. "Yug. It's hollow."

She held up it up. There was nothing inside of it. Mine was empty, too. I put a piece in my mouth. It tasted dry.

"No one will ever know we ate these," Rosemary said. "He won't remember how many he put out."

Rosemary's knee nudged mine as she ate. She ate the whole egg and scraped and licked at the foil paper. When she was done, she crumpled it up into a ball and threw it far from her into the trees.

"There's a kind of bird that catches shiny things and builds her nests with them," she said. She reached for the bunny. "This better be chocolate through and through."

Rosemary was humming as she unwrapped the bunny's ears. She sniffed them and then broke them off.

"These are good."

She handed me an ear. I sucked on it. It was deeper and richer than the other chocolate. Rosemary leaned back against a tree and stretched out her legs.

"What are you thinking about?" she said. "I often wonder what babies are thinking about. Not anything, I suppose."

"I'm not a baby," I said.

There was a sudden rushing noise. I looked up fearfully. The wind blew the tops of the trees hard and they shook. I put my chocolate down. I stood up. A cloud passed over the sun. It got dark, and cold.

"Let's go," I said.

"Robbie!" Rosemary said. "You promised! It isn't anything. Only babies get afraid of the wind."

"Say hello to me!" I said to the sky. I stared straight up. "Say hello to me."

"I'm not saying hello to anybody."

"Say hello to me," I said to the bushes. I was laughing. "Say hello!"

I got up and walked around.

"What's this?" I said.

I picked up a metal thing off the ground.

"That's part of a can," Rosemary said. "Calm down. Do you want the rest of your chocolate?"

"Yes."

"Don't leave it there, then."

I looked over at Rosemary and her face was turned up to me. She was another girl. The cloud shadows fell over her choppy hair, and then the sun shined on her face, and she didn't look like Rosemary at all.

I went and got my chocolate and walked over to her.

"Here," I said. I put it in her lap.

"Thank you," Rosemary said politely.

I kissed her on the forehead and then jumped back.

Rosemary stared at me. Her eyes were big and dark. The red spots came back on her cheeks. She opened her mouth and then closed it. She looked down at her chocolate.

I suddenly wanted her to chase me. I started to run up the hill on the little dirt path.

"Where are you going?" Rosemary cried.

I kept on running. There was a secret excitement in me that came from the sky.

"Say hello!" I said. "Say hello!"

I heard Rosemary scrambling up behind me. I went past cans and stones and bottles on the ground. I kept running and running up the hill to the sky. I got to the top. There was a wooden table there. The trees stopped. Looking out, I could see the tops of the houses and the cold blue sky. I turned around and around. The wind came up and blew in my eyes.

Rosemary staggered up the hill out of breath. She sat down at the wooden table. "Robbie, what's gotten into you?"

I ran over to her and threw my arms around her.

Rosemary held me tight.

"You're the only one who loves me," she said.

We sat at the table. She squeezed me. She rocked me back and forth. I buried my face in her neck. Her skin smelled like chocolate.

I could barely talk. I looked up at her. Her face was fierce as she hugged me. She kissed my forehead.

"There's a kiss for you," she said. "That's all you get!"

Her choppy hair tickled my nose. She hugged me tight.

"I'll never let you go. Never!"

I closed my eyes and she held onto me. After a while it began to get very cold and we had to go home. We walked down the hill together.

"Be prepared," Rosemary said. "They're going to get mad. But I'll take the blame. I don't think they'll spank you. They don't spank you very much. That's where that rash comes in handy."

There were long shadows that came out from the garages and fell over the stony alley. The fences were very quiet. Our footsteps seemed very loud.

The spotted white dog walked out from the side of a garage. He stood right in the middle of the alley. His pink tongue was hanging out, and he was panting. He looked at us. His head came up. His ears flipped forward.

Rosemary froze.

"Oh," she said. "Oh, oh. Oh, Robbie."

She started backing up. Her eyes were wide on her face. Her mouth was wide open. "Run!" she screamed.

She turned around and started running, and in a flash the spotted dog took off after her. It flew by me and crouched down low and began leaping and nipping at Rosemary's heels as she tried to dance away from it.

She was shrieking and crying. The dog jumped with its paws curled in the air and snapped with its mouth. Rosemary had her hands out and was hitting the air and the dog was snapping at her hands. She kept turning around in a circle but everywhere she turned the dog was there.

There was a big stick on the ground near me, and I picked it up and ran at the dog. I hit it hard on the back. Bad dog! I hit it again. It backed away and barked at me, and I ran at it and hit it again. The dog grrrred with its mouth, but I wasn't afraid. I twisted into the jumping and yelling and barking and hit as hard as I could. I wasn't afraid of that bad dog.

I hit the stick on the ground after the dog ran away.

"Go away!" I screamed.

The cold wind rushed through me.

"Robbie!"

Rosemary was leaning against the fence crying. I grabbed her hand and we ran away together, down the alley to our house. We got to our backyard and went through the hole in the fence and kept running until we got into our front yard.

We were back where we started from. We sat down on the steps. The sky was turning blue and black. Across the street, Goodie and her brother came out on their steps and sat down. They looked across at us. Rosemary and I sat together. There was mud all over Rosemary's white legs. Her hair curled up in little tangles on her head. She scratched it and then propped her elbows up on her knees and put her face down in her hands.

She sighed.

9.

It was very hot in our room. I was sitting on the bed while Rosemary played on the floor with Goodie.

Rosemary wore a short dress that looked like a sack. It had straps that went up to her shoulders. Her skin was pink and sweaty. She took clay and patted it and put it into cake pans.

Goodie put a pan in a little white oven and switched on the dial. Her face was red and her glasses were shiny. She looked over her shoulder at me.

"Can't you get rid of him?"

"He's all right," said Rosemary.

"He keeps staring at me."

"Maybe he's your sweetheart."

Goodie made a face at me. She took some clay in her hands and held it out. "Here. Have some cake. Mmmm-good!"

I stared at her. She had tight curly blonde hair and her face was thin. She was very small.

She turned her head away.

"Look at the way he's looking at me. See what I mean? He's a big problem."

Rosemary puffed her cheeks and blew out. There were shadows under her eyes.

Mommy came in and stood at the doorway.

"Is it hotter out there or in here?" she said.

"It's hot everywhere," said Rosemary.

"When I was a little girl we set up lemonade stands on the sidewalk on hot days," Mommy said. "I guess you wouldn't be interested in that, though, huh?"

"No," said Goodie. "It's too hot."

"I don't blame you," Mommy said. "How 'bout you, champ?"

I looked at Rosemary.

"I don't know," I said.

Mommy laughed.

"You know, if you leave the room, she won't disappear."

"He's been following me ever since he found out I'm going to school in the fall," Rosemary said.

"We went to school last year," Goodie said.

"But only in the morning. First grade is all the time. He's going to be by himself."

"Rosie, don't be mean," Mommy said.

Rosemary turned to me.

"Who's going to take care of you when I'm gone and Mommy writes her poems?"

"Mommy will."

"Mommy won't."

"Daddy will come home," I said.

Goodie gave a little laugh, and Rosemary did, too.

"He's just fooling himself," Goodie said.

"Hey!" said Mommy.

"He has that awful skin condition and he doesn't make friends," Rosemary said. "Now he's paying for it."

"Rosemary, that's enough!"

Rosemary threw her clay down.

The Snow Train

"It's boring in here," she said. "When is the Good Humor coming?"

"I'm going home," said Goodie. She stood and picked up her doll.

"Why?" said Rosemary.

"Because there's nothing to do here."

"There's nothing to do there, either."

"Come with me anyway."

"I don't want to come with you to your dumb old house and your dumb old brother," Rosemary said.

"Okay," Mommy said. "Enough."

"He's not any dumber than your brother."

"Hah!"

"Both of you," said Mommy. "Goodie, maybe it is time for you to go home for a while. You'll see Rosie when the Good Humor comes."

"I was going anyway," Goodie said.

She walked out of the room. We heard the screen door slam.

"Someone's a very big crab today," Mommy said. "And someone should remember her birthday is just around the corner."

She left. I looked at Rosemary.

"Someone's a big crab today," she said. She picked up the front of her dress and lifted it away from her. She blew down her neck. "Yuck."

She climbed up next to me on the bed and knelt up and stuck herself way out the window. Her bum wiggled. I could see her head through the glass. She put her tongue out and held it between her lips. She seemed to be tasting the air. Her hair lay flat on her neck. "Listen," I heard her say.

The birds chirped. There was a sound like humming. I thought a car might be going by.

Rosemary pulled her head back in and wiped off her forehead.

"Why are you staring? Please stop staring! I'm sorry I was mean."

"I don't care," I said.

"I'm going outside to wait on the porch," Rosemary said.

I followed her. On the way out, we stopped and looked in Mommy's room. It was very dark. Mommy was lying down on the bed. She had her eyes closed.

"Mommy, we're going to wait outside for the Good Humor," Rosemary said.

"That's fine," Mommy said.

I walked into her room and looked at her on the bed. There were crumpled-up pieces of paper all around her.

"Are you sick?" I said.

"No, sweetie, Mommy's just resting. You go with Rosie, okay?"

"Can we take some dimes?" Rosemary asked.

"Take three, Rosie," Mommy said. Her eyes were closed. "Get me something vanilla, all right?"

Rosemary took some dimes from Mommy's desk and we went into the living room. Gretl was stretched out on the top of the old couch. Her paws hung down. Her head was out flat. Her tail didn't move. We pushed open the door and went out on the porch and sat down on the top step. The houses across the street were very bright. The heat hit us. It burned the tips of my ears. I stretched my legs out over the sunny steps. I looked down at the bright red sores. I felt the sun bite into them. The sun hurt the rash in a way that felt good.

The Snow Train

"Ick," Rosemary said. "You should wear long pants."

She looked up and down the street. The air around her wavered. She wrapped her arms around herself.

"This is just too much!"

She got up and walked around the porch. She leaned on the railing and stared down at the prickly bushes. She pushed herself up on her hands. She hung there. Her face got redder. She grimaced. Her feet dangled. Finally, she let herself down.

"I can't stand this."

She came back and sat down on the steps. She took out her dimes and put them in a little stack on the sunny step.

"They'll burn up," she said. "When the Good Humor man gets them he'll get a burn for being so late!"

She looked up the street.

The rash was burning my legs. My skin began to crawl.

I felt Rosemary breathing next to me. Her breath was so hot. It rose in a cloud off her body. I looked up at the sky. It was white. Even the black leaves of the big tree had white twinkles showing through them. My eyes glared and hurt and I squeezed them closed.

"Listen!" said Rosemary.

I heard the tinkling noise. It was soft at first and then it got louder. I opened my eyes. Rosemary stood up. Her face caught the sound. Her eyes jumped. I stood up next to her.

Across the street, Goodie's door opened. She came out with her brother and they stood on their porch. She waved at Rosemary, but Rosemary didn't wave back. She bent down on the steps and took her handkerchief and pushed the hot dimes into it. She held it by the top like a little bundle. She shook it. She laughed.

The Good Humor truck appeared. It was a little white truck. Its bell was shaking and ringing. It came faster and faster.

"Stop," yelled Rosemary. "You better stop!"

The bell got inside of me. It shook me up. I started to jump up and down. Across the street other kids were coming out on their lawns and running down their driveways. Rosemary started down the steps.

"Wait!" I grabbed her dress. "I'll go with."

"Stop it," Rosemary said. She pushed my hand away. "I'll get in line for us. I'll be first in line!"

She leapt off the steps. Kids were running down the sidewalk, but Rosemary raced past them with her knees up high. I saw her handkerchief swinging from her hand.

The door opened behind me and Mommy came out and stood there blinking. She put her hand up to her forehead.

Rosemary's short hair flew. A dog jumped at her. She twisted and kept running.

I watched. She got farther and farther away.

"Rosemary!" Mommy said. She went down the steps and stood on the grass. "*Rosemary!*"

Rosemary stopped and looked back. I couldn't see what she looked like. She was too far away. The light made her shine too bright. My eyes hurt and I blinked them. I pushed my hands into them.

"Hang on a sec, Rosie," said Mommy.

She started to walk down the sidewalk.

Rosemary watched her. Then she turned and started running again.

"Darn that child," said Mommy.

She stood with her hands on her hips.

The Good Humor truck stopped under the shade of one of the big trees. The man got out and went to the back of the truck.

The Snow Train

Rosemary was ahead of all the other kids. She cut down a driveway. She shouted something at the Good Humor man. She held up her hand.

Mommy yelled.

A big car went by on the street. It went by Mommy and me and all the running kids. Suddenly there was a screeching and a big bang. The car lurched back. Its front bounced up and down. Then it stopped. It was quiet. There was a little smoke. Mommy stood on the sidewalk with her hands to her mouth. Then she started running.

Everything was very far away. Mommy ran out on the street. She knelt down.

I got off the porch and walked down the sidewalk. I was a good boy, I was very careful. All the kids were in the middle of the street, but their mommies started coming out and trying to grab them. Some of them ran away from their mommies. Some of them had their hands in their pockets. Some of them were jumping up and down to see.

I kept walking. I got up to all the kids. Suddenly I heard Mommy. She sounded like a car was inside of her. She sounded like a horn honking.

"Mommy," I said.

I stood there on the curb. All the little kids backed up around me. They looked at me. The light came down bright and black. The tall black trees twinkled.

I stared. I put my hands in my pockets. Rosemary was lying on the pavement between the Good Humor truck and the car. Mommy was kneeling there. Rosemary's head was flat out. Her baby face stared up. Her cheeks were so fat. There was black stuff by her.

An old lady was crying and shaking. Mommy flew up and hit the old lady. The old lady cried out and put her arms over her head. She ran back and tried to get in the car, but Mommy wouldn't let her. She pulled her by her dress. The old lady started screaming. The Good Humor man grabbed Mommy. Goodie's mommy came in and grabbed Mommy and pulled at her.

I looked at Rosemary. She was lying there on the ground. One of her shoes was gone. She was staring off to the side. She wasn't looking at me. I didn't know what she looked like. She was very still. She looked like a big doll. Her black eye stared. Her hair was choppy and wet. She wasn't looking at me.

Part Two: 1957

All Wound Up

I.

The frosted window above the toilet glowed so white from the snow falling outside that the whole room filled with the kind of light that came when the Blessed Mother appeared to children. My mouth opened. It seemed wonderful to me.

"It could happen," I said.

"What could happen?" I replied.

"I just told you."

"What could happen?"

"I just told you!"

I flipped the pages of the photo album. I stared at the pictures of the little girl.

"That's her," I said. "She's bee-u-tee-ful!"

There was a knock on the door.

"Robbie," Mommy said.

"I'm through," I told her.

"Can I come in?"

"No."

"People are waiting, sweetie."

I closed the album and hid it underneath the magazines in their basket. Then I stood up, lifted the toilet seat, and flushed to make her think I had gone. The water gurgled like a little baby. I flushed again just to watch it swirl and splash. The

71

toilet bowl gleamed. The hushed light was like a whisper.

"What are you doing?" I said.

"I just *told* you!"

Suddenly the triplets laughed in their high, tinkly way. I heard Goodie's brother shout. The sound of their voices got me excited. I opened the door and raced down the hall and into the living room. Streamers floated from the ceiling and bright red and green balloons bounced along the floor like big, soft grapes. At the center of the room was a cardtable covered with a paper cloth. My presents were piled high on it. Goodie's brother had opened my new mitt and was pounding his fist into the pocket. The triplets crowded around him, giggling. They had long brown hair that flowed in shiny streams halfway down their backs, and freckles, and very skinny, bony arms. Their crinkly pink party dresses fluffed out and their pointed party hats stuck straight up like little witch hats.

Deanna, the one with the long, pokey chin, held her nose as I ran up.

"He's pee-uuuu!" she said, pointing at Goodie's brother. "Why doesn't he take a bath?"

Goodie's brother banged his fist into the mitt and smiled with his yellow teeth. His thick round glasses shone. His hair was cut so short it looked like his big rock head had thousands of tiny black prickles on it. Fat fell off his stomach and over his belt.

Goodie's mommy came out of the kitchen and put her hands on her hips and stared at me with her crooked smile. She was fat and had short puffy blonde hair and glasses that went up like wings. "Seven years old," she cried. "Imagine!"

She went around turning out the lamps and then came back and cleared off the cardtable and made me sit down at it. She shushed the kids and we waited in the dark. The kitchen door opened and Goodie walked out slowly, carefully holding a chocolate cake with burning candles on it. Her head was down and she was biting her lip. Behind her, Mommy came. She smiled a big smile at me. Her party hat was tilted over her shiny black hair and white forehead.

When Goodie put the cake down in front of me, flames licked her cheeks and her chin flared bright yellow. The candles sent shadows like mountains high up the walls. Her mommy waved her arms up and down and began singing "Happy Birthday" in a strange high voice. Everyone joined in.

I looked out the window while they were singing. The snow rushed past like a cloud of white dust. It seemed so bright from the dark room. The branches of the big tree in our front yard lifted up and shook.

Mommy put her long, cool hands on my shoulders.

"Wish for something you want more than anything else in the world," she said.

I sucked in air to blow out the candles.

"Stop!" cried Goodie.

I blew them all out in one puff. Trails of smoke drifted up and the triplets clapped very hard. Goodie walked up and stood very close to me. She was holding a big flat present wrapped in silver paper. Her new glasses curled up just like her mommy's. Her blonde hair was cut exactly the same.

"Did you make a wish?" she said. "I didn't see you make a wish."

Her eyes were pale blue. She blinked over and over again. She poked me with her present. "Open this!"

I ripped the paper off. Inside was a watercolor in a thin black frame. It was of the little girl. She had short brown hair and a round face. She was floating up from the sidewalk in a little white cloud. A big sun shone in the blue sky above her. On the sidewalk beneath her, two little kids stared up, a boy and a girl. There was a spotted animal next to them that looked like a cat.

"It's from me," Goodie said. "I did it."

"Oh, Goodie," Mommy said. She knelt down and wrapped her in a hug. "That's so sweet."

I put the picture down on the table.

"I'm going to the hospital," I said to the triplets.

I pushed up the sleeve of my flannel shirt. There was thick red skin at my wrist, and white flakes over the redness like fish scales.

The triplets opened their mouths all at once. Goodie's brother moved closer.

Goodie's mommy came over and tried to hug me, but I ducked away from her. She squeezed her hands together at her chest like she was saying a prayer. "Such a brave little boy. You don't cry! You don't complain!"

"I knew you had that," Deanna said.

"They're taking out my blood," I told her. "They're taking the old blood out and putting new blood in."

"Robbie," Mommy said.

The doorbell rang and my heart jumped. I ran to the door and opened it. Aunt Cecilia stood there in a gust of cold wind that froze my face. She had on a big silver fur coat.

"Aunt Cecilia! Aunt Cecilia!" I cried. She smelled like perfume and cold, cold air. Her eyes were bright and her lips were red. I hugged her hard. I pressed my face into her coat. Her smells were all over me. The snow smell was so fresh I sneezed.

"Oops," she said. She pushed the door shut behind her.

"Aunt Cecilia," I said.

"That's my name," she laughed. "Don't wear it out." She kissed my cheek. "Oooh, you're warm. You're a warm, warm, cozy kid, aren't you?"

We went into the living room. Aunt Cecilia held my hand. In her other hand she had her purse and a little suitcase.

She and Mommy kissed cheeks.

"Mmmm-smack!" said Aunt Cecilia. She took off her scarf and shook her red hair and shiny drops flew off it. All the kids stared at her.

"You've met Tom's sister, Cecilia?" Mommy asked Goodie's mommy.

"Hello, Mary Elizabeth," Aunt Cecilia said.

"Hello, hello," said Goodie's mommy. She patted at her hair. "What a nice thing that you could come."

"I snuck out," said Aunt Cecilia. "They'll kill me, but who cares?"

She sat down on the couch and I sat next to her. She pushed her coat off her shoulders and it fell open on the cushion. The inside of it was black and shimmery and I reached out and slowly rubbed my hand over it. Aunt Cecilia picked a cigarette out of her silver case, tapped it and lit it with a little green lighter that looked like it was made out of one of my swirly marbles. She threw her head back and smoke drifted around her bright hair.

Goodie's mommy crouched down near Aunt Cecilia's feet and picked up scraps of wrapping paper. Her face was red.

"I think we're a little combustible around here," she said.

"You bet we are," said Aunt Cecilia. She smiled at Goodie and the triplets, who pushed close. The triplet who stuttered put her thumb in her mouth and reached out and stroked Aunt Cecilia's smooth green dress.

"How tall are you?" Deanna said.

Aunt Cecilia laughed.

"I am exactly five-foot-ten and three-quarter inches tall."

"That's t-t-tall," said the stutterer.

"It sure is." Aunt Cecilia leaned over and tapped her on the nose. "T-t-too tall!"

The triplets all giggled at once. They twisted their bodies back and forth and stared at Aunt Cecilia with their eyes wide.

Goodie's brother came up and tugged my shirt.

"This is for girls," he whispered. "Come on!"

I followed him out of the room and down the hall. He went into the bathroom. I stopped at the door, but he pulled me in.

"Come on!"

When we got inside, he closed the door and took down his pants and sat on the toilet. The soft white light was all over the bathroom, but he didn't seem to notice.

"When I have to make a turd, I like somebody I can talk to," he said. "Sit down."

I sat on the edge of the bathtub and stared at him. His thick jeans were around his ankles, and his striped shirt was pulled up. His belly hung out. He grunted. He looked down between his legs.

"God, it's a big one." He laughed. "And it's still coming out! Take a look."

"I don't want to."

"Come on!" His face was all red. "Oh, God!"

"No."

"Baby."

He grunted some more. His eyes became slits. "There!" he said, finally. He stared down between his legs. "Don't you hate it when it splashes up and hits your legs?"

I didn't say anything. I felt hot. The room was filled with a bad turd smell. Goodie's brother was looking at me funny.

"You've had that crud on you since you were little."

"It doesn't go away," I said. "I have it all the time."

The white light shined down on Goodie's brother, but it just made him uglier.

"Do you ever let people see you completely naked with it?"

"My mommy sees it," I said. "The doctor sees it."

Goodie's brother laughed. His big rock head fell back. His mouth opened. "Your mommy sees it! Does your mommy wipe your butt, too?"

The pit of my stomach began to hurt.

"I wipe my own butt," Goodie's brother said.

He stood up and pulled some toilet paper off the roll and bunched it up. Then he bent over and wiped himself. Little brown pieces of turd hung from the paper. He threw it into the toilet and stared at it. Then he took some more paper and squatted down and wiped harder. He threw that in, and flushed and pulled up his pants. He sniffed his fingers. I got up and started to go out, but he caught my sleeve.

"Somebody better set you straight!" he said. "You shouldn't hang around with Goodie so much. She's just a little goody-two-shoes. Boys who hang out with girls are babies."

He pushed me a little bit. I nearly fell. He stood up close to me. His skin smelled thick and funny, a little bit like glue.

"You're just a little kid," he said, "but already nobody wants to play with you. I'm just telling you this for your own good.

Maybe you noticed how you never walk home from school with anybody. And how you're always by yourself at recess?"

I didn't say anything. I felt his eyes flicking at me.

"Let me see that crud."

"I don't want to."

"No?" His black eyes widened behind his glasses. He snorted. He danced back and began ducking his shoulders and weaving his big rock head from side to side.

"Mommy!" I called.

Goodie's brother threw a punch. I put my arms up to cover my face, but his fist stopped before it hit me.

Goodie's brother laughed. He jumped up and down.

"He don't cry! He don't complain!"

He opened the door and ran back into the living room. I stood there in the white light for a second, trying not to cry. My stomach hurt so much I thought there was some kind of flame burning inside of me. I gritted my teeth and clenched my fists. Finally, I went out again. All the girls were gathered in a circle around Deanna. They were clapping their hands. Aunt Cecilia had put a handkerchief around Deanna's eyes. She had her by the shoulders and was spinning her.

Deanna wobbled with her arms out. The girls bent over and shrieked. They threw their hair in the air. They were laughing as hard as they could.

Aunt Cecilia twirled Deanna around and around, faster and faster.

"Whee, Deanna!" she cried.

Deanna looked like she was dancing. She teetered and spun. Her chin was firm and her fists were clenched and she tried to step her feet carefully, but she nearly toppled. Aunt Cecilia gave her a little push and she wandered through the chairs with her hands in front of her and her swirly crisp dress sticking out, crunching wrapping paper with her black buckle shoes. Goodie's brother ran up and made pig noises in her ear and she jumped. The girls screamed.

Deanna turned and darted at me. I tried to duck but I fell down and she fell down on top of me.

"She's looking!" Goodie cried.

I tried to get her off of me. We were rolling in the wrapping paper and then she kissed me. Her mouth was right up against mine and it smelled like cake and her lips were round and cool. I pushed away from her and got up, wiping off my mouth.

Goodie stared at Deanna in astonishment.

"Did you see that?" she said.

Deanna stood up and pulled off her blindfold. Her thin face was red. Her sisters giggled behind their hands.

"It's a g-g-good thing M-m-mommy isn't here," said the one who stuttered.

"She kissed him," Goodie said. She kept blinking.

I could still feel Deanna's lips on my lips, the way they pushed in at me. Goodie's brother was staring at me.

"I think it's time for everyone to leave," Goodie said.

"You're not in charge," said Deanna.

"Actually," said Goodie's mom, looking at Aunt Cecilia. "It probably is time to break it up."

"It was just getting to be fun," Aunt Cecilia said. She went into the kitchen. I heard her and Mommy laughing, and then Aunt Cecilia came back with an armful of boots and winter coats. The triplets sat down on the floor and wiggled while they put on their leggings. They kicked their legs high up in the air and their crinkly dresses popped over the woolly pants.

The Snow Train

Goodie's brother grunted as he pulled his black boots on. He grabbed his coat and jammed his hat onto his head.

"Sissy," he said to me.

He headed for the door.

"Wait for us," called Goodie's mommy, but he was already outside. The door slammed.

"We don't have to go yet," said Goodie. She stamped her foot. Her mommy grabbed her by the arm and whispered hard in her ear.

I ran to the window. It was nearly dark outside. I could barely see Goodie's brother jumping from one snow pile to another. He kept diving into them and rolling around. He looked like a black dog romping.

Deanna came and stood next to me. She was so bundled up she had to move her whole body around just to look at me. Her long hair was tucked inside her collar, and her pokey chin was hidden by her scarf. Her freckles were very faint on her thin face. I looked at her lips. They looked puffy. I thought of them kissing me. I touched my lips. They felt very light and smooth.

"I don't care that you have that stuff on you," Deanna said. She turned and ran out the door. I watched from the window as she and her sisters followed Goodie and her mommy single file down our sidewalk. Deanna seemed like some kind of little bird to me. Her head was tucked into her chest as the wind blew snow around her. She disappeared into the dark.

I turned back from the window. Aunt Cecilia sat on the old green couch smoking a cigarette. Mommy was next to her with her shoes off and her feet stretched out on the coffee table.

"It's so funny how that whole family wears glasses," Aunt Cecilia said. "Even that dreadful little boy."

"He's a moron!" I told her.

Mommy laughed. "Come over here, birthday boy." I walked over and sat down and she ruffled my hair and kissed my head. "Did you have a good birthday?"

"Yes," I said. I leaned back against her and closed my eyes.

Mommy hugged me. "Guess who's staying over tonight? Just guess!"

I looked at Aunt Cecilia, who was smiling at me.

"Yay!" I said. "Yay!"

I got up and jumped up and down. The room jiggled pleasantly at me. The paper crunched underfoot. I was laughing.

"It's bee-u-tee-ful!" I shouted.

Aunt Cecilia laughed. "He sounds just like Sam."

"Did Sam teach you to say that?" Mommy said.

"Yes," I said.

"Speaking of which," Aunt Cecilia said, "Have you heard from either of those two?"

"Tom's supposed to call tonight," said Mommy.

"We'll see," she said. "A convention of car salesmen in Los Angeles. God, what a cliché! High-priced ladies of the night, fancy scotch. They've probably destroyed the place already."

"Celia," Mommy frowned. She pointed at me.

"Oops," said Aunt Cecilia. "Oops, oops, oops."

"Oops," I said. "Oops, oops, oops!"

I ran up and to her and stuck my face up close to hers. "Oops, oops, oops!"

"Rob, hey," Aunt Cecilia said. She ducked away.

Mommy got up, knelt down next to me, and took my arm.

"Sweetie, calm down."

"I'm not doing anything."

The Snow Train

"What you can do for me now is take your presents into your room. Okay?"

"Mommy!"

"Robbie," she said in her warning voice.

I wouldn't look at her. I felt all hot inside.

"I think you're a little wound up, don't you?" she said.

I kept my face turned away. I felt her next to me like a rock or a black stick lying on the ground.

"C'mon, Jeannie," Aunt Cecilia said softly.

"Even birthday boys need rules," said Mommy.

I could hardly look up. I wanted to tear at myself. My rash bit into me, with little nips and snaps. I scooped up as many of my presents as I could and ran down the hallway into my room and dropped them hard into my toy box.

It was quiet and smelled cool in the room. I stood by the window and stared outside. The snow blew down in the backyard and the wind pushed against the house. I couldn't even see as far as the back fence and the alleyway. I sat down on my bed and scratched my arms through my shirt. I stared over at the other bed. The two dolls in their long dresses sat against the pillow, staring straight ahead. Their shadows fell across the floor.

I got up and went to the doorway and stood listening. Aunt Cecilia and Mommy were in the kitchen, washing and drying the dishes and talking to each other. I went quietly down the hallway and into the bathroom and shut the door. It still smelled a little bad from Goodie's brother, and the white light had gone away. I sat down on the toilet and closed my eyes. The water stopped running and Mommy and Aunt Cecilia came out.

"It's just—it's just time, now," said Mommy.

"Shhh, Jeannie. It's wonderful news. There's no question."

Their footsteps went into the living room. I sat there. It was cold and I shivered. I reached over into the straw basket and picked up the photo album. It was so big I needed two hands. I held it in my lap and flopped it open. The pages were made out of thick black paper.

The little girl in the cowboy hat and blue jeans and pigtails stared straight out from the photo. She was holding onto the hand of a baby boy. He was sucking his thumb.

I peered at the girl in the dim light. Her dark eyes looked into mine but they weren't really looking at me. I twisted and tilted the album and held my nose up almost against the picture, just to make the girl look at me, but she wouldn't.

After dinner we all put on our pajamas and sat down in the living room. I was staying up late because Daddy was calling from California. Mommy sat curled up in her rocking chair by the window. She was wearing her blue robe. Her face was scrubby and pink.

Aunt Cecilia sat on the couch with her feet up on the coffee table. She wore a long white bathrobe that said Detroit Yacht Club on it and she had a furry white towel wrapped in a cone around her head. She had on a pair of shiny white pajamas. Her feet were very long and narrow and her toenails were red. She was drinking a brown drink in a wide glass and trying to tell me why the time was different where Daddy was. "Okay: picture the country. Picture America. Can you do that? Have you seen a map?"

"Uh-huh," I said.

Aunt Cecilia took her open hand and curved it through the air.

"The sun rises in the east," she said. "In New York. And rises. And sails up through the sky." Her hand was high up in the air. "And then it starts to go down. It descends, as they say.

Down and down. And it sinks into the ocean behind Los Angeles. Okay?"

"Okay," I said.

"So the sun has left us behind. It's not here anymore. That's why, when it's nine o'clock here in Detroit, it's only six o'clock in Los Angeles. The sun hasn't gotten all the way there yet. It's the same *actual* time, if you understand what I mean. We just call it by a different *hour*. Because of the sun."

I just looked at her.

"God," said Aunt Cecilia. "Is there an encyclopedia around here?"

"What if it sticks to him?" I said.

"What if what sticks to who?" said Aunt Cecilia. She took a drink. "Or to *whom*, should I say?"

"To Daddy," I said. "The time. What if he comes back and it's dinnertime for him but 9 o'clock for me. I'll be too hungry. How will we—"

"No," said Mommy. "No, no."

"But it could happen!"

"No," Mommy said. "Now listen: it could *not* happen. There are certain things that can*not* happen."

I turned to Aunt Cecilia. "But wouldn't it be funny? If it was time for my bedtime and no one knew it, so I got to stay up? Or if Daddy forgot to get up in the morning? Hah!"

I laughed harder. I stood up. I threw out my chest.

"Daddy, you'd better get up!" I said. "It's time to go to work!"

"No, it's not! Leave me alone!" I replied.

I was really laughing and Aunt Cecilia was laughing, too, but Mommy held up her hands.

"Robbie, please," she said. "Enough, okay? We get it."

The phone rang in the kitchen.

"Hey!" I yelled. "Listen!"

I leapt out of my chair and began running. I nearly tripped when I turned the corner into the kitchen, but I caught myself and slid on the floor. The stove and sink and refrigerator were shining in the dark. The phone was on the wall by the sink and I reached up and grabbed it.

"Hi!" I said.

Static hissed and crackled, and I heard a woman's voice. "I have a station-to-station collect call for anyone from Mr. Thomas O'Conor. Do you accept the charges?"

"Yes, he will," I heard Daddy say.

"Yes, I will," I said.

"Happy birthday, pal."

"Wait a minute," I told him.

I climbed up and settled myself up on the tall wooden stool that Mommy sat on when she was talking on the phone or writing grocery lists. I picked up the phone.

"It's snowing!" I said.

"Now, that is really something," Daddy said. "Because here, on this lovely California evening, the windows are wide open—and there are palm trees outside. Can you imagine?"

I stared out the window over the sink. The snow was coming down in big soft flakes that floated in the dark space between our house and Mrs. Beaudell's.

"It's really deep," I said to Daddy.

All of a sudden, I heard other people talking on the line. Their voices were so clear I jumped.

"I don't believe it!" a woman was saying. She had a loud, rough voice.

"Well, it's true," said another woman. "It's God's truth!"

"Daddy?" I said. "Can you hear them?"

"I sure can," he said. His voice went in and out. It sounded faint. "Listen to those two old biddies!"

"Can they hear us?" I pressed the phone closer to my ear. The women kept talking. "Can you hear us?" I said to them. "Stop it!"

Their voices disappeared.

"It worked!"

Daddy laughed. His voice was back full and deep.

"Long distance is a miracle," he said. "Those're probably two Kansas farmwives stuck in a blizzard. The cows are in the barn, dinner's on the stove, and they're just gossiping away. Now, I wonder what's got them all worked up?"

I told Daddy about all the presents I had gotten for my birthday. While I talked to him I watched the snow. It kept coming down. I thought maybe it was going to snow forever.

I felt someone walk in and I looked up to see Mommy standing next to me. I hugged the phone closer to my face.

"Rob, that's fine," Daddy was saying. "It sounds like you had a great time. Can you put your mom on?"

"Aunt Cecilia's here," I said.

"Well, put her on, too!"

"I can't put them *both* on," I laughed. "There's no room!"

"Well, put *one* of them on, Robbie, okay?"

There was silence on the phone, except for the sound of the static. I waited for him to say something else, but he didn't. I gave Mommy the phone and got down off the stool. She took it and cradled it between her neck and her shoulder.

"Tom," she said. She smiled and stood listening with her arms folded across her chest.

I walked over and opened the refrigerator and stood in the block of white light that came out. The shelves were full of things. There were bottles of milk and pop and bowls covered with wax paper.

"Mmmm," said Mommy. "Yeah."

Gretl walked up from somewhere and rubbed against my legs, purring. I took out a half-open can of cat food and shut the door.

"No, he's been a sweetie," Mommy was saying. She smiled and poked her foot out at me as I went by.

I shook out the food into Gretl's bowl and watched her come over and sniff it. I looked up at the window over the sink. I could see Mommy's reflection in it as she listened on the phone. She was slouched against the counter with her head down. Her hand was closed into a half-fist and she kept brushing her thumb over her fingernails. She nodded her head and opened and closed her mouth.

"You'll just have to wait," she said. She laughed. "Nope."

Standing so near the window, I was too close to see my own reflection, so I backed away into the center of the kitchen. Even then I could only see the top of my head. I crouched down and jumped up and my whole face appeared for a second. I landed with a thump. Gretl raced away from her bowl.

Mommy looked up, startled.

"I don't know *what* he's doing," she said. "He just leapt up and came down with a big bang. Hey, sport?" She was holding out the phone to me. "How 'bout saying goodnight to your dad?"

I jumped again as high as I could, but my socks slipped on the linoleum and my feet went right out from under me. I landed hard on my back. The wind rushed out of me. I rolled over and curled up into a ball.

"Robbie!" cried Mommy. "Tom, hang on!"

She put down the phone and came over and knelt beside me.

I tried to get up, but I couldn't. Aunt Cecilia came running in with her bathrobe flying behind her.

"Oh, my God," she cried. "Did he hit his head?"

I just lay there. I couldn't breathe and I thought I was going to throw up.

"Take little breaths like you're sipping through a straw," Mommy said. "You're all right. You just got the wind knocked out."

She rubbed my back. In a minute I sat up.

"Put your head down between your legs," she said. "Are you going to be sick?"

I shook my head.

"Okay. Wait. Your father's probably going crazy."

She went over to the counter and picked up the phone. "Tom, he's all right. He was just—I don't know. He was jumping around and he fell down pretty hard." She listened for a few seconds. "God, my heart was right in my throat."

Aunt Cecilia helped me get off the floor.

"Come on, kid," she said in a soft voice. "That sounded like one hell of a bang! I heard it all the way in the living room."

"You did?" I said.

I stood up with Aunt Cecilia holding me. My stomach was really sore and I felt tears in my eyes. Mommy helped put me on the stool and I picked up the phone.

"Hi," I said to Daddy. Suddenly my face was wet and I was crying. "I really fell down!"

"I *know* you did," he said. "You've had quite a day!"

"My stomach hurts. Are you coming back?"

I started crying hard. Aunt Cecilia and Mommy were around me. They both tried to hug me. The telephone cord came down through a tangle of their arms. Their bathrobes were all around me. They smelled like soap and powder. I couldn't even see around them.

"I'm coming home as soon as I can," Daddy was saying. "Now, can you be a brave boy for your mom? She needs your help."

"No, she doesn't!"

"Robbie," he said.

"She has all her friends." My tears were hot on my cheeks. "She doesn't need any help from me."

"Robbie," Daddy said.

Aunt Cecilia took the phone out of my hand and started talking to Daddy. Mommy hugged me tight and sat down on a kitchen chair and made me sit in her lap, but I felt too big to sit in her lap. She kept hugging me tight and I finally leaned my head against her shoulder.

"Are you my big boy?" she said.

"I don't know," I said. "No."

"You have to be very, very, careful," she said. "You can't be jumping like that, sweetie. You're too wound up!"

"I know."

"Do you understand me?" she said.

"I know!"

"All right."

She stopped squeezing me so hard, but her face was very close to mine and I couldn't get away from it. It stared straight at me, with a little smile. I ducked my head, but her green eyes followed me. They twisted into me. Finally, I stopped ducking and just stayed still. I stared at Mommy with my eyes blank. I let my eyes loose and Mommy came inside me. Her face become huge and blurry and my forehead began to hurt the same way it did when I ate ice cream too fast. She didn't seem to notice.

She seemed satisfied. She kissed me gently on the top of my head.

"Okay," she said.

She let me off her lap and together we walked down the hall and into the bedroom. I stood in the center of the room and looked around. Everything was waiting for me. The two beds stood side by side in the dark. The wooden toy box had all my toys spilling out of it, and my desk had my books and crayons and construction paper on it. Everything was where it was supposed to be.

The windows were shiny and black, but if I squinted through the blackness I could still see the snow falling.

Mommy switched on the lamp and a yellow circle of light came on over my pillow. We sat down on the side of the bed and she pulled my bathrobe off me, and then helped me take off my pajama top. She took the jar of cream from the bed table and unscrewed the top.

She stared smearing on the medicine. I watched her hands. Her fingers bunched together and rubbed. Sometimes she took her little finger and dabbed the bad places.

"It doesn't do any good," I said.

"Shhh," said Mommy. "It does the best it can."

In the lamplight, my rash was fierce red. In some places, it had the white scales on it. There were places at the crooks of my arms and near my wrists and behind my knees where scabs had formed from scratching. The sides of my legs had long black scabs the size of the big beetles in our backyard.

The cream felt cold and greasy. I shivered.

"It's okay," Mommy said in a soft voice. "Tomorrow we're seeing Dr. Benson."

She was smearing my back and her head was almost behind

me as she talked. "I wish we could get you into that hospital a little sooner. It bothers me that they don't have a bed."

She made me lie face down. She pulled my pajamas to my ankles and smeared the cream on my bottom and all up and down my legs. I buried my face into my pillow and closed my eyes. I felt like I was diving away into a soft pool of water. Mommy's hands made me want to go to sleep. The rash softened under the cream.

I looked back at Mommy over my shoulder. Her head was down. Her forehead was wrinkled up. When she saw me looking at her, she picked up my feet and tickled their bottoms and they jumped and twitched.

I knew I was supposed to laugh, but I felt like crying.

When she was through, I turned back over and she helped me put my pajamas back on. I got under the covers and put my back against the pillows. She screwed the top back on the jar and picked up my hands and looked at my nails.

"You just cut them," I said.

"I know," she sighed. "Sweetie, you have to do me a favor and try not to scratch tonight. Okay?"

"I don't do it on purpose."

"I know you don't." She smiled at me. "You know, I was thinking that you don't really need to go into school tomorrow morning. I'm just going to have to come and get you out to take you to Dr. Benson's. Would you like sleeping a little later in the morning?"

"Okay," I said.

A little feeling of happiness went through me. Tomorrow was a Friday and it meant I wouldn't have to go to school until Monday. And on Saturday, we got to go to the airport to pick up

The Snow Train

Daddy and Sam Sullivan. I began to feel less bad about my rash. I thought that I might even get up early by myself and play with my new toys. While I was thinking this, Mommy leaned down and kissed me and then got up and walked out the door. The medicine felt like a soft, wet blanket on my skin.

I lay there and looked out at the snow. It didn't seem like it would ever stop. I began to think of all the snows I would have to get through before springtime. I thought of big soft flakes falling very slowly, for a long time. I thought of the snow falling until all the weeks ran together and you couldn't tell one day from another. I began to feel warm and sleepy. I burrowed deeper into the covers. I saw the snow falling through a wide, dark, glowing space. A little while later I heard a voice say:

It's true. It's God's truth!

I started up and looked around the room, but it was dark and cold and very quiet.

2.

When I woke up I was on the floor with all my covers around me. The tree outside the window was shining. Its branches were silver and white and they shined so hard my eyes hurt and I had to put my hand up to my face.

The tree gave off the whitest light I had ever seen, whiter even than the bathroom light. I kicked my way out of the tangle of covers and went over and pressed my face against the glass. I squinted my eyes. The sun was coming up just behind the houses across the alley. It shined in a blazing path across the white snow directly to the tree. On either side of the path, the ground was still dark and the snow was colored a deep blue.

The tree lit up the air with its shininess. My breath left little circles on the window. There wasn't anything moving outside at all. The backyard was frozen and quiet. I could feel how cold and hard the snow was and I shivered in my pajamas. My body felt loose, and my arms and legs didn't tug at me when I moved them. I reached down and pulled up my pajamas legs. The rash was red, but not bright red. It wasn't sore. My scabs weren't torn off. There weren't any blood streaks on my legs. I hadn't scratched.

"Yay!" I said. "Yay!"

I jumped up in the air. I walked back over and sat down on my bed. I pulled up my pajamas and looked at my legs again.

The Snow Train

"Yay," I said, but more to myself.

I ran my fingers lightly over the rash. It felt different in different places. Some of the really red skin was smooth, but hot. The scabs were cold and rough and bumpy and hard. If I touched the scaly skin lightly it made me shiver all over.

Sometimes there were scabs that were ready to come off all by themselves. I picked at one on my ankle. It seemed loose when I just touched it.

I thought of what Mommy had said about scratching. I rubbed my fingers very lightly over my legs as I thought about her. I stared out the window at the shining silvery tree.

She had come into my bedroom a few weeks ago and sat down next to me on the bed and put her arm around me.

"We have to make a deal," she said.

"What?"

It seemed to me the white light was growing brighter. I got up and walked over to the window and looked out again.

"Such a brave boy," I said. I leaned my head against the window. The sun burst into my eyes. "He don't cry. He don't complain!"

"What?" I said.

Mommy had kissed me. "You're much braver than *anyone* could be! You really are, sweetie. But you just have to—well, you just have to not scratch for one night! That's all. Just try it! You'll wake up in the morning feeling so fine and good. And then if you don't scratch the *next* night, why, you'll even feel that much better."

"And pretty soon," I said. "And pretty soon!"

I went back over to the bed and sat down. It was time for breakfast and I was hungry. I rested my chin on my knee and pushed up my pajama leg and took my two fingers and pulled at the scab near my ankle. The scab was black and hard and it didn't stick when it came off. I just felt a little rip and then a coolness on the spot where it had been. I put the scab down on the bedspread and scratched my fingers lightly around the edges of the sore. It tickled. I scratched a little harder.

"Oh," I said.

The scratching felt like letting out my breath after I had held it for a while.

I picked up the scab and rolled it in my fingers. It shredded into little bits as I pressed my fingers harder and harder together.

"He don't cry," I said.

I picked at another scab on the side of my leg. I closed my eyes. I scratched just a little more, and then some more. When I opened my eyes there was blood on my fingers. I looked over at the empty bed by the other window. The dolls were sitting on it, by the pillow. There were two of them, in long dresses, with round hats on. I went over and sat down and reached up and touched the window glass. It was cold and slick. The sun hadn't come around the corner of the house yet. The air was dark and the snow was grey.

I looked down at my hands. I wondered if I was going to cry.

I went over to the toy box and got out an armful of my toys and brought them back and threw them on the bed. I sat down with the toys scattered all around me on the covers. There was my submarine and a pile of my new Civil War soldiers, and my new mitt. But they weren't in the right order. I put the mitt in the center of the bed. The submarine was right next to it. In fact, the mitt held the submarine. I opened the mitt up and put the submarine in bottom first, so that its conning tower and periscope stuck out from the mitt's fingers.

The Snow Train

The soldiers were all around. They had little caps and knapsacks. I gathered them up and put them on the blanket, far away from me. They hid in the folds and watched.

One of the toys that had come up by mistake with the others was a little puppy dog with a blue ribbon around its neck. One of its black eyes was gone, and the other was loose. I took it and stared at it. It was so thick and stupid. I shook it and threw it on the blanket next to the soldiers.

I looked at the toys around me on the bed. They seemed to be fine. They were in the right place. I felt better. The mitt hugged the submarine. The soldiers lay on their sides. Their faces were frozen. They could be alive or dead and they looked the same.

"Hey, you."

A voice was talking to me.

"What?" I said.

Mommy had just sat down next to me on the bed. "Good morning, sweetie."

She was wearing her blue bathrobe and she leaned back and looked at me. Her eyes were so good. She reached out and squeezed me tight and I squeezed her back. She smelled so good. We sat back and looked at each other. I liked it when I first saw her in the morning, before she had a chance to get mad or not let me alone. I liked looking at her. Her cheeks were round, and her black bangs stuck up in little tangles because she slept on her tummy with her head pushed into her pillow.

In the morning I thought she might be a fairy, or maybe even a little girl who had got lost. She was quieter than she usually was.

She smiled at me. "What are you playing?"

"Nothing," I said. "I'm just putting them together."

She was quiet for a second and then she reached over for the puppy. "Haven't seen him for a long time."

I didn't say anything. Mommy kissed the puppy on the nose and put him down. She reached behind me and picked up the two dolls that were sitting on the pillow. She tugged at their dresses and played with their hats.

"I hope we're not going to leave out Janet and Eleanor."

"They don't play," I said.

"They don't play? But they're so beautiful."

"I don't play with them."

Mommy put the dolls down and took my hands in hers. She stared at the blood on them.

"Oh, my," she said. I tried to close them into fists, but Mommy held them open and kissed them and then pressed her cheek against them.

She raised her head up. Her cheeks were wet. She was holding my hands very tight. "Sweetie, do you ever think about Rosie?"

I didn't say anything.

"I have dreams about her," Mommy said. She looked at me. "You were very little."

"I don't know," I said.

Mommy stared at me.

"I'll just bet you remember," she said. "I'll just bet." She brushed my hair back from my head. She put her fingers to my chin and held my face up. "What would you think about having a new brother or sister?"

I felt hot and twisty inside. I pulled away from her. I took the submarine out of the mitt and slid it along the bedspread.

"You're probably mad at me," she said. "Deep inside, you've never forgiven me. That's what the books say. Have you forgiven me?"

The Snow Train

I picked up some soldiers and put them in a fold in the blanket.

"Think about it, sweetie. A little brother or sister. It would be someone for you to pal around with and take care of, the way Rosie took care of you."

"No one can take care of me," I said.

Mommy didn't say anything, and I looked up at her. Her face seemed very soft. She looked out the window and I felt her sigh. She picked up one of the dolls and fluffed its hair.

All of a sudden, she laughed. "Hey! Wouldn't it be something if time would just disappear?" She snapped her fingers. "Just like that!"

I laughed, too.

"That idea just came to me," Mommy said. "I don't know why."

"No one would know what time it was," I said.

"That's exactly right," Mommy said. "Time would just disappear! Boom!"

She put the doll down and reached over and brushed my cheek with her fingers. Her fingers felt very smooth and warm.

"Sweetie, do you want me to put Janet and Eleanor away now? Maybe it's time we put them with the rest of Rosemary's things."

"I don't know," I said. I got down off the bed and went to the door and looked down the hallway. The lights were on in the living room. "Is Aunt Cecilia awake?"

"She's having breakfast," Mommy said. She came up next to me and put her arm around me and we walked down the hallway and into the kitchen.

Aunt Cecilia was leaning against the sink eating a piece of thin toast. She had her hair up tight on top of her head and her round silver earrings on and an apron over her dress. I sat down at the table. There was a glass of milk and a bowl of oatmeal at my place. Aunt Cecilia ate the last bite of her toast and washed her hands off in the sink and then dried them on a dishtowel. She reached up into the cupboard and got out a little box. I watched her pour white powder into a glass of juice and stir it up with a spoon.

She took a deep breath, blew it out, and then swallowed the whole glass in one gulp.

"*Bleh!*" she cried. "*Ack!*" Her body shivered and her black shoes made a clattery sound on the floor.

Mommy laughed. "Cecilia, that's ghastly stuff."

Aunt Cecilia rolled her eyes. I drank my milk and watched her. Her funny-shaped purse was on the counter. It looked like a black log with a handle on top. She opened it and took out a little round case.

"It's the diet drink of the stars," she said. She flipped the case open and ducked her head to look at herself. "By dint of this simple powder, Grace Kelly keeps her youthful figure." She snapped the case shut and took off her apron. "I'm off. The curse of the working girl."

"*Bleh, ack!*" I said.

"*Tres charmant*, Roberto," Aunt Cecilia said. "*Tu es un jeune homme extraordinaire.*"

I stuck out my tongue at her.

Aunt Cecilia bent down and kissed me and a little circle of red hair fell out of where it was piled up. It bobbed on her forehead.

"Bye-bye," I said.

She and Mommy left the kitchen together.

I felt a pang in my heart, but I ignored it. I took a little spoonful of my oatmeal. There was brown sugar on it and it tasted sweet and warm. I ate a little bit more. I heard Mommy and Aunt Cecilia talking and then the front door slammed. Mommy came back into the kitchen and put some more toast in the toaster. She sat down and picked up the newspaper.

Suddenly I felt like crying.

"Wait," I said. "Stop!"

I got down from my chair and ran out into the living room.

"She's gone, sweetie," Mommy said.

I ran over to the window and looked out. Aunt Cecilia's car was down at the end of the block, at the stop sign. Blue smoke came out of its tailpipe. It turned the corner and was gone. I kept staring out the window, even though there was nothing to look at. It seemed to me that all the sunlight outside was making me sad, but I didn't know why.

I felt very thin. It was like I was the window glass and the sun was shining through me.

I walked back into the kitchen and sat down and looked at my oatmeal. I heard Mommy in the bathroom, running my bath. For some reason, I thought there might be a small bird at the kitchen window, just pecking at the glass. I looked, but there wasn't.

Mommy came back in and took me into the bathroom and sat down on the toilet to help me unbutton my pajamas. Water was pouring into the bathtub and steam rose up. Feathery prickles went up and down my body as my pajamas came off. The rash seemed to be shifting and waking up. It was like tiny little hairs standing straight up all over me.

There was a full-length mirror on the back of the bathroom door. I turned my head away from it. There was an ugly boy who lived in it who had something crawling all over him that was red and black and smelled like blood.

Mommy gave me a big towel to wrap myself up in and leaned down to feel the water. She was humming to herself. I snuck a look in the mirror and pulled my head away. The ugly boy was surrounded by clouds of steam. He had a rough red face, and a red knee sticking out of the towel. His shoulders and the top of his chest were covered with red blotches. He was staring at me, then the steam covered him up.

"Stop it right now," I said.

"What?" Mommy said. She had the bottle of purple stuff and was pouring it into the bath. The purple stuff was the stuff that was supposed to make my skin feel better in the water, but it didn't. It came in a thick brown bottle. It made the water feel very slick.

I watched the purple stuff float up under the water and spread out like a cloud of ink. Mommy stood up and pulled the towel away from me. The ugly boy appeared dimly in the mirror. All of a sudden, he crouched down and hugged himself. I squeezed my eyes shut. I felt with my arms out for the bathtub.

'Robbie!" Mommy said. "What are you doing?"

"I can't see."

"Well, open your eyes! You're going to hurt yourself."

I touched the edge of the bathtub with my hands and got into the bath quickly and sat down fast. The water felt slick and warm. I slid down up to my neck. Mommy gave me the brown soap. I slowly soaped my body. I washed the purple water up and down my arms and watched it slide in and around my rash.

After a while I decided to sit completely still. The water stopped moving. It seemed like a smooth gleaming piece of purple glass. Mommy sat on the toilet seat holding the big towel. She was whistling softly and staring at herself in the steamy mirror. I watched her reach up and touch her black hair. She had a white pin in it that was shaped like a butterfly.

I brought my toe up underneath the purple water and stirred slowly. The purple glass rippled. I stopped moving. The water splashed softly against the sides of the bathtub, then stopped. When it got quiet enough, I was able to think about the ugly boy who lived in the mirror. He was walking away from the cloudy front of the glass, back into the clear distance, into the blue mirror air. I thought that it would be like opening a window and walking out onto the sky. I closed my eyes. I wondered how far he would walk.

In the car on the way to the doctor's office, the snow was deep on the streets and piled up high around the curbs. The sun was bright, but it was so cold nothing was melting. The wheels of the car hissed as we got on the expressway that went downtown to the doctor's office. The snow had been shoveled off it and Mommy drove fast. She moved her legs up and down and looked into the mirror. She tapped her fingers on the steering wheel. Her eyes darted. We got off the expressway and went up another road and there were big buildings on either side of us and people crowding the sidewalks and spilling over into the streets. We stopped at a red light. A woman stood at the corner waving. I waved back at her. She ignored me. I waved again.

"I think she's looking for a cab, sweetie," Mommy said.

"Then she shouldn't be waving," I said.

We finally parked the car in a big lot and got out into the cold air. It was so fresh and sharp I could feel my scabs give a little tug. It was like they tightened up. Mommy took my hand and we walked together through all the rows of cars.

"My rash hurts," I said.

"We'll be there soon."

"It bites." It felt like a little animal was nipping and tugging at spots on me.

We came to a tall building and pushed into a revolving door that jerked around and spun us out into a big room that clattered with noise from all the people walking back and forth across its shiny floor. Men and women in thick coats stood in clumps and talked to each other and smoked cigarettes. The ceiling was way up high and there was blue smoke floating everywhere in the sunshine that came down from somewhere I couldn't see.

We went over and stood in front of a row of elevators. I liked the thing that had the floor numbers on it. It looked like half a clock. A big metal arrow told where the elevator was. It would catch on a number and then click down, catch and click down. I kept watching it.

Mommy was watching it, too. She smiled at me. "This is quite suspenseful, isn't it?"

The elevator opened and we crowded in. We had to push. I shoved ahead until Mommy grabbed me. "Wait. Stop it!"

She put her hands on my shoulders and turned me around and put me in front of her.

"I'm sorry," I heard her say to someone.

People pushed in after us and I was crowded back into Mommy. The elevator jerked up and my stomach sank. We went up and up and up. My ears got a tight feeling. It felt like all the air was coming into them through a pinhole. Then the elevator opened and we pushed our way out into a long corridor. It was very quiet, like the hallways at school between classes. There were doors up and down it that had white frosted glass tops with black letters on them. Across from the doors were windows that looked out onto a square empty place that wasn't outside and wasn't inside. It was just a place of air, where the building opened up. The air had strange grey light to it.

I ran over to the window and looked down before Mommy could stop me. As far as I could see there was nothing but the grey air and row after row of windows. I looked up, and I could see more windows. Way up, the air seemed to get lighter. The last time I was here, I had seen a pigeon circling and swooping. I looked for it now, but I didn't see it. I wondered if it had ever gotten out. I thought of it floating by itself in the grey air.

We walked down to the very end of the hallway and Mommy pushed a door open into a room that was twice as big our living room, with couches and chairs and big plants in the corners, and coffee tables full of bright magazines. There were kids all over, sitting with their mommies or playing on the floor, coloring or pushing toys. They were yelling and laughing and crying.

Two little boys ran past me to the drinking fountain. One of them nearly knocked me over and when he looked back at me I could see that he had a big purple place on his cheek that spread up to his eye and around to his ear.

Mommy and I went over and sat down on a couch near a tall green plant that had big flat leaves. There was a boy sitting next to us with crumbs stuck all over his cheeks. He picked at them. He was sucking his thumb and crying. His mommy put her head down and talked to him. She tried to take his thumb out of his mouth. The boy jerked it back. He had a crew cut and he was wearing a green flannel shirt and black pants and white socks.

He stared at me meanly. He looked like Goodie's brother would if he had crumbs on his face.

Mommy told me in a whisper to stop staring.

"He's staring!"

"Shhh."

I watched the crumb boy out of the corner of my eye. When his mommy wasn't looking he pulled off some of his crumbs and hid them under his chair cushion.

Mommy started reading a magazine. I got up and put my hands in my pockets and walked around the room. A little baby girl wobbled by, with her arms out and her fat knees shaky. Her mommy was following her. Her round cheeks shook and her eyes bulged. She smiled a silly smile. She had red corkscrew curls that stuck straight out. Her butt looked fat with her diapers.

My throat choked and I felt a funny tingling in my stomach. I wanted to hit her.

The little baby girl walked up to me with her arms held up high. Her face smiled wide. My mouth tasted like I had put a penny in it. She stumbled and her mommy reached down and swooped her up into her arms and carried her away. The baby girl didn't look back at me. She was cooing and playing with her mommy's hair.

I went back to the couch. Mommy was still reading. I sat down and kept thinking about the baby girl. I thought she was like some little animal that you could kill. I started to laugh. She was such a baby.

I heard the crumb boy snicker. I looked up to see a boy who was maybe two years younger than me standing in front of me. He had thin blond hair that was so light and yellow and fluffy he almost looked like a baby chick. He was wearing brown corduroy pants and a white long-sleeved shirt.

He held out a tractor to me.

The boy's face was a bright red. So were his hands. His skin all over was as red as a tomato. It was very smooth. There were no scabs or scratches or scales on it. It was just bright red, like he was sunburned.

His eyes were light blue. He stood there, holding out the tractor.

"Mommy," I said.

Mommy looked up and I felt her jump a little.

"Who's this?" she said. Then she smiled.

I didn't say anything. The red boy kept staring at me.

"Robbie, he's giving you something."

"I don't like him."

"Robbie!"

I took the tractor and held it. The red boy smiled. A tall brown-skinned woman in a checkered dress came up next to him and took his hand.

"Frederick," she said quietly. She spoke to Mommy. "Sorry. He don't really talk."

"Don't worry about it," said Mommy. "He wasn't bothering us."

I handed the tractor back to the red boy and he held it and looked at it as if he hadn't seen it before. I noticed that even the top of his scalp, under his hair, was red. As he walked away, holding onto the woman's hand, he looked back at me over his shoulder. He made me feel funny.

When they were gone, the crumb boy's mommy leaned over and whispered to Mommy, "They're from the Home."

"The Home?"

"Northville," the woman said. She sat back and nodded her head.

Mommy stared after the little boy. "He looks like an angel. A little boiled angel."

"He'll be a ward of the state all his life," the crumb boy's mommy said.

The red boy had gone back to sit with some other boys and girls his age. They were all wearing brown corduroy pants and white shirts, even the girls. They were quieter than the other children. The brown-skinned woman and a brown-skinned man were looking after them.

I watched Mommy watch them.

"What's Northville?" I asked.

Mommy shifted in her seat. She sighed.

"It's where children who are retarded go," she said. "They have something the matter with them when they're born. So they stay there."

"Don't they stay with their mommy and daddy?"

"Some of them don't have mommies or daddies, sweetie. And some of them need special help their mommies and daddies can't give them."

I snuck a look across the room at the red boy, who had his head down and was looking at his tractor. The little baby girl who could hardly walk waddled past him like a duck and picked a leaf off a plant and stuffed it into her mouth. Her mommy came running up and grabbed the leaf out of her mouth. The red boy didn't even look up.

I started laughing. Two stupid people! A woman standing across the room looked up and smiled at me. I saw that it was Nurse Nelda. She put a folder under her arm and walked over to us. I started to tingle inside. She knelt down in front of me.

"It looks like someone's in a good mood," she said.

She wore a white uniform that was crisp and clean and she smelled so fresh, like fresh sheets or pillowcases. Her hair was wavy and black, and her cheeks were pink. Her eyes glittered when they looked at me. I felt like curling up inside of myself.

The Snow Train

My skin leapt alive and began to crawl on me. I couldn't stop looking at her.

"I have a feeling he's quite glad to see you," Mommy said.

"That's just the way I like 'em," Nurse Nelda said. She held out her hand and I took it and stood up. We walked by the crumb boy, who squinted at us. It looked like his face had been mashed into a toaster. I was glad he could see me with Nurse Nelda.

We went through a door and down a short corridor that had little rooms going off of it. Inside them were boys or girls waiting on metal tables, wearing white paper robes. Their mommies were with them. Nurses came in and out the of rooms, carrying trays. Some of the doors were shut. From behind one of them, I could hear a boy crying. Someone was talking to him in a low voice.

We finally went into a room at the end of the corridor. It smelled like medicine. There was a metal table at the center of the room that had a white piece of paper over it. There were white open cupboards where all kinds of bottles and shiny metal objects lay on white towels. There was a white sink with a silver mirror above it.

The sun shined in through the window. I ran over and looked out. The view made me breathe faster. I could see the blue sky and the buildings across the blue sky from us and, far away, the dark river. I could see the bridge that went across to Canada. Canada looked very flat, with buildings that weren't as tall as ours, and a big wide plain that stretched out as far as I could see.

I loved being up high and on top of everything. It made me excited. I loved seeing Canada. I pressed my face hard against the window until I could almost see straight down to the little cars and people going by far below us.

"Open the window," I said.

Nurse Nelda and Mommy were standing talking. Nurse Nelda was showing Mommy her hand, where she had a big shiny ring.

"It's gorgeous," Mommy said.

"Open the window," I said to them.

"Nurse Nelda is getting married," Mommy said to me. "To a doctor like Dr. Benson."

"That's too bad."

They both laughed and I laughed, too. Nurse Nelda came up to me and put her hand on my head.

"Don't you want to congratulate me?"

"Congrats!" I held out my hand like Daddy's friend Sam Sullivan would. Nurse Nelda took it and I shook her hand really hard. I stuck out my chest.

"Open the window."

Nurse Nelda and Mommy laughed.

"Open it!"

"No one's opening any windows," Nurse Nelda said. She sat me up on the metal table and started pulling up my sweater. "Off," she said.

I started to laugh. I felt excited. The sweater went over my head.

"Open it!" I cried into the dark. My sweater came off and then Mommy helped Nurse Nelda take off the rest of my clothes. I felt like I was being tugged and pulled and jerked. My shirt came off and then my pants. I started to laugh when my undershirt caught on my head. Nurse Nelda laughed, too. She tugged and tugged. It got caught on my chin. It turned into a balloon. Finally, it popped off. My feet bounced up when my shoes and socks came off and my hands went up over my head to get my shirt off. I was like a little puppet. I began waving my arms around.

The Snow Train

"Shhhh," Mommy said to me.

I just had my underpants on. I watched Nurse Nelda. I could smell the nice way she smelled. I saw her dark eyes looking at me. She walked behind me. I felt her fingers touching my back light-ly. She pressed and poked a little, and I heard her sigh. My skin felt so good when she touched it. She was so clean.

She went into a drawer and got out one of the white robes and put it over my head. My rash shrank when the crinkly mate-rial touched it. The door opened and Dr. Benson came in. He was short and thick and he had white hair in a crewcut. He walked very fast towards us with his left hand over his chest pocket, which was full of pens and pencils. He always walked like that, as if he was afraid they were going to fall out all over the floor.

"Hello, Doctor," said Mommy.

"Hi," I said.

Dr. Benson came right up close to me and held out his hand in a very serious way. I shook hands with him.

"Hello, Clark Kent," he said, which was what he always called me. He was smiling a big smile. His teeth were very large. His skin was pink. He reached up and switched on a light that hung down from the ceiling above the table. It was very bright. He took my chin in his hand and bent down to look at my face. Mommy walked up close to us. She had her arms folded around her chest. She looked at me along with Dr. Benson.

"Jeannie, we're trying as fast as we can about that bed."

"It's just awful," Mommy said. "He's up half the night scratch-ing himself. He's stiff and sore all over. I can't let him out to play with the other boys. They tease him. I won't have him subjected to ridicule."

Dr. Benson didn't say anything, but he cleared his throat. He made me lie down and pulled up the gown to my waist. He picked up my legs, one at a time, and bent and moved them slowly back and forth. Then he got down very close and looked at my rash. The bright light made me squint. I turned my eyes away. I felt his smooth hands touching my feet.

"He's so brave," Mommy said. "Aren't you?"

Dr. Benson sat me up again. He pulled the top of the gown down. and looked at my shoulders. His head was close to mine. I felt his soft, warm breath on me. His hair brushed my ear. It felt dry and stiff, like the fur of a little dog. He picked up my arm and stroked his thumb along it. My rash shuddered. It was scaly by my elbows, and hard, like a dinosaur's skin.

Dr. Benson seemed to be thinking. He held my arm and squinted at it. The air in the room began to feel cold. The sharp bitter medicine smell made the rash hurt. I began to shiver, and Dr. Benson put my arm down and went over to the sink and began washing his hands with brown powder soap that frothed up over his big, thick thumbs and palms. He washed very carefully. I could hear him scouring his hands. It sounded like he was grinding them together.

He turned around with his hands wet and Nurse Nelda handed him a towel and then came over with my clothes and helped take off the paper gown. She put on my pants and shirt while Mommy and Dr. Benson talked in low voices.

Nurse Nelda had a quiet look on her face. She smiled at me but she didn't say anything, and her eyes weren't as bright as before. She tied my shoes as I sat on the table, and then leaned down and kissed me on the forehead.

"Bye-bye, sweetie."

"Okay," I said.

The Snow Train

She left the room and Dr. Benson and Mommy came over and stood by the table I was sitting on. Mommy put her hand on my shoulder as Dr. Benson started talking.

"Rob, this thing has been a monkey on your back for a long time, hasn't it?" he said. "You can't really play outside. You can't enjoy yourself. You can't even sleep at night. It's good we're doing something about it."

"It's just gotten to that point," said Mommy.

"I won't kid you, Rob," Dr. Benson said. "You've always been straight with me and I'll be straight with you. Your skin is an especially tough problem. We don't know why, really. We're guessing you don't have the things that keep these rashes away. What we call immunities. Remember I told you about them? They're what make Superman tick. They give him his power. Without his immunities, the kryptonite gets Superman. He's gotta have 'em.

"Right now, Rob, if you were Superman you'd be feeling pretty low. You'd be in a fairly weak state. That's why I'm recommending this blood-changing procedure, which is a very new thing. You'll be the first in this area to benefit from it. By taking the old blood out and putting the new blood in, we'll be able to add fresh, strong immunities to your system. You'll be leaping tall buildings at a single bound in no time."

He smiled his white smile at Mommy.

"Where does the blood come from?" I said.

"There's a pool," Dr. Benson said. "People donate theirs."

"Will it hurt when it goes in?" I said.

Dr. Benson snorted through his nose. He swiped his hand in the air like he was trying to grab a mosquito. "Hurt? Nonsense. You'll just feel—" He stopped and looked at Mommy. "Help me out here, Jeannie, you're the language expert."

Mommy seemed confused.

"Well, I don't know," she said. "I suppose it's basically like a transfusion, isn't it? You might just feel sort of a flowing."

"A flowing!" Dr. Benson said. "Perfect." He smiled with his white teeth. He patted his pens and pencils.

"Does it whoosh through?" I said.

"A whoosh?" Dr. Benson asked.

"It may not even be——" said Mommy.

"It'll be very quiet," Dr. Benson said. "We might even give you something to make you a little sleepy."

"I'm not afraid."

"Well, that's good," said Dr. Benson. He looked at his watch. "Since when is Superman afraid? And you'll be the envy of the other kids there. When they see how well this thing works, they'll all want it."

"What kids?" I said.

"On the ward. In the hospital. You'll have a lot of fun. There'll be kids in your situation to play with."

I thought of all the torn-up looking kids in the waiting room. I thought of the crumb boy and the red boy. I wondered if they would be there. My stomach began to hurt. Mommy helped me down off the table and went to get my coat. I walked over to the window and looked out again. Across from us there was another building with people walking around in it. I could see into a room with a lot of desks. There were men sitting at them with their shirtsleeves rolled up. They were wearing hats and typing. One of them looked just like Daddy. I waved at him, but he didn't see me.

I thought of people living in a room in the middle of the sky. I thought about walking across the sky to them.

Mommy and I said goodbye to Dr. Benson at the door.

The Snow Train

"No later than the middle of next week, Jeannie," he said. "I promise."

When we walked through the waiting room, the crumb boy wasn't there anymore, but I saw the red boy sitting with the other children from the Home. He looked up at me, and then immediately looked down. Then he looked back up again.

"Wave at him, sweetie," Mommy whispered. "He likes you."

I gave him a wave, because she made me. He didn't wave back, but he stared at me with his blue eyes wide.

Back at home, Mommy gave me a peanut butter and jelly sandwich and some pop, and I sat down on the old green couch with my pillows and my blanket. I had all my books around me and also my gun and my submarine.

"All set?" said Mommy.

"Okay."

She walked around and pulled the curtains and then turned off the lamps, except for the big one next to the couch. It gave off a circle of light that came down right on the couch's arm. I put my sandwich and pop inside the circle.

The coffee table caught my attention. Little dark glitters twinkled off its flat, black top. They seemed to come from inside it. I watched them carefully.

Mommy knelt in front of me. She cocked her head.

"Why so sad, sport?"

I didn't say anything.

"Robbie?"

I felt my eyes tear up.

"Sweetie, I need a little time to write now. It's only fair. Mommy spent the whole morning with you."

"I know," I said. I felt like sobbing. I gulped a little.

Mommy knelt down next to me. "I'm going in now. Tonight, I'll read you my poem. Would you like that? You're my best critic. We'll have dinner and you can give me your opinion."

There was a loud metallic click, followed by a hushed, hollow explosion—a *whoomph!* My heart jumped.

"What's that?" I cried.

Mommy laughed. "Sweetie, it's just the furnace starting up! My God, you're spooky today." She ran her hands through her hair. "I feel so guilty! I'll just be in the bedroom! I'm not going to the North Pole."

"I know," I said.

She pushed her face against mine. She nuzzled my cheek. "Can you ever forgive me? Oh, dahling, say you will!"

Her hair filled my face. I laughed and ducked my head. As soon as I laughed, she kissed me and got up and left. I heard her walking down the hallway, and then her door shut. I ate some of my sandwich. Typing came from Mommy's room. It went *tap-tap, tap-tap*, and then there was a single *tap*, and then it stopped.

I put my sandwich down and slid off the couch and stood in the center of the dark room, listening. The coffee table was shining. The glassy pictures on the wall gleamed with a dark gleam. I looked at the rocking chair and the overstuffed armchair. They were being very quiet. I started to go down the hallway towards the bathroom, but a long burst of typing came from Mommy's room. I froze. It seemed to go on and on, *tappity-tappity, tap-tap-tap-tap-tap, tappity-tappity-tappity, tap-tap-tap-tap-tap*.

She was in there with her hair tangled up, hunched over the big black typewriter. Her face was all closed in, and she was squinting at the paper like she was mad. Her fingers were flying.

The Snow Train

When the typing stopped, I went into the bathroom and got the photo album and brought it back out onto the couch with me. I took a bite of my sandwich and opened the album up on my lap. The light from the lamp streaked from picture to picture as I turned the pages. I stopped at one that I liked. The little girl was kneeling down and holding onto a playpen with both hands. She had a big rosy face. Her pigtails hung down over her shoulders. She was smiling at the little boy in the playpen. The little boy held a stuffed puppy. He was staring at her, with his mouth wide open. There were smears on his cheeks that looked like jam. His eyes were wide. He watched the little girl like he was amazed.

I wrapped the blanket close around me. I felt cold. The *whoomph!* came again. There was a rumbling in the basement and I trembled inside my stomach. The house began to breathe, I heard its breath rushing through the walls. The house had a heart. I could hear it beating. If I put my bare feet down, I would be able to feel it thumping through the floor.

I looked around the dark room. When the little girl was alive, the armchair and the couch and the coffee table had all been animals. They turned into furniture just to hide from me. But they could become alive again at any moment.

The coffee table was hard and black and flat. It could be some kind of strange thing, like a shark or an alligator.

A grunt or a sigh seemed to come from the rocking chair. As soon as I turned my head, I heard a dry, scraping sound from the coffee table. I knew without looking that it was moving towards me.

I blinked and saw that the rocking chair was rocking back and forth, fast. I stood up on the couch with the blanket around me. My heart was pounding.

"Oh, Mommy," I cried. "Mommy, Mommy!"

The doorbell rang. I couldn't move. It rang again. Mommy came running down the hallway. A pencil was sticking out of her hair above her ear. She opened the door and cold light burst in. Goodie was standing there wearing her big winter coat. Her cheeks looked rosy red.

"I'm here," she said. She smiled a big smile and walked past Mommy into the living room.

"Yes, you are," Mommy said. She stayed by the door.

Goodie stood in front of me. "Are you having a snack? Does your mommy let you stand on the couch?'

"Was this expected?" Mommy said.

Goodie looked down and blushed. "Yes," she said in a small voice.

Mommy closed the door. "I think it's nice you're visiting, Goodie. But you have to play very quietly. I'm doing some work in my room." She looked over at me. "Robbie, can you please sit down?"

I sat down.

"I'll take care of him," said Goodie. "I'll be very quiet."

Mommy went back to her room. Goodie took her coat off.

"Do you want to offer me a cookie?"

"We don't have any."

"That's a terrible lie." She walked around the room. "It's so dark in here. Dark and grim."

She stopped in front of the coffee table and raised her hands above her head and twirled slowly around.

"I might be a dancer." She smiled at me over her shoulder. "I think your Aunt Cecilia is so beautiful. She's like a model in a movie magazine. And she buys clothes for Hudson's Department Store! How glamorous!"

Typing came from Mommy's room, a soft *tap, tap-tap-tap, tap.*

The Snow Train

"You have such a glamorous family and you don't even appreciate them," Goodie continued. "Your mommy publishes poetry in the Detroit *Catholic*. Your father is *very* handsome! Hey, there's the painting I gave you! Why didn't you put it up in your room?"

Goodie walked over and took the painting from where it was leaning against the wall. She blew on it as she walked back. "It's dusty already."

She leaned the painting against the coffee table and sat down next to me on the couch. "Was your birthday wish for Rosie to come back? I know it was! Tell me the truth!"

"I don't like wishes," I said.

"If you wish hard enough, anything can happen," Goodie sighed. "Rosie and I used to play so much! We were the best of friends. We played and we played. I was playing with her on the day she died!"

She put her chin to her hands and stared at the picture. "She was a sweetheart!"

I didn't say anything. Goodie got up and went down the hallway. When she came back, she had a white towel over her arm. She knelt down on the floor in front of the painting and draped the towel over her head. She bowed her head and folded her hands and put them to her chin.

"Oh, Blessed Mother," she said. "Bring us back to our lives that we used to lead a long time ago. Help this doubting boy to cure his skin. He doesn't believe in you. Show us your way, please!"

She raised her hands in the air. Despite myself, I stared at the painting. The little girl floated high above the children on the sidewalk. Her eyes were open and she was staring up into the sky.

"Please, oh so long ago," Goodie moaned. "Please help us."

Mommy typed a little, just a *tap-tap*. Goodie folded the towel down off her head and got up from her knees. She sat down next to me on the couch and took the album onto her lap and spread it open.

"There she is." She smiled. "My mother said it at the funeral: an angel from heaven."

The little girl sat on a tricycle in front of a Christmas tree. She had pigtails with white bows at the ends. Her arms were twisted and her head was down. Her mouth was open. She looked like she was riding the bike as fast as she could, even though she was sitting still.

Goodie sighed a deep sigh.

"You were very little, Robbie. There were so many people there. Everyone was crying. Even the priest was crying! I was with her on her last day. She was going out to get ice cream. Bang! She's a little angel now."

Goodie looked sadly down at the pictures of the little girl. "I saw her in her coffin. Her head was swollen up and it had big stitches like railroad tracks! You were there."

"No, I wasn't."

"You were in a daze. All you could do was hold onto your mommy." Goodie lowered her voice. "The poor woman was never the same after that, they say."

She pointed to another photo. The little girl stood with a little blonde girl by the backyard fence. They were both very little, almost as little as the little baby girl in Dr. Benson's office. They had their hands up to their faces and were squinting in the sun.

"There I am!" said Goodie. "That was before you were born. That's how long I knew her. I know a saint!"

"No, you don't."

Goodie turned sharply to me. "Of course I do. Rosemary's a saint. What else could she be? She was baptized, wasn't she? She didn't do anybody any wrong. She's a saint! The Blessed Mother picks all the little girl saints." Goodie stared at the album. "She's a saint in heaven watching us right now. Can't you feel it? Ooohh!" She hunched her neck down and shook herself. "Her eyes are on us like tingles!"

The little girl stared out at me from the picture, but the sun hid her eyes. I reached over and shook the album a little. Goodie snatched it away. "Hey, what are you doing?"

"She's not looking," I said.

"What do you mean, she's not looking? She's looking!"

Goodie flipped through the album until almost the end. She pointed to a picture on the page: "There!"

The little girl held a basket of eggs. Her hair was cut short and her cheeks were fat and puffy. She stared straight at the camera, but she wasn't looking at anything.

Goodie put the album down and got down on the floor on her knees again. She pulled the towel around her head.

"Stop it," I said.

"Oh, Blessed Mother, please send this little girl back to earth to help her brother. She is a saint who can do anything. He's a sickly little boy who misses too much school with his bad skin problems. Other children laugh at him. He's never had any friends. He's horrible to look at."

Goodie's glasses gleamed. She began whispering. Her mouth was down to the tips of her folded hands. I couldn't hear what she said.

Mommy typed hard in her room. It was the sharp fast pecking kind of typing, *tack-tack, tack-tack, tack-tack, tack-tack*. It sounded like she was stabbing the paper.

Goodie pointed to a picture of the little girl sitting on the back of a pony. She wore a brown corduroy jumper over a white blouse with big collars. Mommy held the reins. They were both waving. I thought that the little girl looked heavy and mean.

Goodie held up the album to me. "Try and look at her picture. Just try it and say a prayer."

I ignored her.

"What if you die?" she said. "What if you die while they're changing your blood!"

My stomach felt hollow.

"It's possible," said Goodie. "Sometimes death runs in families. Sometimes God picks out the children to take back first. And you haven't even made your First Communion!"

Goodie knelt back on her heels. Her blue eyes moved softly behind her glasses. Her mouth opened halfway. "If you die, you'll go where Rosie went. Both of you to the same part of heaven. You'll join the holy orphans of heaven." Goodie bowed her head again. She folded her hands. She squeezed her eyes tight. "Please, Blessed Mother."

"It's time for you to go," I said.

Goodie looked like she was having a dream.

"The best time for you to die, though, is just *after* you make your First Communion. The second after! You're so pure."

"You don't know anything!"

Goodie got up and began walking around again. She picked up what was left of my sandwich and sniffed it.

"You don't like Deanna, do you?" she said.

"I like her better than you."

"I can't kiss you because you're younger than me and you have that awful skin condition. Otherwise, I might do it."

"I don't want you to kiss me."

Goodie turned red and dropped the sandwich. "I forgot that I wanted to tell you something. My mom says your mom swallowed a seed and is having another baby. Maybe it'll be Rosemary. Maybe she's coming back to punish you for being so mean to me!"

"That's not true."

Goodie laughed. "That's how much you know. Your mom has a baby moving in her stomach right now."

"I don't care."

"Yes, you do!" said Goodie. "It might be Rosie. Watch out!"

We were both quiet for a while. Then Goodie got up and walked over to the window and poked her head through the curtains.

"Why do you keep it so dark in here?"

She pulled the curtains around her so that I couldn't see her. She was just a bulge.

"Oooooh," she said. "I'm a ghost!"

The bulge wiggled. I got up and went over and hit it hard with my fist. There was a gasping sound. The curtains started wrinkling and shaking. Goodie's head poked out. Her face was beet red. She was hunched over and holding her cheek. Her glasses were half off her face. She got up and walked in a crouch over to the couch and sat down on the edge of it.

"My head hurts," she moaned.

I didn't know what to say. The typing came out from Mommy's room louder and faster, *tack-tack-tack-tack*, *tack-tack-tack*, *tackety-tackety-tack*, over and over again. Goodie pushed herself off the couch with one arm and grabbed her coat. She walked over to the door, still holding her face. Tears were spilling down her hand. She tugged at the handle, but she couldn't get it open. I went over, but she gasped and backed away from me.

"I'm not doing anything," I said.

I opened the door for her and she ran out. I watched her go.

She headed straight across the snowy street to her house, not even looking for cars. She stumbled as she ran up her front steps.

That night I sat on the couch next to Gretl, waiting for Mommy to come in. Gretl sat very close to me with her paws tucked underneath her and her whiskers brushing my pajama leg.

Gretl was a calico cat. She was black and orange and white in patches all over her. She even had little black patches on the pink insides of her ears. The tip of her tail and her paws were white. When she walked, she disappeared into her patches and you couldn't see her at all, just her colors moving.

I petted her hard and made her eyes roll back in her head. I put my hand under her chin and held it up. Her eyes looked like they were floating in water. She pulled her head away and stared at me out of the corner of her eye. I leaned down and touched her nose with my nose. She jerked away.

Mommy came into the room with her blue bathrobe on. I watched her stomach to see if I could see it move, but there was nothing but her thick robe. She was carrying a piece of paper in one hand and a drink in the other. She put the drink down on the coffee table and stood in front of me.

"Ahem," she said. "Are you ready?"

"No!"

"Very droll." Mommy put her glasses on and looked at me over the top of them. "Constructive criticism only, please. This is called 'Don't Forget the Salt.' It's for the Cooking & Home page of the Detroit *Catholic.*"

She began to read:

The Snow Train

The ancient Etruscans used it
So did the barbaric Galt.
Celtics and Carthaginians
Druids, Scots, and dread Numinians
Called upon their savage gods—
For just a pinch of salt!

The fierce and mighty Cook Islanders,
Cannibals to a man,
Relished just a dash of salt
To perk up their frying pan!
The proud and handsome Amazons
When the cooking pots were brought
Were known to turn their baleful eyes
Upon the keeper of the salt!

I hear you call, barbarians,
From your feasting in the sky.
I watch your wrinkled brows
As you raise your heavy goblets high:
You can forget the pepper, the cumin or the malt
But whatever you do, my saucy lass
Don't forget the salt!

Mommy finished reading and took off her glasses. She did a little bow. I didn't say anything.

"It's supposed to be light humor. I didn't hear you laughing, pal."

"Look, see the pretty children go," I said.

Mommy stuck her fingers in her hair and pushed it back on top of her head and held it there, like she did when she was amazed. She stared at me. "Where did you hear that?"

"What?" I said.

"Those words you just said."

"I don't know."

I didn't know. The words seemed to come to me in a voice I knew, a voice I always knew. But I didn't know whose voice it was.

Mommy seemed very serious. She looked down at the poem and frowned. "Oh, well."

"What words are they, Mommy?" I asked her.

Mommy dropped her hair and it flopped back down over her forehead. "That's amazing, really, It's the beginning of an old poem of mine. You must have heard me say it sometime."

"Say it for me now," I said.

Mommy shook her head. "I don't write poems like that anymore," she said. "I just write funny ones."

I didn't say anything. I actually didn't see what was so funny about her poem. I liked the way the other words sounded better.

"Were they really cannibals?" I said.

"The Cook Islanders?" Mommy came and sat down and took a sip of her drink. "I believe they were."

She reached up to her ear for her pencil, but it wasn't there. She looked around the room. Her eyes had a blank expression. She began stroking Gretl from her head to her tail, very hard. Without warning, Gretl jumped off the couch and ran under the dining room table and stood there, staring back at us.

Mommy put her little finger to her lip and bit at her nail. "Cats want to be friends, but they're very stubborn."

"You were petting her too hard."

Mommy drank from her glass and didn't say anything.

"They like to be petted just right," I told her.

"I've been petting that cat since before you were born," she said. "It was my cat to begin with, buster."

"Can we watch television now?"

She put the paper down and sighed. "I guess we can." She

looked over at me. "How are you feeling? Are you sore?"

"I'm okay."

She put her arm around me and pulled me close to her. "Nothing is going to happen to you, you know that? *I'm* not going to let it."

I thought about what Goodie said. I thought of me dying in a coffin with my head swollen up. I snuggled in tighter against Mommy. I felt cold all over.

"It just breaks my heart to see you like this," Mommy whispered. She kissed the top of my head. "It simply breaks my heart. And we're going to do something about it."

Mommy got up and went over and turned on the television. She came back and sat down next to me and put her arm around me again and I leaned into her. I thought of Mommy swallowing a seed and having a baby inside her. I wondered when she could have done it without me knowing. I knew that Goodie was lying, but I pressed my head against her side, anyway. I heard gurgling and squeaking noises. I wondered if that was a baby talking. To get away from the noises, I snuggled further down and put my head in Mommy's lap. A loud man with a straw hat was talking on the television. Mommy scratched my head lightly with her fingernails. I could feel the roughness of her bathrobe against my face. The tv flickered up and down. Blue shadows floated over us. I closed my eyes.

"Look, sweetie," I heard Mommy say. "Sweetie, look!"

I raised my head up. A man with a monkey was on the television. The monkey was on a leash and the man was making him hop from a stool to the floor and then back again. That's all the monkey did. It kept jumping in the flickering blue light. Another monkey came out wearing a skirt. It hit the other monkey on the head with a little umbrella. The monkeys began running around in circles. The audience was laughing.

I couldn't stand the monkeys. The expressions on their faces reminded me of the crumb boy. I sat up. When I did, Mommy put her elbows on her knees and her face in her hands and leaned forward to stare at the television. I watched her. I thought for a second that I didn't recognize her. She had her head turned and she didn't seem like anybody I knew.

Sometimes I wondered how I knew everybody I knew. Mommy and Daddy, Aunt Cecilia and Sam Sullivan. I wondered what they were like before I knew them, and where and how it had all gotten started.

Grown-ups like Aunt Cecilia just acted like they knew you and you knew them, but how had it all started? At what point did everybody become familiar?

Mommy got up and turned off the television. She stood and yawned and stretched. "I don't know why I get such a big kick out of those chimps."

"I think they're stupid."

"And I think it's time for you to get to sleep. We've got a big day tomorrow with Daddy coming home."

"I liked your poem," I said.

She smiled at me. "I don't know if you did or not. To be perfectly truthful with you."

Her eyes started to poke inside of me. I turned my head away.

"I liked the barbarians," I said.

"That figures."

We went into the bedroom. After she put my medicine on, she kissed me and turned off the light and went out, closing the door behind her so that there was just a crack open. I lay and looked at all the dark shapes around me. They never changed. Every night I lay there, and every night it was the same—it might as well be the same night. I thought of Mommy saying this morning, time should just disappear. No one would know what time it was.

I thought of the long-time-ago past. It stretched back. It was like a long blank space, like the empty air where the pigeon floated outside Dr. Benson's office. The words came to me again: *Look, see the pretty children go.* They wouldn't go out of my head. *Look.* I could hear Mommy moving around. Water was running. A few minutes later, I thought I heard talking. Once I heard her laugh. I was mad at her for talking to Daddy without me, but then I fell asleep.

After a while there was cool air flying through the bedroom from the crack in the door, the cool dark air that the house sent out at night, after everyone was in bed, sent out directly to me.

There was something coming at me in the dark.

"Huh!" I said. I hunched up. The moving thing came through the dark room very quickly, but just as it got to me, it disappeared. I could feel the air that it moved when it disappeared.

After a while I heard my voice. It woke me up, but it wasn't really me talking. It was just my mouth moving.

Where did the little girl live? I was saying. *She lived by herself. She lived behind the couch with her dolls.*

My words wouldn't stop. They tumbled out of me. I twisted and tossed to wake up.

She came out when no one was at home. She lifted her chin and stared out the window. Her chin was grumpy. She was by herself and put her hands high on the glass to see out. Look see. Look see!

I was swimming up from inside a sleep that was holding on to me with fierce hands. I finally broke the surface, and realized that I had stopped talking. The words I was saying floated back down deep into the place where I had been sleeping, where the fierce hands were.

3.

Daddy and Sam Sullivan's plane, when it finally came down from the sky, was grey and had a big nose. It was fatter than I thought it would be, fat like a bumblebee was fat. When it stopped and turned around, it swung its tail behind it first. Its propellers were going very fast, but the plane moved very slowly. It just crept along. It stopped right underneath us.

Aunt Cecilia and I were upstairs in the glassed-in place where people watched the planes coming in. Mommy was downstairs at the gate, waiting.

"It seems like they could devise a way to get people off airplanes faster," said Aunt Cecilia. "The longest part of this whole business is waiting for the stairs to wheel up and the door to open. It's enough to make you want to strangle somebody."

She dropped her cigarette on the floor and snubbed it out with her shoe. She jammed her hands into the pockets of her fur coat.

"Maybe they could just rip open the top and pull them out with a crane," she said. "What do you think?"

"I don't know," I told her.

Two men in overalls pushed the stairs up against the plane. They were long steel stairs with a curving railing and black steps with rubber on them. One of the men climbed up and knocked on the door with a wrench. A woman wearing a little narrow hat

opened it and said something to him and they both laughed.
Breath like grey smoke came out of their mouths. I noticed that
it was very grey everywhere. The runway and the sky and the
planes that hummed down from the sky were all grey. I blinked.
I reached out and touched the window. I thought that maybe the
glass itself was grey.

Aunt Cecilia lifted her hair out of her collar with both hands
and let it fall down her back. It looked like a shiny red river of
hair. She pulled out the little mirror from her purse and made a
face at herself and said: "Cripes." She snapped the mirror shut and
grabbed my hand. "Let's mosey, shall we?"

We went down the stairs and stopped halfway to the bottom
so we could see out over the heads of the crowd of people waiting. They were shifting back and forth on their feet and craning
their necks and talking to each other. The passengers started to
come through the door from outside. They were mostly men, with
hats on their heads and coats over their arms and briefcases. The
crowd made a little corridor to let them go through.

I thought that the men seemed aware of everybody watching
them. They kept their heads down and some of them whispered
to each other and smiled, as if they had a secret they had brought
with them from where they had traveled, a secret that none of the
people waiting knew about.

I saw Daddy. He had his hat thrown back on his head and
his white raincoat over his arm.

"There's your pa, but where's our man Sam?" Aunt Cecilia
asked.

Daddy walked a little apart from the other men. He was shorter
than they were, and he stood very straight, with his chin held up.
When he got into the middle of the crowd, he stopped, put his

briefcase down and took off his hat. He looked around. The lights made his black hair shine.

"Shit!" said Aunt Cecilia.

She was looking at the plane, which was standing with its propellers still in the grey air. I saw Sam Sullivan walking down the steel stairway talking to the woman wearing the narrow hat. He was holding her arm.

I looked back at Daddy and saw Mommy standing right next to him. I didn't know where she came from. She threw her arms around him and gave him a quick kiss. He squeezed her tight with both arms and said something in her ear.

I jumped from the steps and dodged through the crowd. I lost sight of Mommy and Daddy and got caught in all the people. I had to start shoving to get through. By the time I got to them, I was out of breath.

"Hi!" I said to Daddy. He was holding hands with Mommy.

"Hi, champ." He put his other hand on my shoulder and squeezed it. Standing up close to him, I could see that his suit was rumpled, and that his face looked rough. But he smiled at me. I started to put my arms up, but then he didn't hug me and I put them down. I stood there a second, and then started talking.

"Look," I said. I jumped high in the air. "Yay!"

"Rob, you're rarin' to go," Daddy said.

"I'm all wound up," I told him.

Mommy stared at the doorway. "Where did Sam go off to?"

"He's coming down from the plane," I said. "I saw him talking to that woman."

"What woman?" Mommy craned her neck. "Where?"

I started to feel stirred up inside. I wanted to tell Daddy a lot of things, but when I opened my mouth, I didn't know what to say.

"Look what I got for my birthday, Daddy."

"What's that, Rob?"

He stared down at me.

"I didn't mean to say that. I meant, *guess* what I got for my birthday?"

I jumped in front of him and walked backwards. Then I came back and leaned up against him and put my head on his side for a second. "I got a lot of stuff."

"I know you did."

"Here he is," Mommy said.

Sam Sullivan came through the door still talking with the woman. He was holding a bottle that had a red ribbon around its neck. The woman gave him a wave and walked past us carrying a little round suitcase. I could smell her perfume.

Sam came up. He was very big and tall and had a lumpy red face and bright blue eyes. When he saw me he smiled and threw his arms out wide.

"Bee-u-tee-ful," he said. "Kid, you're a sight for sore ones."

He squeezed me to him hard. I could feel his stomach going up and down. His shirt smelled sweet and smooth and warm. He pushed me back and stood with his hands on his hips. He took off his hat and brushed his brown hair off his forehead.

"He's the cat's canary, ain't he?" Sam looked at me and slowly shook his head. "He's the real tuna."

"I'm not a tuna!"

"You're the *big* tuna," Sam said. He lifted his chin. "Where's Celia?"

"No doubt in the ladies' room," Mommy said. "What's the occasion?" She pulled the bottle out of his hand and looked at its label.

"Midwest Regional Ford Salesman of the Year," Daddy said. "Slick here took all honors."

Mommy held the bottle up. "The finest California champagne!"

"What's she doing way over there?" said Sam.

Aunt Cecilia stood across the corridor from us in another waiting place. She had her arms folded tight around her. She was smoking a cigarette as she watched people get off a plane.

"Those aren't the right people," I said.

Sam Sullivan sighed. He picked up his briefcase and walked over to her. He took her by the elbow and tried to kiss her, but she jerked away. She kept her elbows folded and smoked her cigarette in short little jabs.

"Why does she have to make such a fuss?" Daddy said.

"Why does he have to manhandle stewardesses right in front of her?" Mommy said.

Daddy laughed. "That's just Sam. He can't help himself."

Aunt Cecilia had put out her cigarette and was talking very fast to Sam while he shuffled his feet and stared at the floor.

"Well, he's being reminded of just that right now," Mommy said.

But by the time we got the suitcases, Aunt Cecilia and Sam had already made up. They were walking at the same time as hugging each other, and they kept bumping into each other.

"Hey you two," Daddy said in a gruff voice. "Break that up!"

They laughed. Aunt Cecilia ducked her head into Sam's neck. He brushed his brown hair back from his eyes. They were both so big. They had big hands and feet and their overcoats were thick on them. They took up a lot of space.

Next to them, Mommy and Daddy looked like small, dark, miniature people, with little mouths and noses, like my toy soldiers, neat and trim.

The Snow Train

We went out the doors into the cold grey air. Aunt Cecilia and Sam both stopped and lit cigarettes, and then kept on walking, holding hands. I walked between Mommy and Daddy. The world was filled with everyone going places. The planes flew in so low that I thought I could see the people in the lighted windows staring down at us through the grey air. Cars stopped and people leapt out and ran into the airport. Horns honked. I liked it all. I liked looking at everything, and having everything fill up my head.

We got to our car and put the luggage in the trunk. Mommy gave Daddy the car keys and they sat in front, and I jumped into the back with Aunt Cecilia and Sam on either side of me. We drove out of the parking lot and pretty soon we were on the main road. Aunt Cecilia and Sam shifted and pressed their legs against me. Their coats felt smooth and thick. Both of them yawned and stretched at the same time, and I heard Aunt Cecilia giggle. They breathed so much the windows were a little steamy, even with the heater on. I leaned my head back and realized they had their arms locked behind me on the top of the seat.

We were out by the farms, and there was white snow frozen in the ruts in the fields. Cars carrying people from the airport were all around us. They were crowded with kids and suitcases. One car even had a black and white dog pressing its face against the back window. The men driving the cars leaned forward intently and stared at the road. We all drove along like this for a while. I wanted the cars never to leave us. I thought that we were all keeping each other company. I thought that maybe we could all be one family driving together, forever.

Snow started falling. Daddy turned on his windshield wipers and his headlights. The farmhouses were little bunched-up dark buildings far away from the road. Sometimes there was a light on, and I wondered if a family was there together, sitting in a room and watching tv.

I wondered if it was possible for all of us in our car to be a family. I thought maybe that Mommy and Aunt Cecilia and Daddy and Sam Sullivan could all be my parents and that I could be their kid.

I began to feel warm inside. I felt like talking.

"There's that hill where we go sledding sometimes," I said to Sam. "In California do they have any sledding? There probably isn't any snow."

"There isn't any snow, but they go sledding anyway," Sam said. "They can't slide down those rocky hills that fast, though. The rocks get in the way. The rocks come up and bump them hard."

In my mind I saw the kids bumping down rocky hills on their Flyers.

"It makes an awful noise," Sam told me. "They scrape something fierce." He put a cigarette to his mouth and lit it and cracked the window. "Squeaking and scraping. The kids just pop straight up in the air like popcorn."

"Wow."

I felt Aunt Cecilia's leg move next to mine. "Give me a butt, Charlie."

"His name isn't Charlie."

"Tall-tale Charlie, give me a butt," Aunt Cecilia repeated. "What other tall California tales have you got, Slick?"

Sam Sullivan grinned and turned red. He searched through his pockets and handed her a cigarette and a book of matches. Up in the front of the car, Mommy and Daddy were sitting close together, their small dark heads staring forward without saying anything.

The Snow Train

Usually, Mommy sat on her own side of the car, but today she was huddled up next to Daddy. I could see part of her face in the rearview mirror. It looked round and sly. Her eyes seemed to be half-closed.

I sat back against the seat and watched Aunt Cecilia put her cigarette to her lips and suck smoke in, and then blow it out. Her hands were long and white, with red nails. On her right hand, she had a small ring with green and white jewels in it. it looked like a little checkerboard, only in a circle. The cigarette smoke curled around me. I loved its warm, dry smell. I kept watching Aunt Cecilia's hands. I began to think about what it would be like if she were Mommy and she was putting medicine on me. My eyes closed. Mommy's hands were wrinkled, but Aunt Cecilia's were smooth. I thought about her rubbing the medicine in, stroking me in circular motions. I was lying on the bed. Maybe the rash would just disappear, and my skin would be as white and smooth as her hands...

"Champ," somebody whispered. "Hey!"

I opened my eyes. Aunt Cecilia was leaning over me. The car had stopped. It was dark outside and things felt topsy-turvy. I looked through the window and saw a house with a roof that rose to a peak. Snow-covered bushes surrounded a little front porch. There was a person already walking up the walk, bundled in a coat, and I realized that it was Mommy. We were home.

I let Aunt Cecilia help me out, and we walked to the door as Daddy and Sam Sullivan drove the car further up the driveway. When we got inside, Aunt Cecilia went into the kitchen and I took off my coat and sat down on the couch. I felt my rash changing on my body, like it always did when I went from cold to warm. It loosened and began to prickle and itch. I rubbed my pants legs with both hands until Daddy and Sam Sullivan came in the front door. They took off their coats and put them in the front closet and came and sat down. Sam lit a cigarette.

Daddy sat on the edge of his chair and reached out to the coffee table and picked up a magazine. "I missed my *Life*," he said, flipping through it.

I went and stood by his chair and looked over his shoulder. "There's a lot of pictures in that one," I told him. "That's the one with the kids that have the big treehouses. Look."

There were some kids in Florida whose father had built them treehouses in their backyard. The trees had moss hanging from them and were very big and old. The treehouses looked just like regular little houses, and they were connected by wooden walkways with railings. Each of the three kids had his own treehouse, and they would go back and forth and visit with each other on the walkways.

I watched Daddy looking at the pictures.

"It took him three years to do it," I said. "He worked on weekends, but you have a job on weekends."

"He's a very handy guy, apparently."

"I wish we had even just one."

Daddy laughed. "I wish I could build you treehouses like this, Rob, but it would take me from now until Kingdom come."

"Still, I would like it."

"I know, Rob, I know."

He started leafing through the rest of the magazine. I leaned against the side of the chair and watched to see what pictures he looked at. There was a picture of the President meeting and shaking hands with someone, and he stopped and looked at that for a second. There were a lot of ads for big shiny cars, but he didn't really pay any attention to those, like I thought he would.

The Snow Train

For some reason he stopped at an ad of a woman wearing an apron and holding a box of cereal. She was standing in a sunny kitchen in front of a table where a little boy and girl were having breakfast. The kids were blonde and their faces looked like apples. Their mother was smiling a big smile, as if something she was seeing made her very happy.

Daddy held the ad up to the light. The sunlight in the kitchen was amazingly yellow. The page glowed under the lamp.

Daddy seemed strange sitting there holding the magazine so stiffly, with his elbows in the air. I reached out and tried to turn the page for him.

"Rob," Daddy said.

"There's nothing on that page."

"I'm looking at that breakfast nook. What if we moved and you had a kitchen with one of those?"

"I don't think we're moving, are we?"

Aunt Cecilia carried in a big silver tray with bottles and glasses and a pitcher full of ice on it and put it down on the coffee table. Daddy came over to make the drinks. I stood next to him and watched him. First he rolled up his sleeves. Then he poured from the bottles into a little silver cup, and then poured from the cup into the pitcher.

"Can I go to the lot with you tomorrow?" I asked him.

"Sure you can, pal. There won't be much going on there in this weather, though."

"That's all right."

Mommy came in with a bowl of potato chips and a plate of cheese and crackers. She handed me a glass of Coke. I grabbed it and drank as fast as I could. It felt cold and harsh going down. When I was done with half of it, I burped.

"Ahhh," I said. I sat down on the couch.

"Sweetie, let Sam sit where you are," Mommy said. "You sit in the middle. He needs the ashtray."

I was in my favorite spot by the arm of the couch and the big floor lamp.

"He can reach," I said.

"Robbie!"

I slid over to the middle and Sam and Aunt Cecilia sat on either side of me. I didn't like it. There was nothing to lean against and the middle cushion was too soft. I felt like I was sinking in. I had to reach too far for my Coke.

Daddy put a little metal strainer over the top of the pitcher and carefully poured into four glasses. He put olives in three glasses and a little onion in one. He picked the olive glasses up by his fingertips and handed them one by one to Sam and Mommy and Aunt Cecilia. He kept the onion for himself. They all smiled at each other and drank from their glasses. I did, too.

"Here's mud in your eye," said Sam.

It was quiet for a second.

"Well—" Mommy started to say.

"Mommy wrote a poem," I said.

"That's great," Daddy said.

"I did, too," said Sam. He stretched his big shoes out in front of him and hooked them under the coffee table. "There was an old lady from Flint, so poor she was constantly skint—"

"Sam!" both Mommy and Aunt Cecilia said.

"She went to the bank, gave the teller a yank, said there, that's worth a mint!"

I started laughing and Sam reached over and tickled me.

"Hey!" I said.

"No more," Mommy said. "I mean it, Sam."

"All right, all right," said Sam. He winked at me. "It's poetry. I thought you'd appreciate it, Jeannie."

Mommy made a face. "It's not any poetry I've ever heard of."

Aunt Cecilia was watching Sam. She took a drink of her drink. "See any movie stars out there in sunny California?" she said to Daddy.

"Well, Slick here met Audrey Hepburn," Daddy said. He lifted his chin and popped his onion into his mouth.

"He did not," Mommy said.

Sam grinned.

"Oh, God," said Aunt Cecilia. "You did not!"

Sam Sullivan poured himself another drink. "She got out of her limo, and I happened to be standing in front of the hotel. I just said hello to her."

"Why didn't you sell her a car, Mr. Midwest Regional Ford Salesman of the Year?" Mommy said.

"I was too busy admiring her."

Aunt Cecilia had a little smile on her lips. "While you were so busy, did you happen to notice what she was wearing?"

Sam stared at his drink. "No, actually, I didn't. A long evening dress and some kind of jacket, I think."

"What designer? Givenchy?"

Sam pursed his lips and looked at me sideways. "You're the expert," he said.

Aunt Cecilia crossed her legs and tugged at her skirt. Her face looked very long and skinny.

"Everyone's some kind of expert to him," she said to Daddy. "According to him, the world is full of experts."

"He's a car expert!" I said.

"That's right," said Sam. "I am."

"So what kind of shape was she in, Mr. Expert? Nice chassis? Motor run good?"

Daddy smiled at me. "I haven't seen those birthday presents of yours yet, Rob."

I jumped up. "I'll go get them."

"Why don't we go see them in your room?"

As we walked down the hallway, I heard Aunt Cecilia laughing hard.

"Your Aunt Cecilia is one of the moodiest creatures I've ever known," Daddy said. "She jumps from one to the next, bing-bang-boom!"

We came to my room and went inside. Daddy turned on the light switch.

"When she was a little girl was she like that?"

"I think she was actually worse when she was a little girl. She's calmed down a bit."

I went over to my toy box and brought out a bunch of my toys and spread them out on my bed. I put out the soldiers and the mitt and the submarine. I looked up to see Daddy walking around the room. He seemed nervous to me. He bent down and pushed the curtain aside to look out the window. Then he sat down on the other bed and picked up one of the dolls and held it in his hand and rubbed its head with his thumb.

"Don't you want to see these presents?" I said.

"Whoops," Daddy said. "Sorry."

He came over and sat down at the foot of the bed. I showed him how the Civil War soldiers had bayonets on their rifles, and how some of them were made lying down, so they could hide better, and how some of them were squatting. Daddy looked at everything and smiled. He agreed with everything I said, although he didn't play with anything by himself. We could hear laughter from the living room. When we were done talking, Daddy smiled and walked over to the window and looked out again.

"Are we going to move?" I said.

"I didn't know you were so attached to this old barn, Rob."

"I like it here."

"We all like it here, but we're going to need more room."

"I don't think that we are. I like it here."

"Sure you do."

"Then why would we move?"

Daddy turned away from the window and pinched his nose between his fingers. His face seemed dark and sharp. "There might be some memories here that are better off left memories," he said, finally. He turned to me and shoved his hands into his pockets. "It might be good for all of us if we got away from this house, Rob. It might be that this is the time for us to do that."

"What about me?"

Daddy looked at me. "What about you? You're coming with us, Rob. Do you think you're staying here by yourself? Setting up house?"

Before I could say anything, there was a crash from the living room. It sounded like a dish. I heard Sam shout something, and Aunt Cecilia laugh.

"Why don't we go check out what this crew is up to?" Daddy said. "We may be the only sober ones in the bunch."

When we got to the living room, Aunt Cecilia was sitting where I had been sitting on the couch. She had her shoes off and her feet curled underneath her. She and Mommy were talking in loud voices. Sam was standing by the coffee table shaking the cocktail pitcher. He saw us and shook it harder and harder. The ice rattled and clinked. Sam shuffled his feet.

"Comin' right up, suh!" he said. "Uh-huh! Uh-huh!"

"What I don't understand is why it's *anyone's* business," Aunt Cecilia said to Mommy. Her cheeks had pink spots in them. "Why don't they just——"

"Celia, they're sensitive to——" Mommy said.

"Sensitive people are morons," Aunt Cecilia said. She leaned forward and held out her empty glass towards Sam. "They get in the way! They muck up the works!"

"Celia, they're your mother and father."

Sam poured a drink into Aunt Cecilia's glass. He did it very carefully. His face was flushed. "I think what she's saying, Jeannie, is that whenever certain O'Conor elders get together, they confab about why Sam and Cecilia ain't hitched. It gets to be——"

"Well, why ain't you hitched, Sis?" said Daddy.

Aunt Cecilia squinted at him. She brushed smoke away from her face.

"We're not married because we're not married," she said. "That's not the point. The point is——"

"I understand very well your point," Mommy said.

"And your point is, you agree with them," Aunt Cecilia said. She flopped back against the couch. Her drink splashed up in her glass. "That's so typical. Married women want everyone to get married. It's insulting!"

"Now, gals," said Daddy.

"There was a young gal from LaSalle," Sam began, "in need of a chum or a pal——"

"Christ!" Mommy said. She put down her drink and got up and went into the kitchen. Daddy went in after her. I stood there in the living room. I heard Mommy and Daddy talking loudly in the kitchen. Smoke curled around past my face. Aunt Cecilia came up to me and put her arms around me. "Aww, Robbie, I'm a jerk. Give me a hug."

"It's okay," I said, but she hugged me anyway. She hugged me too tight. She smelled very sweet.

"You're my favorite, you know that?" she said.

Mommy called her and she went into the kitchen.

Sam was sitting on the couch looking at the page in *Life* that Daddy had liked, the one with the sunny kitchen and the rosy kids and their mommy.

He snorted. "Look at these chumps."

I laughed. "They're morons!"

"I'll say!"

Sam kept reading the magazine. Aunt Cecilia came out into the dining room wearing an apron. She started putting dishes on the table. I got up and went into the bathroom and shut the door and sat down on the toilet. I took the album out from the magazine basket and flopped it open on my lap. I looked for one picture that I didn't usually look at a lot. In it, the little girl was sitting on Daddy's lap and smiling a wide smile. She had her pajamas on and her feet stuck straight out.

Daddy had his arms around her. His chin rested on top of her head. He was smiling straight out at the camera.

I held the picture close to my face and stared at the little girl. This time, she was looking at me. Her eyes stared into mine. She was smiling, but her eyes were hard. They had little white pieces of light in them. I kept looking at her. She kept staring at me.

My heart started pounding. I dropped the album on the floor.

When dinner was over, I took the dishes out into the kitchen while they all talked in the dining room. After I stacked them up in the sink, I went down the steps into the little room by the back door, where everyone's boots were kept, and where our winter coats and hats and scarves hung on pegs. It was cool there, and I could feel the nighttime outside. Below me the long stairs stretched down to the dark basement.

I pressed my hand against the glass in the door. I could feel the cold from outside. I could smell it growing under the door, seeping in. It was like a little ghost coming in, a ghost of cold air.

I stared at the door. The thought came to me that it was very old. I touched its wood with my fingers.

I walked back up the steps and into the kitchen. The plates full of chicken on the counter looked like animals had been at then, the meat all broken down with the bones sticking out. I went over and stood in the dining room doorway. I could see the side of Mommy's face where she was sitting on her chair. She laughed. Her face gleamed like snow. Daddy smiled at her.

Sam Sullivan stood up and held his glass high.

"The ladies!" he cried. His face was big and puffy. "Long may they reign!"

Mommy and Daddy threw their heads back. Their mouths were wide open. Aunt Cecilia wiped her eyes. Her face was red.

Daddy saw me standing there. He looked at Mommy. She turned to me and smiled. "It's about that time, sweetie."

"I know," I said, but I didn't go anywhere.

They all looked at me now. They had smiles on their faces. Their smiles held as they stared at me. When I was gone, they would go back to talking and laughing and drinking.

"Brush your teeth good, sweetie. I'll be there in a sec."

The Snow Train

Sam Sullivan was reaching for a cigarette and I caught his eye. He winked at me.

"Good-night," I said.

"Sleep tight, pal," he said. Aunt Cecilia blew me a kiss.

I stood there for a second longer, then walked away through the kitchen. I heard somebody say something in a whisper. Aunt Cecilia laughed.

In the bathroom, I stood at the sink and brushed my teeth and thought of them all together in the dining room. Their laughter seemed to get louder. In my mind, I saw that they were all like animals. Mommy and Daddy were little dark animals, Aunt Cecilia and Sam were big, sloppy animals. None of them cared about anything but themselves. They just did whatever they wanted to do. They didn't ask me, they just decided for themselves. They pretended to listen to me, but they didn't.

I thought of the car ride home from the airport and how I thought they could all be my family. It was a joke and I was stupid. How could I be their boy?

I spat out into the sink. As I did, I noticed that the white porcelain was gleaming. I thought maybe the hushed white light was coming back. I looked around the room and thought there might be a glow spreading. I couldn't tell for sure. It was possible.

"It could happen," I said.

As I watched the water swirl around the sink, I thought of new blood in me. I thought of it flowing through me and of how I would feel when my old blood was washed away. I thought of myself without any scabs or sores. I thought of myself flying.

I turned suddenly to look at the full-length mirror on the door. I surprised the ugly boy in it. He tried to duck, but froze when he saw me looking at him.

I saw the scratches and scabs on his forehead. I saw his big blocky head. I saw his eyes that stared at everything.

I could hear the animals outside. They had moved into the living room, and their sounds even closer, their roaring sounds. I saw the roaring and the smoke coming out of their mouths. Their laughing was like smoke.

I walked closer to the mirror. The ugly boy had on a pair of blue jeans rolled at the cuffs and a blue flannel shirt with black checks. The cuts and scabs were like little red and black zippers on his face. The long thin scratches were from the nails of animals.

"It's all right," I told him.

He was smiling, now. He looked surprised.

I woke up suddenly in the middle of the night. A strange shudder went through my rash. The room was very dark, and the covers were on the floor again. I was freezing cold and I needed to go to the bathroom. I got up and went out the door and down the hallway. The light was on in the living room. I stopped and listened and thought that I heard a whispery noise, like sighing. I tiptoed past the bathroom and peeked into the living room. Sam was sitting on the couch and Aunt Cecilia was sitting on his lap. She had an apron on and her hair was up in a bun. The whispery sound was them kissing and their clothes rustling. Sam had his mouth up like a little baby bird and Aunt Cecilia was leaning down and kissing him with little sighs.

Sam's face was bright red. His hair was rumpled.

I watched them for a while. Aunt Cecilia hummed as she kissed Sam. She pulled up his chin with her hand and gave him soft kisses on his forehead and eyebrows and on the tip of his nose.

"Little baby kisses," she said. She played with his hair and twisted it into curls. "Baby baby kisses."

Sam grabbed her by the back of the neck and kissed her very hard. They were pushing their mouths against each other.

"Hey," I said.

They didn't hear me. Sam fell over and pressed Aunt Cecilia back into the couch cushions. Her legs went up in the air and she giggled. Sam reached down and pulled at her dress. She hit his hand. He rubbed her bottom and started pulling at her dress again.

"You'd better stop that," I said.

"Huh?" Sam said. He looked up, but he didn't see me. His eyes were like they were blind.

"Shhh," Aunt Cecilia said to him. She wrapped her arms around him and began kissing him hard.

I turned around and walked back into the bathroom. I stood by the toilet and tried to pee, but I couldn't go. The tip of my thing was starting to hurt. I stomped my foot. Finally, a little came out, and then some more. I began to feel better as my pee filled the bowl up. When I was done, I flushed and went out the door. I heard a scramble from the living room, and then Aunt Cecilia peeked her head around into the hallway.

"Robbie, what in God's name—"

"I had to go to the bathroom," I said.

She walked up to me. She was smoothing her dress with her hands.

"Oh," she said. "Well, that's all right."

She swayed a little bit. Her hair was falling out of her bun, and her lips looked smeary. "Sam and I are just getting ready to leave," she said. "Your mom and dad went to bed."

"I know," I said. "What are you doing?"

"We're talking, sweetheart. Isn't it time for you to go to bed? We're going to wake up your mom and dad."

"*You* might wake them up. I'm not going to wake them up. I'm not making noise."

"Shhh-shhh, sweetie, I know that. Do you want me to tuck you in?"

"Where's Sam?"

"He's getting ready to go, hon. C'mon, let's get you to bed."

She put her hand on my shoulder and tried to turn me around, but I shrugged her off.

"You shouldn't have been kissing him."

"Robbie!"

"He's not a baby," I said. "Why were you giving him baby kisses?"

Aunt Cecilia turned bright red. Sam Sullivan came out behind her with his hair all rumpled up. "What's going on, sport?"

"He's upset," Aunt Cecilia said.

"I'm not!"

"Shhh!"

They both tried to grab me, but I turned around and went back into my room. I shut the door behind me hard and got under the covers and huddled up with them tight around me. I heard whispering and thought they might try to come in. But in a little while the front door closed and Aunt Cecilia's car started up on the street. I closed my eyes and tried not to think about anything.

4.

The next day was Sunday and Mommy and Daddy and I got up early to go to Mass. After I got dressed, I walked into the living room and looked at the couch. It looked deep and rumpled to me. I thought I could still smell Aunt Cecilia's perfume.

There was so much snow outside the window it seemed like we were stuck at the North Pole. Mommy and Daddy came in with their coffee and sat down on the couch. They had their good church clothes on, Daddy with his dark suit and Mommy with her long rustling blue dress. I thought they looked like strangers dressed up to go out.

They leaned forward and put their cups on the table at the same time. Daddy cleared his throat and started to say something, but Mommy interrupted him and reached out her hand. "Robbie, come sit."

I went and sat down next to them and she leaned over and gave me a kiss and put her arm around me. Her face had the round moon satisfied look it got when she had a secret she liked.

"Sweetie," she said, "remember when I asked you if you'd like to have a new brother or sister?"

"No."

"Come on, now. In the bedroom the other morning after Aunt Cecilia spent the night?"

"Yes," I said.

"What did I say?"

"You said it would be somebody for me to play with."

"That's right," said Mommy. "But more than that, it would be somebody you could show the ropes to. Sort of take care of. Remember?"

I didn't say anything.

Mommy took a deep breath. "Robbie, I'm going to have a baby. Just think! It's wonderful news!"

"Why?" I said. There was a burning in my chest.

"Because we want to have another child to love just as much as we love you," Mommy said.

"Families are brothers and sisters," Daddy said. "Rosemary died, but we need to be a family again. You need to have a brother or a sister, Rob. It's not good to grow up an only child."

I began to see a baby in my mind. It looked like the little baby girl in Dr. Benson's office. I started to laugh. "Would it be a little girl?"

Mommy smiled at me. "It might. Would you like a little sister? Deanna Starling *has* become his little friend," Mommy said to Daddy. "Did I tell you about that?"

"The little girl in the pictures," I said.

"What?" Daddy said.

Mommy squeezed me close to her. "Sweetie, I know you wonder about Rosie and think about her. You like to look at her pictures. And that's fine. You just have to—" She stopped. "Well, you know, sweetie. It's perfectly okay if you want to talk about her."

"I don't look at any pictures."

"Sweetie, you've got the album there in the bathroom."

The Snow Train

"I don't look at anything!" I shouted.

"Hey, buster," Daddy said. "Just calm down now."

"Okay, okay," said Mommy. "Stop. Everybody." She looked at Daddy. "This is big news all around. I think we all need a little time to digest it." She stood up and glanced at her watch. "We're going to be late for Mass, Tom."

Dad stood up, too. He seemed mad to me. He put his hands on his hips. They were both looking down at me. They smelled like their church clothes.

"The little girl—" I said, and then stopped. I was trying to explain it, but I couldn't. It was just a joke.

"I was just kidding," I said.

Mommy leaned down and hugged me and held me tight. She kissed me hard on the forehead. "Stop being so serious."

When we went outside it was like opening the door of a giant freezer and stepping in. Everything was white and frozen. People were coming out of houses up and down the street, all bundled up in hats and coats and scarfs. The dads got into the cars to warm them up first, and then the moms and the kids came down the steps and climbed in.

Mommy came out and stood next to me on the porch, puffing little clouds of air. She was wearing her bright red coat with the fur collar, and she had a black purse that hung from a long strap. She had her little white round church hat on, and the tips of her ears were red. She smiled and waved across the street at Goodie and her family. They were standing there while their daddy brushed snow off the car.

Goodie's mommy waved back, but Goodie and her brother didn't. I suddenly remembered hitting Goodie. Her brother stared at me with his hands stiff at his sides. I could see his big rock head, all prickly with his black hair. I thought of his fists flying at me in our bathroom.

There was a rumbling as Daddy pulled the car down the driveway. He honked the horn and we went down and got inside. I scooted along the back seat, which was was icy cold. The car seemed big and hollow. Daddy backed us out and we bumped up the street through the snow ruts. All around us, the brick houses looked like they had been pelted with snow, like a thousand kids had thrown snowballs at them. The pine trees and green hedges were so full of snow they could barely stand up.

Mommy turned around from the front seat and put her chin down on her folded arms and looked at me. Her eyes twinkled under her hat. I could tell that she wanted me to be in a good mood.

"Aunt Cecilia and Sam were kissing on the couch last night," I said to her.

"What?" Mommy laughed and looked at Daddy.

"I saw them! She was giving little baby kisses. Baby kisses! Mmmm-smack!"

"Don't look at me," Daddy said. "I thought they'd already left."

"He was lying on top of her," I said. "Bee-u-tee-ful!"

"Robbie, that's quite enough." Mommy's face didn't look moon round anymore. She turned around and sat down hard in her seat and we didn't say anything more until we got to the church parking lot. We pulled in behind a long line of cars and drove slowly across the icy cement. As we waited our turn, I looked across the street at the black cinder school playground, and the school building, made of old red brick. It looked cold and hard, hard enough to break my head against. I saw the incinerator where the janitors burned the garbage and felt a knot of fear in my stomach. The incinerator was made of grey cement blocks and shaped like a little hut, with a door and a smokestack but no windows. It was full of black ashes and broken glass. It was where kids went to fight, where the Sisters couldn't see them.

One time I watched two kids fight. The bigger one pushed the other one in there, climbed in, and slammed the door shut behind them. After a while, the big one came out and dusted his hands and walked away. He was followed by the little boy, who was crying. His shirt was ripped and covered with soot. His tie was pulled tight so that the knot was very small. When one kid beat up another, that was what he did, to show that he had won.

We finally parked and got out of the car. Families walked past us, with their heads up and their faces rosy. Their voices were hard in the cold air, and their boots made a crunching noise in the snow and ice. Car tires squeaked all around us. Daddy kept stopping and talking to everyone he knew. Mommy smiled at them, but didn't say much, and I could tell she was still mad at me. I tried walking very close to her as we went up the church walk, but she didn't pay any attention to me. One time I grabbed her coat, but she pulled her arm away.

Inside the door of the church were the red-faced old men in suits. Daddy shook hands with them, and they patted his back and smiled at me and Mommy. We took holy water from the big stone bowls and put it on our foreheads. It felt thick and smooth and heavier than water usually felt. The church was dark and glowing at the same time. Dull gold lights hung along the walls, and the air smelled like smoke and incense.

Mommy and Daddy walked down the aisle, past the confessionals, and got into the pew right behind Goodie's family.

Goodie's daddy half-turned to Daddy and gave a little wave with his hand. He smiled at Mommy and winked at me. He had black hair cut into little prickles like his son, and a chunky face like a chipmunk. He had thick black glasses.

Goodie knelt up on the kneeler. She knelt very still in her yellow dress. She had her hands folded straight up. Her brother turned around and pretended to be getting his prayer book, but when Mommy and Daddy weren't looking he shook his fist at me. His eyes were black and shiny. He elbowed Goodie and whispered something and she turned just a little sideways and looked at me with just one eye. It was watery and red. It flicked at me.

At the back of the church a woman began singing, and everyone stood up. The priest came out from behind the altar, followed by the altar boys. They walked fast, with their robes flying. The priest stood with his arms raised. A strange voice saying hard words came out of him, and the altar boys knelt and bowed their heads.

I looked at Mommy. I saw that her hand covered Daddy's hand on the pew. I watched their hands together. Mommy had a little ring with a diamond on it. Daddy had his big gold and red college ring. The rings gleamed together. Their hands were plain and white and still.

Goodie stood in front of me holding a white-and-blue prayer book tight in her hands. There was a ribbon in her hair. She was tiny and blonde. Her brother hunched over next to her.

I felt like I was floating. I looked off to the side at the little dark altar where the Blessed Mother stood. In front of her was a black iron stand with glowing candles in red and green glass holders. The Blessed Mother had her arms outspread and her head cocked in a funny way, almost like it was resting on her own shoulder. Her eyes were half-closed, and she smiled a little smile.

She looked like a moron.

When we sat down for the sermon, the Blessed Mother started shining inside her stone and the light that came from her was like the light in our bathroom. I felt a tingle down my spine. The priest's words were very strange. I thought he might be talking to me. I tried not to look at the Blessed Mother. I looked at Goodie sitting in front of me. I counted the hairs fuzzing up on her head. She had a halo of light blonde hairs above her regular hairs. Her hair was so shiny. It glowed like the deep gold lights on the church wall.

I felt everyone around me moving, standing up and sitting down, and I did just what they did, but I was staring at Goodie.

When I looked at the altar again the priest was holding the Host way up high. His sleeves fell back from his arms. A bell rang. It rang inside of me and shook me up. The priest began eating the Host. It was very big so he broke it first, and then stuck the jagged edges of it into his teeth. It was so quiet I could hear it crunching. It was like a bone he was snapping inside his mouth.

The altar boy held a gold tray under the priest's chin. The priest drank some wine, wiped his teeth off with a cloth, and threw the cloth to the altar boy. I looked over at the Blessed Mother again and she was still smiling like a moron.

The bell rang again, and everybody put their prayer books down and started leaving the pews to go to Communion. They did it like they were sleepwalking. Row by row, they went out into the aisles, walked to the back of the church, and then came back up the center aisle, heading for the altar. They walked very slowly, with their heads down and their hands folded.

Goodie's family went out of their pew, and then it was Mommy and Daddy's turn. They left without even saying goodbye. They shuffled with everyone else. Mommy had her head down, but Daddy stood very straight, with only his chin bent down.

The only people left in the pews were some very old people and a few kids like me who hadn't made their First Communion. I watched the priest move slowly from person to person at the altar rail. It was making me sleepy, the way he did it, over and over again. The people started coming back from communion with their mouths full and their eyes very sad. They were very silent. Their cheeks were sucked in. They looked far away.

I started looking at a little girl who was walking up the aisle, putting one foot in front of the other very carefully. She had her head so far down she was staring straight at the floor. Her folded hands covered her face. Her brown pigtails hung over her shoulders. They had two little white ribbons at their ends. Her frilly pink dress stopped at her knees and I could see the pink socks on her legs, and her shiny white shoes.

She turned to look at me, and her pigtails swung, but her face was still covered by her hands. I wondered how she could walk with her face covered up like that, and why she didn't bump into anything.

I closed my eyes. When I opened them again, the little girl was sitting at the end of our pew. She was staring down at a big book she had open on her lap. Her pigtails hung down straight and stiff like they were frozen. They didn't move at all. The book didn't move. The book didn't seem to have any pages. It seemed frozen in her hand. Her mouth was frozen, too. Her lips seemed very thick to me. Her eyes looked blank.

She didn't move, just like the statue. She was a little statue sitting there.

The Snow Train

The kneeler shook and sagged as Mommy and Daddy knelt down next to me.

"Sweetie," Mommy mumbled. "Move over!"

She was mumbling because she had the Host in her mouth. She nudged me.

"Stop it," I said.

Goodie and her whole family came back and knelt down in front of us. Goodie looked at me as she went by, just with her one eye, and I nodded at the little girl. "Look! Look!"

Goodie frowned at me fiercely. Her lips started moving. She looked like she was sucking on her cheeks. She turned red. I wondered why the little girl bothered her so much. I turned around to see, but the little girl was gone.

When the Mass was over, we walked along the cold sidewalk outside the church with Goodie's family. Goodie kept flicking her eye at me. Her brother walked behind me and started stepping on my heels.

The grownups were ahead of us in a little clump. Goodie's brother came up very close behind me. "Moron, I'm going to kill you," he whispered.

"I didn't do anything," I said.

Goodie's daddy put a pipe in his mouth and smoke smelling like cherries drifted back to us. He walked with his hands behind his back. He was a teacher at the high school, and he and Goodie's brother worked on projects together in their backyard.

"Congratulations are in order," I heard him say.

"A blessed event," Daddy said.

"Wait until those diapers," Goodie's mommy said. "Not so blessed then."

Mommy smiled and shook her head. "It's blessed. I don't care how many diapers."

"Of course it is, Jeannie," Goodie's mommy said. "Of course it is."

Mommy turned to look back at Goodie. "Have you heard the news, Goodie?"

"It's very nice, Mrs. O'Conor," said Goodie. "Rosie is going to be so proud!"

The grownups were silent for a second, and then Daddy said, "I'll bet that's right. I'll bet she would be proud."

"She's looking down from heaven right now, isn't she?" Goodie said to Mommy.

"I suppose," Mommy said. She seemed mad. She pulled her coat tighter around her and walked on ahead. Goodie's brother pushed in closer to me. He kept squeezing in on me. I could smell his thick smell, it was full of meat, he smelled like the steaks when Mommy put them out on the counter before dinner.

He shoved me and I nearly fell over. Before I could say anything he grabbed my arm tight and dug into it with his fingers.

"Stop it," I said. "Let go."

I struggled to pull my arm away from him, but he wouldn't let me. There were people all around us, walking to the parking lot, but no one paid any attention. The clump of grownups got farther away. Goodie stopped from a distance, and watched us with the flash of her hard tiny eye.

Goodie's brother pushed me again, and then let go.

"Tomorrow I'm going to beat you up at lunch hour," he said. He seemed almost friendly, like we were both in it together. He was smiling. He slapped and rubbed his gloves together.

"You're bigger than me." I could hear the tears in my voice.

The Snow Train

"You're in the fifth grade!"

"It has to happen," Goodie's brother said.

"I didn't do anything."

"You punched my sister."

"No, I didn't."

Goodie's brother shoved me again and this time I fell over. I hit the snowy sidewalk hard and a sharp pain went up my elbow. A woman walking beside me on the sidewalk jumped out of the way.

"Hey, you two!" Goodie's mommy yelled from way up the sidewalk. "Stop roughhousing! Let's get a move on!"

Goodie's brother ran away. I got up slowly and brushed myself off. Grownups walked all around me. They didn't look at me. I knew that none of them could protect me. I huddled into my coat on the sidewalk. I felt like turning and running into the street.

I raised my head and saw Mommy standing by herself in the parking lot, looking back at me. I could tell she was wondering what I was doing. I ran as fast as I could, and caught up with her. I threw myself against her.

Her arms came around me. Tears started up in my eyes. I knew that Goodie's brother would be watching, but I didn't care.

"Hey," Mommy said. "I love you, you know." She hugged me very tight. "Both of us get good and mad, don't we?" She laughed a little bit to herself. "Your sister was the same way."

I wished she wouldn't laugh. I pressed against her red coat. The whole sky had somehow gotten inside my head, and was spinning there.

"Just because I have another child doesn't mean I won't love you just as much, Robbie," she said softly. "In fact, I'll love you even more. I'll have to depend on you."

"That's not true!" I said into her coat.

"Yes, it is true." She pushed me away from her and held me

at arm's length. She took my chin in her hand and wouldn't let go of it. "Look at me."

I twisted my head away.

"C'mon, look at me."

Her fingers pushed my chin up. I stared at her. She was staring down at me with a question in her green eyes. "What little girl were you talking about this morning?"

I ducked away again, but her hand forced me up.

"Nothing," I said.

Mommy let go of me. She pushed my hat firmly down on my head. "Are you sick?" She zipped my jacket up tight. "You're acting so oddly. Do you feel okay to go to work with Daddy?"

I looked across the parking lot full of frozen cars. There were white clouds tumbling under the grey sky. The sky seemed too wide.

"I don't know," I said.

"Sweetie, you know what? It's good for you to be with your Dad sometimes. Why don't you go along with him."

There was nothing I could do. I stood there as Mommy got into the car with Goodie and Goodie's family. She sat in the front seat with Goodie's daddy. Goodie's mommy sat in back with the kids. Goodie's daddy backed the car out with his pipe in his mouth. Mommy turned around gave us a little wave, and smiled.

Daddy and I walked over to our car. The parking lot was very quiet now. I could hear singing coming from inside the church. The voices were faint. Daddy stood there for a second listening with his chin raised high in the grey air, as if the singing was coming from the clouds.

On the way to the lot, the sun flashed out of the grey clouds and into our dirty windshield. It went right into my eyes and made me squeeze them shut. When I opened them it had gone away, and the streets looked even greyer. Dirty snow was piled up high on the curbs. We passed the old wooden stores owned by the Italians, the tiny little stores and the wooden houses behind them where they lived. They had little statues in the front yards, all spreading their hands to the sky.

Daddy turned the car into the lot and we parked and got out. The dealership was a long flat building with big picture windows. Inside, I could see the shapes of the new cars. In the back lot, the used cars sat covered with snow. The wind was starting to blow hard and the blue and white flags on the light poles made a buzzing, flapping noise.

When we got inside, I stood by the door while Daddy pressed some switches and the bright ceiling lights came on with a strange crackling sound. Streaks of light swirled through the big cars on the floor. The cars were red and black and blue. Some of them had white tops and bands of silver chrome down their sides. They were packed in very closely, with yellow pieces of paper pasted to their side windows.

Across from the cars was a row of little offices, very tiny ones. They only had room for a desk and a chair and a filing cabinet, which were all made of grey metal. The offices were where Daddy's salesmen sat.

Daddy went into his office, which was at the very end of the row and twice the size of the others. He sat down and opened his briefcase, still wearing his coat and hat. He turned on the lamp.

"The heat'll kick in in just a second, Rob," he yelled.

He took some papers from a tray and put them in front of him. The light kept him in its bright little circle and made his skin look very pale. He didn't look up again.

I walked over to my favorite car, which was called the Skyliner. It was colored white and blue and it was on a turntable, with spotlights that made it glow. Sam Sullivan had once told me it was his favorite car, too. It had big round red taillights like cherries and its top folded like an accordion onto the back hood. Its steering wheel caved in like a big deep bowl, with the horn right in the center.

On the turntable was a life-sized cardboard cutout of a woman wearing a flowing dress. She seemed to be dancing. A balloon came out of her mouth that said, "Try the Skyliner! America's most *romantic* convertible!"

I climbed up on the turntable and opened the Skyliner's door and sat down behind the wheel. The car smelled sharp and new. I sat there and held the wheel. Sounds came from the quiet and got inside of me. Daddy's adding machine clicked. A car whooshed by on the street. The road seemed to hiss a long time after the car was gone. It made me feel sleepy. I lay down on the seat. Above me, through the front windshield, I could see the cutout woman smiling out the window with her arm in the air. She seemed very real to me. I waved my hand at her. I thought her smile got bigger. I closed my eyes.

I woke up to the sound of voices and saw Sam Sullivan talking to Daddy in his office. I watched them through the windshield of the Skyliner. It had gotten almost dark outside, and the light on Daddy's desk glowed yellow. I got out of the car and walked over and stood in the doorway.

Sam was puffing a little. His face was redder than usual, and spikes of his hair stuck out from under his hat. He had his coat pulled tight around him.

"Oh, to be in sunny California," he said.

Daddy smiled. "You're back in the Midwest now, son. This is where things get serious."

"Things are very serious at the moment, old chap," Sam said. He rubbed his face with both hands, and his skin folded up like rubber. Daddy laughed and shook his head.

Sam looked over at me. "How goes it, sport?"

"I'm okay," I said.

"Good. Any coffee around here?"

"There might be some in back," Daddy said. "What time did you kids leave last night?"

"Way too late." Sam went out the door and down the hallway. I followed him to the back of the dealership, where there was an old coffee pot sitting on a hot plate. He picked up the pot, but dropped it. It clanged on the floor. Coffee grounds fell out.

"Bee-u-tee-ful," he said. He wiped his forehead with his hand. "Jesus H. Christ."

"Are you sick?" I said.

He jumped. "Don't scare me like that, Rob."

"I'm sorry."

Sam stood there slumped a bit with his coat still on, looking down at the coffee pot. He finally pushed it under a desk with his foot and reached into his overcoat pocket, and brought out a small bottle. He poured some into a paper cup. He took a drink of it and made a face. I walked up close to him and looked at the bottle. It had reddish brown liquid inside of it. The label had a picture of a king on it. I picked the bottle up. It was heavier than I thought it would be.

"Careful, kid," Sam said. "You could drop that."

He took the bottle from me and put it in his pocket. He

stood there for a second staring down at the cup on the table. He took off his hat and pushed his fingers through his hair, which looked greasy. I watched his face. It had folds in it that flopped over, like the skin on a dog's face.

Sam took another drink from the cup and smacked his lips. He bumped his hand against his chest and gagged. His face flared red.

"Excuse me," he said. "Oh, shit."

He put his hand to his mouth and hurried out of the room and around the corner. I heard the door to the bathroom slam. I waited a little while, listening to the click of Daddy's adding machine. Then I walked around the corner and went into the bathroom. It was just a little bathroom, with one urinal, a toilet stall, and a sink. As soon as I was inside I smelled a bitter, sharp smell. I saw the soles of Sam's shoes under the door of the stall.

There was a great big sound, like an "Awww." I heard Sam talking to himself. It sounded like he was crying. I leaned against the wall and waited for him. After a while, the toilet flushed. The shoes moved and then the stall door opened.

Sam Sullivan came out covered with sweat. It was dripping off his face. It had soaked into his shirt under his open coat. In the tiny bathroom he seemed even bigger than he usual. He staggered to the sink, braced himself, and looked in the mirror. He shook his head. His hair was all over the place. He turned on the faucet and washed his face and then rinsed water into his mouth and spat it out.

He turned around and nearly bumped into me when he went to get a paper towel.

"Robbie, God," he said. "You're following me today."

"Are you sick?"

"Not feeling too well, I must admit, chief."

"You should go home."

The Snow Train

"Don't tell your Dad, okay, Rob? He might just get worried."

"I saw you and Aunt Cecilia kissing last night," I said.

He rubbed his face hard with the paper towel. His cheeks looked burned. "Yeah, I guess," he said. He laughed. "God, we must have put on a show—"

"You shouldn't have been kissing like that."

Sam was looking at me differently.

"Robbie," he said.

"I tried to stop you, but you didn't hear me."

"Robbie, you may be a little young to understand this, but—"

"You were on top of her!" I yelled. He was making me very angry.

"Okay," Sam said. "Okay. Shhh."

He came over and crouched down and looked his face into mine. He smelled sharp and acidy. His eyes were curious. He put his arm out and touched my shoulder. "Robbie, what's the matter, huh? What is it?"

I didn't want to, but I started to cry. I put my arms around him and hugged him tight. He patted my back. "Hey, champ. Hey, now. What's goin' on here?"

I kept on crying. It just poured out of me.

"What is it, kiddo?"

He had his arm around my shoulder. The rash on my face hurt from pressing it against him. I broke away. I wiped my eyes with my sleeves. I couldn't look at him.

"There's a kid who wants to beat me up," I said.

"Oh," said Sam. "Aha!"

He seemed happy, for some reason. He nodded his head up and down.

"A big kid," I said. "Bigger than me."

"That jerk! Why is he after you?"

"He says I beat up his sister."

"Did you?"

"I didn't touch her! He just wants to beat me up. And he's a lot bigger than me. He's in the fifth grade!"

Sam shook his head. "That's not fair. That's a guy who's a bully."

"He is!"

"That's right, he is. The question is, what are we going to do about it?"

"He's going to beat me up at lunch hour tomorrow," I said.

"Now, that's no way to think, Rob. You gotta think positive. You gotta think you're gonna beat *him* up!"

"Why don't *you* come and beat him up? Daddy would let you out."

"I can't do that, Rob. You've got to learn to fight your own fights."

Anger filled me. I felt like I was going to start shaking. He didn't understand. It was so easy for him to say.

"No, I don't," I said. "I can't. He's going to hurt me."

Sam shifted nervously. He put his hands in his pocket. They hit against the bottle he had in there. He pulled it out and looked at it, and then put it back in. He took off his coat and hung it over the door of the stall. He was wearing a green sweater underneath and khaki pants. He pushed up the sweater sleeves and crouched down. "Robbie, I'll tell you what—"

"No," I said.

"Wait a minute, let me tell you. How about if I teach you a few punches? A way to box? That way you won't be so scared. You'll be able to fight back."

167

"I don't like to fight."

Sam stayed in his crouch. He put up his fists. "Look. This is the basic defensive stance. When he comes at you, this is what you do."

"What good will that do?"

Sam crouched down lower. He started to circle around me.

"Stop it!"

"Robbie, I'm not doing anything." He held his fists up high. "Put your fists up. You can't fight without putting your fists up."

I put my fists up. He reached out and turned them around so that my knuckles were facing him. "Higher," he said.

I held them up higher, until they almost covered my face. Sam circled me with his fists moving just a little bit. I backed up.

"Not back, around," Sam said. "Circle."

I circled, but I bumped into the sink. He seemed to get closer to me. His eyes moved and a light tap landed on my right fist.

"Hey," I said.

"Hit me," he said. "Go ahead."

I slapped his fist and started laughing. I backed away.

"No," Sam said. "Try to punch me."

His hand reached out and tapped my shoulder.

"C'mon, Rob. Just toss me one."

I hit his fists a couple more times. They were like big rocks at the end of his arms.

"That's right, sport. You got it!"

Sam reached out and suddenly his fist was right in my face. He just touched my cheek. He did it with his other fist. I felt his cold knuckles tap me.

"Stop it," I said. I put my fists down. Tears came up in me. "Why are you hitting me?"

Sam stood up. He put his hands on his hips. "Rob, when someone's coming at you, you have to hit him or be hit. Now, what's it gonna be?"

We stared at each other. I didn't know what to say. It seemed hopeless to me. The door opened and Daddy walked in. Sam smiled nervously.

"Can anyone come to this conference?" Daddy said. Then he wrinkled his nose. "Robbie, are you okay?"

"It's me, Tom," Sam said. "I had to let go of some lunch."

Daddy scratched his head. "Jesus, Sam."

Sam's face turned redder. "No more of those martoonis, pal."

"I guess not," Daddy said.

"We were just having a little learner's boxing match," Sam told him.

Daddy looked surprised. "Is that right?"

"I guess," I said.

"He's a regular little scrapper, isn't he?" Daddy said.

"He's going to be fine." Sam smiled at me.

"Rob, if you're done with your lesson, your Mom is going to be wondering why we're not home," Daddy said.

"Okay."

We walked out of the bathroom together, with Sam following us. The cars on the floor seemed to shine very bright. We put on our coats and Daddy packed up his briefcase.

"Turn out the lights when you go," he said to Sam. "And lock up."

Sam laughed.

"Yessir," he said. "Yassuh!"

Daddy and I walked outside. It was very dark and cold. We got into the car and Daddy started the engine and let it sit to warm up a bit. Through the big window of the dealership, we saw Sam walk out onto the floor and stop by the Skyliner. He reached under the turntable and pulled the switch. The big car started moving around in slow circles. Sam touched it with the tips of his fingers as it went past.

Daddy smiled. "He does love that car, doesn't he, Rob?"

I watched Sam. He put his hand in his coat and pulled out his bottle and drank from it. He was staring at the cardboard woman in the flowing dress. Dad gave the horn a honk, and Sam jumped and ducked. Even through the window I could see that his face was red. It was like he had been caught in another world.

5.

The next morning I tried to get Mommy to laugh, but she wasn't in a very good mood. I sang to her as she sat at the kitchen table and read her newspaper.

On top of old Smo-key,
I had me some fun.
I shot my poor tea-cher,
With a sub-ma-chine gun!

I went to her fune-ral,
I went to her grave.
Some people threw flo-wers,
I threw a gre-nade!

When I got to her cof-fin,
She wasn't quite dead.
So I took a ba-zoo-ka,
And blew off her head!

When I finished my throat was dry and I took a drink of milk. Mommy put down the paper and shook her head.

"Where in God's name did you learn such a gruesome song?" She looked up at the clock and sighed. "Sweetie, please don't dawdle so much. What in the world is the matter with you?"

I put down my spoon and stared at my oatmeal. The truth

was, I was cold right down to my bones. I had been cold under the covers in the early morning and had gotten up cold and looked out at the bare trees and the dark frozen backyard and knew I wasn't going to get any warmer all day. It seemed hopeless to me.

"I might be sick," I said.

"No, you might not be," Mommy said, but she leaned over and put her palm on my forehead. She frowned. "Well, you do seem a little warm."

"See?"

She smiled, but her eyes looked tired. "Listen, if you start to feel sick at school, just tell the Sisters and they'll call Mrs. Beaudell next door. Okay? She'll come and get you."

She got up and took her plate to the sink. A stab of fear went through me.

"Why can't I call you?"

"Robbie, I told you twice last night. I'm going to be at the doctor's for a checkup, and then I'm having lunch with my writing pals."

"But I was going to come home for lunch."

"We went through this last night. Don't you listen anymore? I'm not going to be here. You can't come home for lunch!"

She jerked open the refrigerator door and reached in and pulled out a paper bag. She slapped it down on the table in front of me and took away my bowl. "Here! Already made! Christ!"

Tears filled my eyes. When she saw them, she put down the bowl and crouched by my chair.

"Robbie, God, I'm sorry." She tried to hug me, but I twisted away. She stood up. "I'm just a little tired today. I've been sick this morning."

I looked at her in alarm.

"No, you're not," I said.

"Sweetie, sometimes having a baby makes you feel sick, until you get used to it. That's why I need you to try to be really good to me, for a while. I need you to listen to me when we talk, okay?"

She walked over to the sink. The side of my empty glass was coated with a slick white rinse of milk that was sliding slowly to the bottom. Watching it made me my stomach lurch. What if I threw up in front of the whole class?

"If I'm sick you can come and get me," I said to her.

She was hanging her apron on a hook in the broom closet. She slammed the door shut and walked fast over to me and crouched down next to me. I flinched.

"Listen to me. Do you want a spanking? I don't care about your skin, I'll wallop you good! Do you hear me?"

"Yes," I said.

"Now——" She stopped and took a deep breath. "I've already told you that I'm not going to be here. I am always here, but today, for *two* minutes, I am *not* going to be here. Would you mind repeating that for me?"

"You're not going to be here."

"That's correct. You win the prize. I am not going to be here!"

She stomped down the stairs to the landing. I heard her banging things around. She came back with my coat and my boots.

"I don't like you that much in the morning," I said.

"Well, I don't like you that much, either." She clapped her hands together. "Move! Chop-chop!"

We went out into the living room. I put on my coat and my boots while Mommy stood there with my books and lunch bag. My coat was made out of some kind of grey material that shined like a rain puddle when it got wet. I had on my billed winter hat with the earflaps down and the chin strap dangling. Mommy knelt down in front of me and fixed the chin strap. It seemed to me her knuckles chucking my chin were little fists. They pinched my skin tight for a second, then let go.

Her green eyes went into me. Her face was large against mine. "You do want to be my good boy, don't you? You want to help Mommy, don't you?"

"Yes."

"Good. Then I'm sorry I got mad at you." Her face softened. "Aren't you going to kiss me goodbye?"

I shook my head. Mommy smiled at me.

"One of these days you're going to get too big to kiss me goodbye, won't you? Are you going to stop kissing your Mommy goodbye one of these days? You'll have a little girlfriend you can kiss goodbye."

Her face smooched down towards me. It was smooth and long. I kissed her cheek. It was white and cold. She handed me my stuff.

"Onward and upward, champ."

She put her hand on top of my head and steered me to the door and opened it. I stepped down the slippery steps of the porch and onto our crunchy, snowy walk. The door shut behind me. It was freezing out and very dark, and a fast wind was blowing the snow across the sidewalks. The branches of the trees looked black and hard in the streetlights. I walked up the block. Most of the houses I passed had their kitchen lights on. It was like nighttime out. The people eating their breakfasts could've been eating dinner.

It was possible the time zone had changed after all.

I stopped and looked back at our house. I didn't recognize it. Its big front window stared blankly at me.

"Where are you going?" I said to myself. I realized that I was shivering.

"I'm going to school."

"But where are you going?"

"I just *told* you!"

The cold bit into me. I decided to take a shortcut through the Tierney's backyard. I cut up their driveway past their coal cellar, where the snow was dotted black with little pieces of coal. I saw Ellen Tierney's mother pass the kitchen window, holding a cup of coffee, but she didn't look out. I ran through their snowy back-yard to their back gate and went out into the alley. It was desert-ed. The wind blew the snow up in little puffs, so that a white mist swirled around me. I walked through the mist and came out onto a block that was very strange to me. The houses were the size of our house, but they seemed newer. No one had been out yet. The snow was white and clean. The air smelled brighter here. I kept on walking. The wind blew cold and crisp into my face. I wiped snow from my eyes and saw a toboggan coming down the center of the street. It was being pulled by a mommy, and on it were three little kids who were too young to go to school. They wore bright red hats and they were talking and waving their arms around. They waved at me and yelled something I couldn't hear.

I closed my eyes. I felt like falling down in the snow. I felt sleepy. The mommy took her kids farther away, running as fast as she could.

The wind blew cold into my ears.

I opened my eyes. I was still in the alley. I hadn't gone any-where. The skin of my face felt hot and I was shivering. The snow blew up all around me. A bunch of big kids passed the mouth of the alley. Goodie's brother was one of them. He kicked and hit at things as he walked. He was the only one not wearing a hat and his black prickly head stuck out against the snowy street. Goodie followed behind, wearing a white hat that looked like half a snowball.

I ducked down next to a garage and waited for a long time. Then I tried to throw up. I stuck my mitten in my mouth. I tried to gag so that I would throw up right on my shiny jacket, so that I could run home with pieces of oatmeal coming off me.

But I couldn't throw up. I finally left the alley and went up the street. I didn't see Goodie's brother anymore, but all around me kids were coming out of houses. They came down the sidewalk in ones and twos and clumps of four or five. They were all bundled up. The boys carried their binders and books under their arms, and the girls hugged them to their chests. Some of the boys tried to slide on the slick sidewalk, with their arms out for balance. They'd come up short and have to take a hop-step to keep from falling, and then they'd try again.

The kids crowded past me, talking and laughing. Some of them bumped me. I tried to go slower, but their thick winter coats seemed to swell and lift me up and carry me with them. We moved faster and faster. Pretty soon, we could see the school towering above the houses like some kind of strange castle. I tried to stop, but all the kids swirling around me pulled me along like a flood. I was swept by a house where a woman stood in the driveway with a snow shovel and smiled at me. I was carried past a tree that I loved to touch, and a fire hydrant I always jumped over. We came around a corner and then the school was huge in front of us and it pulled us slipping and sliding across the black cinder playground. Some kids fell down on icy patches, but others took their places, and more kids came from other sidewalks, in long streams, until we were all racing across the slick black playground, laughing and yelling, pushing and shoving, kicking out with boots. Iceballs flew in the air. Our breath was like a big raggedy cloud rising into the dark air.

I looked up to see the Sisters staring down at us from the brightly lit windows. The first bell was ringing.

In front of the school, the flood broke into two rivers. The little kids went to the left and the big kids to the right. I looked up and saw Goodie's brother with the big kids. He was leaping around, jumping up and down, trying to see me. I ducked down into a crouch. A few of the kids around me looked at me and laughed. Goodie's brother went into the big kids' door, still jumping up and down.

With my heart pounding, I followed the other little kids into our door. The hallway was dim and shiny. The ceiling lights swayed back and forth as voices echoed and sounds seemed to crash into each other. There were classroom doors up and down the hallway. The walls between were lined with black hooks, and kids stood taking off their coats and hanging them up and putting their boots in pairs underneath.

As I stood outside my classroom looking for an empty hook I saw the triplets coming towards me. They were walking in single file, with Deanna in front. She was wearing a pink wool hat that looked like a thick pancake lying on top of her head, and a plain blue coat that had big white buttons. She had pink mittens with dangling tassels. She came up to me and stood very close.

"Goodie says that you hit her. Did you?"

Her sisters took off their boots and coats, but watched us out of the corners of their eyes.

"She—" I stopped. I didn't know what to say.

Deanna lifted her hat off her head with both hands. Some

strands of her long brown hair stuck to it like spiderwebs, and she pulled them away one by one.

"My mother says Goodie spends too much time with younger children," she said, staring down at her hat. "She might make me mad, too. Especially if I had to go to the hospital."

The second bell rang. The hallway was emptying out all around us. Deanna and her sisters stood in a row in their white blouses and blue uniform skirts.

"You don't have to fight with her brother, do you?" Deanna said. She seemed almost pleading.

"I don't know." The fact that she knew about it made it more real. Fear jumped in me. "Who told you?"

"Everyone's talking about it," Deanna said. "All the little kids know. It's not fair, he's too big."

The one who stuttered began to cry. She put her chin down."That's t-t-too bad for you!" she sobbed.

Deanna shushed her. The final bell rang. She looked at me and whispered, "You're very brave."

She led her sisters into the classroom and I walked in behind them. Most of the kids were in their seats already, with their hands folded on their desks, looking up at Sister Emelda as she wrote things on the blackboard with a clicking piece of chalk. I went over to my desk by the window and sat down. I looked around and saw some of the kids staring at me. When I stared back at them, they ducked their heads away.

The room was warm and bright. There were red pieces of construction paper cut into the shape of numbers or the letters of the alphabet and pasted on the walls. Next to them were crayon pictures of little kids playing in snow forts or sledding down hills. The rough, chunky map of America hung above the blackboard.

Sister Emelda started talking, but I didn't really listen. I kept looking out the window. I could see a bunch of house roofs and the lines from the telephone poles going across them. A few flakes of snow drifted down. The sky had turned a soft, puffy grey. A gnawing started in the pit of my stomach.

I watched Sister Emelda. She stood in front of the room with her hands in her pockets, rocking back and forth on her heels and jingling her keys. She was little and round, and wore small steel glasses. There was a rosary wrapped around her waist like a belt. All of a sudden, her eyes looked over at me. Her mouth opened and closed.

She put her hands on her hips and stared. Everyone turned in my direction.

"Did you hear what I said, Robert?"

"No, Sister."

"Are you all right?"

"Can I go to the rest room?" I said. "I think I'm sick."

Someone giggled and Sister Emelda gave the class a hard look, then she pointed at the door. "Go on."

I got up with everyone's eyes on me and went out. The minute I got out into the dim hallway, I felt a cold and clammy feeling come over my body. Something twisted inside my stomach, and I burped, and then my throat started burning. I ran to the rest room and burst through the door. It was cold and empty. The black and white tiles looked like they were made out of ice. I hurried into a stall and threw up as hard as I could.

When I was finally done, I stood up and went over to the sinks and washed my mouth out. My shirt was soaked through like Sam Sullivan's. I wiped my face with paper towels that scraped my rash and made my face burn. After a few minutes I left the rest room and walked out into the hallway. The rows of coats looked like the empty shells of little kids hanging from the walls in the dim light. Way down at the end of the hallway a white light came from the doorway. Instead of going back to my class I walked slowly towards it, past the other classrooms where Sisters were teaching, and where kids sat with their faces turned up and their hands folded in front of them.

I reached the heavy door and saw that the white light was the snow gleaming from where piles of it were plowed up along the edges of the playground. I put my fingers on the steel mesh that covered the door's window and felt the cold air leak from the glass. The church stood across the street. The houses on the same block with the church were quiet. No cars moved. It was the empty time I remembered from when I was little, after the older kids had gone to school. I used to sit in the living room then while Mommy was in her room and stare out the window at the sky.

The skies were always emptiest at this time of day. It was the emptiest time in the world.

I put my forehead against the steel mesh and closed my eyes.

It was freezing by the door, and I shuddered. I thought I felt the loneliest I had ever been. I thought of our empty house. I thought that this was the time of day that called me to come home, to snuggle up tight under the covers with Gretl, or play with my soldiers in my room. Even if Mommy wasn't there, I could go there.

When I got back to the classroom, Sister Emelda told me to put my head down on the desk. I put it into my folded arms and tried not to think about anything. A couple of times my stomach lurched, but I didn't have to throw up again. I started to be half asleep and half awake. I heard the sounds of the classroom all

around me, and Sister Emelda's high-pitched voice asking questions, and sometimes I felt the wind of her robes as she went by
me in the aisle. It was like a dream I was having of being in school,
with everything softened around the edges.

Later, I heard the kids start to talk, and paper bags unwrapping. It was lunchtime, but I was in a little cocoon, far away from
everyone. I daydreamed about the little kids I had seen on the
toboggan this morning. I didn't know who they were or where they
disappeared to, but I knew they looked familiar to me. I drifted
off through the sky, to where the puffy clouds floated, and then
there was a roaring noise like thunder. I woke up with a start and
realized that it was the noise of everyone on the playground laughing and shouting. I lifted my head and looked around the room.
The boys were all gone. All the girls were eating lunch, or talking
quietly. Some of them had their heads down on their desks. Sister
Emelda was out of the room.

Ellen Tierney sat at the desk next to me. She was tall and had
a very flat face and flat brown eyes. She had straight black bangs.
She was eating her sandwich in little nibbles, folding it back up in
waxed paper between each bite. She looked over at me. "Are you
going to run away? I saw you sneak through our backyard this
morning."

I stared at Ellen. One of her blouse buttons was undone and
I could see a little piece of her bare stomach. It was the color of
a peach. Her belly button moved while she talked.

"My big brother says you're going to get taught a lesson."

She unwrapped her sandwich and was about to take another
bite when she saw me staring at her. "What are you looking at?"

I didn't say anything and she looked down. She turned red. She
buttoned her blouse. "Everyone says you're going to run away. You're

a creep, anyway." She said it loudly, and the other girls looked up. They sat very still in their seats. Their eyes watched me. The noise from the playground rose into a roar and it seemed to me that the roar was actually the roar of Goodie's brother, that the shrieking and the yelling and the wild laughter all came from the throat of Goodie's brother screaming with his face twisted in his rocky head.

I turned in my seat and looked back at the triplets. The one who stuttered had her mouth wide open. Deanna watched me with her shining eyes.

I got up. I felt my face burning red. I walked across the front of the room and out the door. Outside the room I put my boots and coat on and went down the hall. I stepped out the door and into all the noise. The cold wind blew in my face. Kids swarmed all over the playground, running and chasing each other. I looked for Goodie's brother but I couldn't see him.

I went and leaned against the empty bike rack. I put my hands in my pockets, but then took them out, in case somebody might hit me when I had them in. I didn't think about anything. I looked at the bare trees that stuck up out from the ground and the sidewalks that went over the black cinders. I looked at the piles of snow.

I heard a high whistle. A group of kids were coming my way. I stood up off the bike rack. I felt like a giant hand was holding my heart. When the kids got closer, I saw that they were Goodie's brother and his friends from the fifth grade.

The big kids stopped in front of me. Their jackets were smeared with snow. They had red and blond and black hair that was thick and rough-looking. They tossed their heads like ponies and breathed fast clouds of air. Their faces were red.

Goodie's brother took off his jacket and gave it to one of his friends and stood there in his blue uniform shirt and black tie and pants. His shoes were thick and brown. He stepped up and pushed me.

"Take off your coat."

"Stop it," I said.

Goodie's brother pushed me again, and laughed. When he laughed, something flared inside of me, and I pushed him back hard in the chest. His eyes flashed behind his glasses and he ducked down into his fighting crouch. Fear went through me like a wind. I turned to run, but he spun me around and hit me in the face. At first it didn't feel like anything, and then it hurt. It felt like there was a brick inside my cheek.

I didn't seem to understand what being hit meant. I tried to walk away, but Goodie's brother came up and hit me on the side of the head, and I sat down. It felt like something had bitten and crushed my ear at the same time. As I sat on the ground I wondered if this was going to stop, or would it go on? There were some kids standing right in front of me, and they backed up and looked at me like I was a million miles away. Goodie's brother came around and said something I couldn't hear. He grabbed my coat and pulled me up so I was standing. Then he ripped the coat over my head and tossed it onto the ground. The zipper sliced my face. The freezing cold air hit me. The wind whipped through my shirt and flapped my tie in my face. I felt very thin.

Goodie's brother circled me. I couldn't look at him. He came at me and hit me in the stomach. I turned around and fell to my knees and hugged myself with both arms. My breath caught inside of me and wouldn't come out.

Goodie's brother knelt down next to me and got me in a tight headlock. He put his thick grunting face right into mine. His glasses were steamed up. He was panting. His thick smell was all over me.

The Snow Train

It was like a wild animal was on me. He picked me up in the head-lock and started dragging me. I dug in my heels. I kicked and hit at him. I pulled at his arms around my neck, but I couldn't get him to stop. I tried to bite him, and he hit me hard on the top of my head with his knuckles, over and over. Stars exploded in my head. I was pushed up against something hard. It was the door of the incinerator. I tried to pull away with all my might, but Goodie's brother punched me in the stomach, and slammed me into the door. It opened and I fell into the burnt, stinking darkness. The door clanged shut. It was pitch black. I started crawling away into the thick darkness. It smelled so thick and burnt I thought I was going to suffocate. Pieces of cans and bottles cut into me. I heard Goodie's brother walking up fast behind me. I curled up with my hands over my head. He reached down, grabbed me hard and jerked me up. His fist hit me on the face and the shoulder and then on the side of the head. Whenever I covered my head he would hit me in the stomach. I began to get so afraid that I thought I would die. I kicked out and flailed with my arms, but he kept knocking my arms away and hitting me.

After a while, Goodie's brother pushed me down onto the freezing black ground and sat on me. His knees in their thick pants were on either side of my face. I could see enough to see his head, his shiny thick glasses, and the smile on his face. He drooled some spit down at me. I twisted my head away and it landed with a warm plop on my cheek.

"Say you're sorry," he said.

"I'm sorry."

"Creep."

He reached down and took my tie and yanked it hard. I thought he was going to tear my head from my neck. He pulled it into a small black knot.

"You ever give my sister any trouble again, I'll kill you. Hear me?"

"Yes," I said.

He got up and walked over and pulled open the door. Cold grey light poured into the incinerator. His friends all tried to look in, but Goodie's brother shut the door with a loud clang. I waited. I was wet and shaking all over. My head felt numb and my stomach was sour and sore. My mouth tasted like blood. The bell rang for the end of lunch hour, and a herd of feet raced by the incinerator. It felt as though the ground was shaking. When it was very quiet and I could no longer hear any footsteps and voices, I got up. I could hardly walk. I felt around the incinerator with my hands on its cold brick walls, and found the metal door. I groped for the doorknob and pulled it open.

The outside light made me dizzy. I stepped out onto the empty playground like I was the last kid alive. I looked across the church parking lot to all the quiet little houses. I walked around the incinerator and stood staring up at the front of the school. Its windows looked back down on me, but no one looked out of them. They were as empty and cold as the sky going by, or the grey empty houses.

Snot and blood poured out of my nose. My pants were ripped at both knees. The rash on my legs had been torn open and bits of cinders were stuck in it. My palms were raw and covered with soot from the incinerator. My face felt like it had been scraped and burned. I couldn't feel my mouth. My jacket was nowhere in sight. I turned around and walked across the playground towards the houses. After a minute, I started running. At first I was stiff and my legs hurt, but then I felt better and I just ran and ran. I raced across the street that was blocked off with SCHOOL signs, turned the corner as fast as I could and kept on running. I ran so far that when I looked back I couldn't even see the school towering over the houses. It was just gone.

I ran through neighborhoods I didn't even know about. I ran past houses that had been in the world forever. I ran so fast the air got thin. I ran through the top of the sky and out the other side.

I finally slowed down and started walking. A car passed. I thought there might be someone in it looking for me, and I ducked down. When I got to a corner, I saw a high wooden fence that had a big tree growing up right alongside it. It had big, thick roots that went right underneath, so that the tree seemed to be growing out of the fence itself. I heard another car coming down the street so I squeezed myself behind the tree.

It was a tight fit. My back was to the fence and my face was pressed against the hard, wet bark. The only way to stay there was to hug the tree. My arms could barely reach around it. It smelled as cold as anything I had ever smelled.

Kittycorner from me across the street a woman with a scarf over her head came out of a house with a dog on a leash. I watched her out of the corner of my eye. She stopped and lit a cigarette. She seemed to be staring right in my direction, so I stayed completely still. After a minute she walked away.

I discovered that if I pushed back against the fence and propped my heels against the tree I felt almost comfortable. I squeezed the tree. I felt a little sleepy. I heard voices and I opened my eyes. Three high school girls were walking past with their books. One of them said, "Look at that strange little boy!"

They laughed. They kept on walking. One of them called back, "You've got bark all over your face."

I stared straight ahead. It seemed perfectly natural for me to be behind the tree, like I had always been there and always would be there, and that when people said things like that to me it was just a part of living behind the tree that I had to accept.

A lot of cars were going past now, and I could see inside them. I watched them calmly. They were just men driving by. They wore hats and wool mufflers and heavy overcoats. They had nothing to do with me. They were going to a world that I could never know about, and I was in a world too small for them to see.

It became very quiet. I stood shivering. My head felt like part of the tree, and its wet, black bark became my skin. I watched the brown little birds that went flying by so fast in the grey sky above me, and the squirrels that hopped on the snowy lawns.

I heard the sound of running footsteps. Deanna raced past the tree, going as fast as she could. She didn't see me.

I called to her, "Deanna."

My voice came out in a croak.

Deanna looked back in a startled way, and quickly ran back to me. She stopped a little ways off.

"Robbie, what are you doing there?"

"I don't know." I turned my head just enough to see her. "I'm scared."

"That big bully isn't around," Deanna said. "But everyone's looking for you. Sister Emelda is calling your house! What are you doing behind here?"

Her face was long and skinny and red from running. Her eyes looked at me anxiously. I realized that I knew Deanna and that she knew me. It seemed strange. Looking at her, I began to wonder again where and when and how everyone had met each other.

"How do I know you?" I said to her.

Deanna stared at me. "Robbie, I've always known you. We live in the same neighborhood. You came to my birthday when we were four."

"But what happened before that?" I said. "When did we meet each other?"

Deanna came closer. "Robbie, you're all bloody. And you're shivering."

I faced the tree again. I didn't feel like saying anything.

"Robbie, talk to me!"

I kept quiet. Out of the corner of my eye, I saw her turn and run away. She looked back at me once, over her shoulder, and then ran back towards the school, as fast as she could.

I closed my eyes. I hugged the tree to me as hard as I could and felt its freezing bark burn into my face. My head felt as light as a balloon. No one else came past. Time went blank and then it passed. Suddenly, it seemed like I needed to get home right away. I pulled myself from behind the tree, and fell down. I started laughing. I got up and kept walking. I fell down again, but I kept on going.

When I got to the corner of my block, I stopped and stared down the street. Everything was hard and sharp, like I was looking through a telescope. The black addresses of the houses leapt out at me. Our house was way down the street, but I could see its empty windows and the chipped red bricks and peaked roof. I looked up at the sky and was amazed by the clouds—they were racing, tumbling against each other, and so low they could've been grey smoke pouring from the houses' chimneys.

The air felt fresh and cold and empty. Inside all the houses the mommies were drinking their coffee. I knew that if they looked out their windows and saw me, they might ask me questions, so I decided that the boiler had broken down at school.

I imagined the boiler breaking, saw it like a huge metal heart collapsing, saw myself racing down the steps to the basement and trying to save the school. It blew up, and got me all black and dirty, but I lived and Sister Emelda told me I could go home early because I didn't have my coat.

I sped up and swung my arms a little. I walked like a boy who had just saved the school. My head was up.

I passed the house of the fireman who had nine children.

I passed the house of the woman who wasn't Catholic.

I passed the house where the man had fallen down the steps and turned purple.

I got to our house and walked up our walk and climbed the steps to the porch and opened the glass door that had the big curly "O" on it. There was the heavy wooden door with three little windows going like steps, and I pushed it open.

There was a little *whoosh*, like a jam jar coming unsealed. I called out, "The boiler broke!"

I thought that in the silence that answered me some noise had just stopped. There was something strange about the living room that made me not want to be in it, so I went through the dining room and into the kitchen. I opened the refrigerator, then shut it. I tried to take off my tie, but I couldn't get it undone because Goodie's brother had pulled it too tight. I decided to go to the bathroom, but when I went in and stood over the toilet I couldn't go, because the room was glowing with such a bright light, so I came back out into the hallway. I felt like I needed to keep moving around. I kept hearing noises in the living room, so I looked in from the hallway and saw the little girl crawling out from behind the couch on her hands and knees.

I decided that I should go back down to my bedroom, where my toys would be, but then I thought I would be trapped there.

"I was crushed instantly," the little girl said. "They carried me inside, and I was dead."

The Snow Train

She was standing in the hallway by the kitchen door looking up at me.

"The driver was very sorry," I told her. "It wasn't her fault, but she was rich and promised to pay for my college education."

"She had too much too drink at her bridge game!" the little girl cried.

We were back in the living room. She was sitting on the couch, dangling her feet, and I was sitting on the floor by the television. I could see what had bothered me about the room before. The house had started to make its own light. A sort of brown smoke was rising from the carpet, and the furniture was beginning to breathe a soft green glow. I could hear the beat of the house's thumping heart.

"Don't you *ever* dart into traffic without looking," the little girl said. Blood came out of her nose and she wiped it away with the back of her hand.

"I'm going to play with my soldiers," I told her.

I got up and left. The hallway down to my bedroom seemed strange, like it was tilting a little, but when I got into my bedroom and sat down on my bed I felt safe. I put some soldiers on the bed and began having them shoot at each other.

I felt a little breeze. When I looked up, the girl was sitting on the other bed. I started to cry a little.

She watched me. She was very thin, with yellow-looking skin and choppy brown hair that hung on her neck. She was wearing a dress that looked like a sack. It hung from her shoulders on two straps. Her knees were scraped and raw. She had little cotton socks on her feet, neatly folded over at the top, but only one shoe, a brown one with the buckle undone. I thought she looked like an orphan.

"You are an orphan when you die," she said. "There aren't any parents there."

"Stop it!" I yelled.

"Why did you tear down the curtains?" she asked me.

I looked around the room. It was true. The curtains were lying in thick piles on the floor, and the curtain rods were dangling from their hooks. The windows looked naked. I could see right out both of them, into our backyard, and next door to the side of Mrs. Beaudell's house.

I saw that it had started to snow again.

"It's your fault," I said.

The phone was ringing in the kitchen and I wished that it would stop. The little girl got up and went over to the window. She put her hands to her mouth and gasped. "Who threw Janet and Eleanor out into the snow?"

The next thing I knew, we were sitting cross-legged on the big bed in Mommy and Daddy's room. The little girl had her head down. I could see the part in her hair running like a twisty white path. Big, rough stitches crisscrossed it. They were red and black.

My shirt was off and I kept running my hands over my chest, the rough scaly skin where my rash was.

"They left me in the funeral home," the little girl said. "I was lying in a room all by myself, and they walked away forever!" She sniffled. "Oh, how my mother cried! She was never the same after that, they say." She looked at me crossly. "Stop scratching that!"

"I'm not scratching," I said. "I'm just feeling it."

I looked around the room. The little girl had taken Mommy's white case and dumped it on the floor. There was a pile of big metal curlers and bobby pins on the oval rug. All the drawers were pulled out of the dresser. Mommy's stockings and slips flopped over their sides. Her typewriter was on its side on the floor. Around it paper was ripped up into little pieces.

"Mommy always was a sloppy girl," said the little girl with a smirk.

"You did that! It wasn't Mommy!"

"Don't you dare talk to me that way!" she exclaimed. "What gives you the right? You're a messy bad little boy with an awful skin condition. You're ungrateful. You lie. You *hit* Goodie! You cause trouble for everyone. Who do you think you're talking to? I *live* behind that couch! I know things! I see what goes on around here!"

"Stop it," I said. "Why is there blood all over?"

It was true. My chest and arms were smeared with blood and it was streaking on my fingers.

"I told you to stop scratching," the little girl said. "But you don't listen. You never listen to anyone."

The little girl got up and started jumping up and down on the bed. She snapped her wrists as if she were whirling a jump rope. I got off the bed. I watched her. My chest was burning. She hopped high in the air, landing on one foot and then the other. The springs creaked. There were moments when she seemed to hover before falling, and I felt my stomach drop.

"You might die in the hospital," said the little girl.

We were sitting at the kitchen table. I was drinking Coke from a glass full of ice. It felt cold and strong going down my throat. It was giving me quick shivers. My teeth were chattering. Gretl came up the stairs from the basement and saw the little girl and turned around and ran back down as fast she could.

"Go away," I told the little girl. I wanted to go to bed.

The little girl took my glass and threw it against the wall above the stove. It shattered all over the place and some of it fell on the burners. It made me want to turn all the burners on, because I had read that glass could melt. I wanted to see the ice melt along with the glass, and sizzle.

"Shhh," the little girl whispered.

She looked up and cocked her head. There was a loud thumping coming from the front of the house.

"I think someone's knocking," I said.

I heard my name being called. It sounded like it came from so far away. I looked down and saw myself with my shirt off and blood all over me. I was freezing.

"It's Sister Emelda," I said. "She's looking for me."

I couldn't see the little girl anywhere. I got up from the chair and ran out into the dining room and peeked through the curtains. Sister Emelda was at the door with Mrs. Beaudell and Deanna. Deanna saw me and pointed with her mouth open. I shut the curtains and ran back into the kitchen. The little girl stood at the stove turning on the gas burners. Little blue-yellow jets of flame sputtered up. She jumped up and down.

"Don't let them catch you!"

The knocking stopped. For a second, all I could hear were the burners hissing. Then the glass started crackling. There were footsteps on the driveway and I saw the top of Sister Emelda's habit at the window, and then her hands grasping for the sill.

"She's going to try to pull herself up!" the little girl cried. She put her hands to her mouth. "She'll see us! She'll come to the back door! You've got to do something, quick!"

I turned and ran out of the kitchen, stumbling down the steps into the landing. I tried to lock the door, but my fingers kept slipping. I felt the little girl's hands on my back. They were so cold they burned handprints into me.

The Snow Train

"The basement!" She danced up and down. "Hurry!"

We raced down the steps into the basement. I looked around at the furnace where it grew up into the house like a big tree and the washing machine and dryer, and Daddy's workbench. There was no place to hide. I heard the back door push open with a bang. Sister Emelda cried out, "Robbie? Where are you?"

"Robbie!" called Deanna.

The little girl and I went over to Daddy's workbench. I heard them walking around upstairs, calling. I realized I was crying and shaking.

"Stop that, you baby!" said the little girl. She stamped her foot and a puff of dust flew up from the cement floor. "Here!"

She went over to the toolbench, reached up, and grabbed a hacksaw that was hanging from the pegboard on a silver hook. She handed it to me. It had a heavy orange wooden handle and a shiny steel blade.

One of the little girl's dress straps had fallen off her shoulder and she pulled it back up again. I saw the stitches in her hair, like staples.

"Go ahead," she said. "Why don't you?"

"It's not my fault!" I yelled at her.

"They'll blame you anyway," she said.

I heard Sister Emelda at the top of the basement steps.

"Robbie? Oh my dear Lord—are you down there?"

The little girl disappeared. I took aim at my right foot and threw the hacksaw down as hard as I could. It stuck and quivered. My foot suddenly felt very full. It seemed to swell up through a split in my black sock, and the blood that came up looked black, too. I watched it pour out of me. It didn't hurt. I decided it was never going to hurt unless I moved. So I stayed still.

Part Three: 1957

The Boiled Angel

I.

Early the very first morning I was in the hospital the little girl pushed in through the white curtains, grabbed the iron bed rails, and shook them so hard they rattled.

"It breaks my heart to see you like this," she said.

Around my bed was the same thick air that had been caught and trapped there when the fat nurse who didn't know how to breathe had pulled the curtains shut the night before.

I turned my head very slowly to look at the girl. She was wearing a brown corduroy jumper over a white blouse that had floppy round collars as big as lily pads. Her face looked tiny and old and wrinkled. She pressed it right up against the rails and stared in at me, smiling. Her eyes were as black as buttons.

"It simply breaks my heart," she repeated in a sad whisper. "Such a brave little boy. He don't cry! He don't complain!"

Go away! I said.

The little girl lowered her head and tried to fit it through the side rails, but it wouldn't go. She stood on tiptoe and pushed with all her might. Suddenly her head burst through. Her face grew redder and redder and swelled up like a red balloon. She was trapped. Her mouth opened wide. Her hands jerked at the bars. Her body jerked, but she was caught.

The iron bed trembled and rattled. I was crying and she was crying.

The Snow Train

"Help me," she said. "Oh, please help!"

Help! I said.

The white curtains came flying apart with a zipping, swishing noise. My heart pounded. My eyes jumped open. The fat nurse said "Hi" to me in her little voice. She was huffing and puffing.

"Are you awake?" she said. "Are you talking in your sleep?"

I was lying in a white, high bed with thick flat pillows. Stiff sheets held my legs in a tight grip. I was covered with sweat. My rash stung all over.

I saw other nurses pulling bed curtains up and down the rows of beds. The air in the long room was grey. I heard noises far off, grown-up voices talking and heavy footsteps and clattering metal sounds.

The fat nurse had a white bathrobe over her arm and a pair of brown slippers in her hand. She laid them on the bed, lowered the side railing and sat down. She stared at me. She had pale skin and small shiny eyes like a bird. She put her warm hand on my forehead.

"I rushed to get here when I heard you crying," she said. "I raced! And now you tell me you're all right."

"I didn't tell you that," I said.

The fat nurse put a thermometer in my mouth. "Your very demeanor tells me that. You're revved up and rarin' to go. I can see it."

She pushed the covers back and helped me sit up and swing my legs over the side of the bed. Then she unbuttoned my pajama top and folded it down over my back and off my arms. My skin felt like it was coming unstuck from itself. I looked down at my chest and arms. The skin there was red and wet and rough, like a sponge. My fingernails had black bits of scabs stuck behind them.

The cool air felt freezing cold and I shivered.

The fat nurse put on a pair of soft white gloves. She took a tube and squeezed cream onto her fingertips. She began rubbing it into my back.

"Why did the moron throw the alarm clock out the window?" she said. "Take your time. Answer from the heart."

The fat nurse rubbed and my skin burned in little hot flashes. I bit down on the thermometer and looked around the room. Men in dirty white coats were setting up cardtables in the long aisle that ran between the beds. Young nurses in striped dresses came out and put trays of food on the tables, and when they did, kids in bathrobes walked out very stiffly and sat down. Their faces looked mean and hurt. None of them said anything. There was one boy who had skin like slush, and a very fat boy who looked like he had pieces of dried leaves stuck all over his face. I saw a brown-skinned girl with pigtails go slowly by holding a Raggedy Ann doll. Her face and arms were covered with pinkish-white splotches shaped like jigsaw puzzle pieces. Over one eye she had a huge star-shaped piece that made her look like an Indian pony.

The fat nurse stood up and took off her gloves and threw them in a white can with a lid that she opened by pressing a pedal with her foot. She reached over and took out the thermometer and then helped me put on the slippers and bathrobe. We walked out to the cardtables. My skin burned with every step. I sat down at a table next to two other kids. One of them was the girl who looked like the Indian pony. The fat nurse said her name was Dawn. The other kid was a tall boy named Billy who was older. He had boils so bad his face was swollen. There were bunches of boils under his cheeks that looked like bumblebee stings. His ears were blistered and red.

The Snow Train

After the fat nurse left, Billy stared at me. His eyes were like holes in his puffy red face.

"You sure got the crud," he said. His voice was very low and slow.

"No, I don't."

His red, crushed face twisted up. "Yes, you do."

"You're a moron," I said. I was starting to shiver again.

Dawn hugged her Raggedy Ann. She looked at both of us.

"You got it worst as I seen," said Billy.

There were trays in front of us with cornflakes and milk in metal bowls and orange juice in paper cups. We each had a banana. Billy peeled his and broke it with his red hands and put the pieces on his cereal. He said "Hah!" for no reason. I turned my head away. The shivering wouldn't let go of me. I picked up my spoon and put it down. I felt someone standing next to me and looked up to see the fat nurse wearing her coat and hat. Her purse hung from her arm.

"You never answered my question," she said. "Why did the moron throw the alarm clock out the window? It's very important!"

"To make time fly!" said Dawn in a small squeaky voice.

"That's right!" said the fat nurse. She shook her fist. She seemed excited. "That's the ticket! That's what we're all looking for."

She bent down close to Dawn and kissed her on the forehead. Dawn giggled as the fat nurse walked past all the beds and out the door. A few minutes later, a tall blonde nurse who wore her white hat stuck high up in her hair like a little cloud stood in the middle of the aisle and clapped her hands together.

"Stand up, children," she said.

This nurse was skinny and had a soft voice. When she clapped her hands they made hardly any sound. She walked by pointing at each of us and counting. A breeze that smelled like lemons came off her. When she finished counting she made us get into a line and led us out the door into a big hallway. It went on so far I couldn't see the end of it. Yellow lamps shaped like fishbowls hung from the ceiling on long iron chains. The wooden floor was dark and shiny. Along the walls there were wooden benches with high backs that made them look like the pews in church. Old men and women in pajamas and robes sat on them reading or talking. Some of them had hard, bright-red rashes on their faces and hands. I saw a very old lady sitting in a wheelchair who had big bandages on both of her ears. It was like they weighed her down and her head hung on her chest. Her eyes were closed and her hair stuck straight up like white weeds. Next to her on one of the benches sat a man with a pipe in his mouth. He was wearing shiny black pajamas and a black shiny bathrobe. His face was huge and swollen and his skin looked like cracked, dry mud. His ankles were as thick as elephant ankles. He seemed to be watching me. When he saw me looking at him, he winked. I turned my head away.

When we got a little further another nurse came up to us and picked all the girls out of line and walked down the hallway with them. The blonde nurse counted the boys again, and then took us through a big white door and into a wide, shiny bathroom. It had black and white tiles on the floor and tall white urinals and toilet stalls that looked like closets. The ceiling was very high. Down the center of the floor were three large bathtubs sitting on little platforms. At the ends where the faucets were there were tangles of little hoses.

We stood there against the wall. On one side of me was a boy with little sacks bobbing from his forehead and cheeks like the heads of fat white worms. His face didn't move. His eyes stared straight ahead. Billy was on my other side. He didn't seem to have anything inside of him that made him stand up straight. His hands hung down. His swollen face stared at the floor.

The blonde nurse went to all three bathtubs and turned on the faucets. Steam started rising up. She put on a pair of rubber gloves and pointed to the first three kids on the bench, who took off their bathrobes and pajamas and hung them on hooks on the wall behind us. I looked at their skins and then didn't look back until they had gotten into the tubs and sat down. The blonde nurse handed each of them a bar of brown soap. The boys rubbed the soap on themselves. Their skin got redder and redder. The blonde nurse went to a wooden shelf and took down a bottle of green-colored shampoo. She came up to one of the boys, poured some shampoo out onto her gloves, and began to wash his hair. Her hands made a wet, squishy sound.

"Close your eyes," she said.

The boy closed his eyes and she rubbed his head roughly, then took one of the hoses and sprayed his hair with it. Green suds dripped past his ears and down his face. He was biting his lip. "It burns!" he said. He got some in his mouth and tried to spit it out. The blonde nurse didn't say anything. She walked to the next bath-tub and shampooed the very fat boy with the scabs stuck to his face like leaves. He hung on tight to the bathtub. His head rolled back and forth under her hands. Tears rolled down his cheeks.

When the blonde nurse was finished, she clapped her soft clap and the boys got out of the bathtubs. She gave them each a white towel and then let the water out of the tubs and began filling them up again. Billy and the sack-faced boy took off their clothes. I took off my bathrobe, but then I couldn't take off the rest. Billy got into one of the tubs, and the sack boy got into another. There was one empty one. I turned my head away. The blonde nurse came up to me. Her lemon smell was all around me. Her hat was sailing high up in her hair. It looked like a ship on top of a wave.

"What are you staring at?" she said. "What's the matter?"

I was standing very straight. I didn't think I could move. I looked the blonde nurse in the eye and her eyes moved away. I wondered if she was afraid to see me. Her face began to get red. She reached out her hand towards me, but stopped as the door of the bathroom opened and the man I had seen on the bench, the man wearing the black bathrobe and the shiny black pajamas, came in. He was smoking his pipe and he had a newspaper under his arm.

The blonde nurse turned around and put her hands on her hips.

"Mr. Topping, how many times have I told you to wait until the children have had their baths before you come in here?"

"I see it's time for their medieval water torture," the man said. His voice was strange-sounding, thick and grumbly. "Doesn't do a bit of damn good as far as I'm concerned. It's just more pain for the poor wee ones."

The man walked through us. His head was very big, and his hair was short and black and parted in the middle. The skin of his face was in hard, grey slabs that fell over each other, like armor, or like a crocodile's skin. His eyes looked buried. As he went past, I saw that there was a bright yellow dragon on the back of his bathrobe. Its mouth had red fire coming out of it.

The man went to a stall and shut the door. We could hear him whistling and then there was a loud fart. Some of the kids laughed. The blonde nurse stared around the room and the boys were quiet. She clapped her hands together. Her face was bright red. "We're leaving right now," she said. "We'll finish this later." She didn't even look at me.

The Snow Train

The nurse took us out of the bathroom and down the long hallway to a big room. The light in the room was bright and grey. There were big windows on all three sides and I could see out into the wide cloudy sky. There were toys lying all over the floor. They were mostly little kid toys, like blocks and dumptrucks and pull-trains on strings. There were wooden shelves in the walls with board games and jigsaw puzzles stacked on them. Next to a big armchair was a little bookcase filled with books.

The girls were already in the room with their faces shiny and their hair wet. Some of them were playing jacks on the floor and others sat at little school desks and read or wrote things on small blackboards. Dawn was at one of the desks playing with her doll, singing something to herself in her squeaky voice.

The boys ran to pick up toys. Billy sat against the wall and zoomed a race car on the rug. The sack-faced boy walked around tossing a red ball in the air. His sacks bobbled. His eyes were very small, almost slits, as he watched the ball go up.

I went and sat up on a wide windowsill and stretched my legs out. The window was divided into two tall windows and each had a little handle that opened it. I turned one handle and felt the sharp cold air hit me. I pressed my face through the open crack. We were very high up. I could see straight down to the front of the hospital. People walked up and down the sidewalk to the main doors. There were piles of snow everywhere. I saw ambulances going by on the street. A car stopped at the curb and a man got out and went to the trunk and took out a wheelchair. He unfolded it and wheeled it around to the back door. He opened the door and helped a lady in a fur coat onto the chair. He pushed her up the walk. People moved around them. Farther away from the hospital, cars crowded together on the expressway, and past that there were rows and rows of houses, as far as I could see. Way on the horizon, down by the river, was a tall metal tower with a red light that blinked over and over again.

I turned from the window and looked back into the room at all the kids playing. The sack boy was crawling on the floor like a white worm. Billy sat at a desk with his head down on his arms and I could see how red and blistered his neck was. A lot of the kids were scratching themselves. I saw little girls running their hands up and down their legs and on their faces were blank looks.

I felt my rash start moving on me. It tightened up and began to crawl. It was like something living on my skin that had nothing to do with me. I couldn't take my mind off of it, and finally I lifted up my pajamas and began to scratch my legs with both hands. I shuddered. It hurt me too much, but I had to keep scratching. All around the room kids were scratching, and I thought that they were all animals. The dragon man came into my mind, breathing blue smoke. The room was crawling with scratching animals. Dawn the pony talked to her doll and giggled. Billy stuck his neck up like a burned turtle and stared through the holes of his eyes. I put my face to the window again and the cold air froze my hot skin.

Later on, in the afternoon, I was sitting by myself on my bed when a crowd of ladies came in. They had purses swinging from their arms and they were wearing thick heavy coats and boots. They waved and smiled. All the kids sat up. The ladies began stopping off at each of the beds and the long room became full of voices.

I didn't even see Mommy until she ran up and gave me a big hug and a kiss. Her perfume made my rash burn, and I tried to pull away from her, but she didn't notice. She finally let go of me and pushed her coat down off her shoulders. She wiped her hair back off her forehead and sighed.

"Now," she said. "Let me look at you!"

"You can't," I said.

"What do you mean, I can't?" She crossed her eyes and pushed her face at me. "There! That's my special look for you!"

I had a feeling like the one I had in Dr. Benson's office when I saw the little baby girl. My chest jerked and quivered. My teeth cut into each other.

"Are you cold?" she said. "Where's your blanket?"

"I don't need a blanket."

"You sure do," she said. "It's freezing out there. The weatherman says a big storm is coming up. There's going to be a ton of snow."

She pulled the blanket from the foot of the bed and spread it out. Around the room, on all the beds, the kids were sitting talking to their mommies. I heard laughter, and I looked up, and it was Billy laughing so hard that he was doubled up on his bed. The lady who was sitting there with him touched her hand to his shoulder, and when he didn't stop laughing she took him in her arms and held him tight. He was shaking.

"Robbie?" Mommy said. She was handing me a white envelope. I didn't know what it was. I took it in my hand and looked down at it. "Go ahead," said Mommy. I opened it up. It was a card with a picture of a clown holding some balloons. Inside it said "Get Better And We'll Throw A Party!" There were all sorts of names written on it.

"The kids at school—" Mommy was saying.

The names jumped around the card in big, jerky letters. They crawled all over it. I saw a big "D" and I followed it and it said "Deanna."

"Deanna?" I said.

Mommy laughed. "Of course, Deanna! You know—your little friend."

"Don't—" I said.

"Sweetie, don't what?"

I threw the card in her face. The corner of it hit her cheek. A red mark came and I laughed. Mommy's eyes flashed in anger, and I thought she was going to hit me. I felt hot all over. I shook my head. Something twisted inside my stomach. I couldn't talk. Mommy reached out and grabbed both my hands and held them very tight. Her hands were white and cold. I watched the red mark on her face.

It seemed to me that if I could just get up and walk out of the long room, I could go into the playroom and sit by the window and watch the snow when it came falling down. And there would be nobody around. But everywhere there were things that kept me from moving. Mommy was one of them. The tight sheets bound me in. My rash kept me from moving. And all the people who were in the room kept me from moving.

"It's okay, it's all right," Mommy was saying. "Listen to me."

"It's all right," I said.

"It is," Mommy said. "I understand. It really is."

I pulled away from her. I couldn't stand the sound of her voice. I heard the girls laughing. Some of them had gotten down from their beds. They were dancing in a circle. Their mommies were standing there smiling at them.

"Hey," I heard Mommy say. "Look."

The blonde nurse was coming down the aisle pushing a little

boy in front of her. He was wearing rough brown corduroy pants and a long-sleeved white shirt. His face was bright red. Behind them was a tall brown-skinned woman carrying a little suitcase.

"That's that little boy," Mommy said. "The one from—"

"I don't want to talk to him," I said.

"Shush!"

The little boy got closer. The blonde nurse had her hand on his shoulder. She stopped him at the bed next to mine and said something to the brown-skinned woman, and then left. The woman reached down and grabbed the little boy under the arms and helped him sit up on the side of the bed. His legs swung down in his blocky brown shoes. His head came up and he looked right at me, and his eyes widened. He didn't take them away from me, even when the woman knelt down to unbutton his shirt. She saw him staring and turned to look over her shoulder at us. "Pleased to see you," she said. She turned back to the boy. "Frederick, do you recall these nice folks?"

The red boy's face shone like a red light bulb.

"Hello, Frederick," Mommy said. She turned to me. "It's the little boy from Dr. Benson's office. Remember? The one who gave you the tractor?" She smiled at the red boy. "Where's your tractor, sweetie?"

The red boy ducked his head and then looked at the little suitcase the woman had put on the bed. She opened it up and pulled a tractor out and handed it to him. He held it up to us and smiled.

"Oh," said Mommy. "Look at that."

The way he was staring at me made me turn my head away. I shifted in my bed. "Mommy!" I said.

"Shhh!"

The blonde nurse came back carrying a bathrobe and a pair of pajamas. She handed them to the brown-skinned woman and began drawing the curtains around the red boy's bed. He kept staring at me even when the curtain slid by his face.

Most of the other mommies went home, but Mommy sat on my bed and talked to the fat nurse while I ate dinner. I was at a table with Billy and the sack-faced boy. We were eating meatloaf that tasted like it had been in a can. I couldn't eat more than a few bites, but Billy and the sack boy gobbled it down. The sack boy's little sacks bobbed as he ate. He didn't seem to know how to hold a fork. He stuck his elbow straight out like a wing and poked the fork at his mouth in a stiff way. I wondered if he did that to keep from hitting his sacks.

Billy ate very fast, with his head almost on top of his plate. Sometimes he said something to the sack boy and the sack boy would laugh, and then they would both look at me. The red boy sat next to Dawn at another table. Dawn hardly ate at all. She kept talking to the red boy, but he never said anything back to her. The minute the nurses came to clear away their trays, he got up and ran over and climbed up onto the chair across from me.

"Oh-ho!" said Billy. His bumpy face smirked up.

The red boy smiled at me. I looked at him sitting there. He was so quiet. His red was like no other red that I'd ever seen. It glowed inside him.

"The red one's uglier than the scabby one, but not by much," Billy said.

I looked at the red boy and he looked at me. His hair was so white on his head, and his head seemed so big, yet soft. His eyes were light blue, so light that I thought I could see through them.

The Snow Train

He's just a baby, I thought. I couldn't get the words out of my head. I didn't know where they came from. *That's just a baby.*

"Someone had a good dinner, it looks like," Mommy said when I came back and got into my bed. She reached to wipe something off my face, but I turned away. She and the fat nurse looked at each other.

"Nurse Kilmer just told me that when she was a little girl, she had asthma so bad she had to go to the hospital a lot," Mommy said.

"I was in and out!" said the fat nurse. She pressed her hand against her chest.

"She knows that it can be very hard when you're little," said Mommy.

"It seems like the world is coming to an end!" said the fat nurse.

"A hospital is a strange place with new faces." Mommy smiled at me.

"I decided after that that I wanted to help children," the fat nurse told me. "To make it my life's work."

I looked over at the red boy, who was lying in his bed with his tractor on his lap. He had closed his eyes. I thought he might be sleeping. The fat nurse saw me looking and she leaned closer to us and lowered her voice.

"He's a poor lost soul," she whispered. "We have him here every six months or so, just to make him comfortable. There's really nothing anyone can do."

"What is it that he's got?" Mommy said.

The fat nurse shrugged her shoulders. "Something very rare. It's an extreme form of psoriasis. He's prone to infections and sometimes catches terrible fevers. He can't even go out into the sunlight, poor thing. He spends all his time indoors."

She smiled over at the red boy. Mommy got up and went to his bed and sat next to him. She reached out and brushed his forehead lightly with her hand. He didn't look up or open his eyes.

I suddenly wondered what it would be like if he was our baby, instead of the baby Mommy was bringing us. I thought maybe it was possible she had picked the wrong baby.

Mommy sat there staring at the red boy. I noticed that most of the kids were standing by their beds now, looking at us. The fat nurse leaned over and pointed to her watch. "Mrs. O'Conor," she whispered. "They're waiting for their story."

"Oh!" Mommy said. "Sorry." She came back over to my bed and picked up her purse and put on her coat. She looked at me, and then back at the red boy.

"He could be our baby," I said.

"Sometimes, I read to them from a story," the fat nurse said. "I think it helps them get to sleep at night."

"What did you say?" Mommy said to me.

"It's a little something extra I like to do," said the fat nurse.

Mommy opened her mouth, then closed it. She seemed very tall standing over the bed in her coat, holding her purse. She leaned down and kissed me on the mouth. "Listen to Nurse Kilmer's story, and then go to bed, sweetie. I have to leave. I'll come back tomorrow with Daddy."

"Okay," I said. "It's okay."

"Sure it is," said the fat nurse.

The fat nurse and I watched Mommy walk down the aisle. She seemed to be a lady walking down a street somewhere.

"You have a very pretty mom," she said. "I'll bet all the boys would like her to be their mom."

The Snow Train

"They never said anything," I told her. I saw that the red boy had woken up and was rubbing his eyes.

"They never do," the fat nurse said.

The fat nurse made all of us get into a line and then she took us out into the hallway, which was very quiet and dark. The kids shuffled in their slippers. It was too dark to see their rashes and they looked just like any other bunch of kids in white bathrobes, except that they walked so slow and stiff. The red boy kept close to me. He took baby steps. He wobbled a little and his eyes opened and closed. Once he almost tripped. He was holding his tractor to his chest.

The fat nurse stood by the door of the playroom while we all went inside. The lamps were on and the room was warm and cozy. A heavy snow was blowing outside the big windows like flapping white sheets. When the kids saw it, they all ran and looked out, but the fat nurse made them sit down on the floor or in the school desks. I sat with my head against the wall underneath one of the windows. I could hear the glass shaking, and feel little trails of cold air around my ears. The radiators began to make a banging, hissing sound.

The fat nurse sat in the big armchair by the bookcase and smiled at us. She pressed a hand against her chest.

"You're all my children," she said. "Did you know that?"

None of the kids said anything.

"When your moms and dads aren't here, it's my job to take care of you. I don't have any kids of my own, so you're my own. I think that's just right, don't you?"

"That's right!" Dawn cried in her squeaky voice. The fat nurse smiled at her and took a book out of the bookcase. It was a big, thick book and she spread it open on her lap and reached into her pocket for a pair of black glasses and put them on. The glasses gleamed in the light, and they were like the windows, shiny and black, with her white snowy skin behind them.

The red boy was curled up at her feet, sound asleep.

"*The Adventures of Roderick, Marian and King Richard the Lion-Hearted on the Third Crusade,*" said the fat nurse. She looked up over her glasses. "When last we visited our two young people, they had been captured by Saracens. Roderick was clubbed by a guard and knocked unconscious. Oh, they're in a tough spot!"

The fat nurse took a deep breath and started reading. "Chapter Seven," she said. "'Bring Me The Infidel Boy!'"

Blackness swirled around me. In a confused dream, half-waked, half-slumbering, I was by the hearthside in Nottingham. I smelled the rich fragrance of my good father's fresh-baked bread and the welcome aroma of my mother's juicy songbird pie.

There was someone kneeling beside me.

"Mother," I murmured. "Fetch me a draught of cool spring water, if it pleases you, and—"

"Hush, Roderick," said a voice, kindly but urgent. "Be still. Your very life depends on it."

A hand shook my shoulder.

"Nay," I said, twisting away. "Let me but slumber here a while longer."

"Roderick, I implore you! Awake!"

The fat nurse paused and stared around her. The kids in their white robes were very still. The girls had their hands to their mouths.

The red boy kept his small head down on the floor. He never moved. I thought that he looked like a little red doll. I stared at the book on the fat nurse's lap. My heart started beating faster.

The Snow Train

The book seemed to get bigger and bigger. It spread its sides like wings.

The fat nurse began reading again.

Slowly I arose from the depths of my dreams and opened my eyes. Peering intently into my face was a Saracen maid dressed in billowing pantaloons. The veil that masked her face rose and fell softly with her breath, and she smelled of some strange and exotic spice. Strings of tiny silver falconer's bells dangled from her neck and wrists, tinkling musically with her slightest movement.

I groaned and started away from this strange vision. My head was afire!

"Roderick! Don't you know me?"

I raised myself dizzily upon my elbows. That dulcet voice, so sweet, so quiet...

"Marian! Dear Marian!" I exclaimed.

For so it was. My own sweet sister, dressed in the outlandish costume of a cruel and pagan land! She threw her arms around my neck and commenced crying as if her heart would at any moment be torn asunder.

"Oh brother, I have been sorely afraid! You have lain so long as one dead. I thought—"

The fat nurse stopped. She sucked in her breath and held it. Her eyes blinked. Something seemed to be shining on her cheeks.

I stared at the book. Its pages fluttered under her small, thick fingers. She began again.

"Hush," I whispered. I comforted her as best I could, with gentle pats and murmurs. My wits were returning and I took in my surroundings. We were in a capacious tent, richly appointed with low couches and soft pillows. There were large carpets of wondrous weave covering the hard-packed floor. Hanging from one wall, the crescent of an executioner's scimitar glinted wickedly in the light from the guttering candles.

Outside, I heard the sound of approaching ponies, and a sudden shout of command.

"Marian, dear sister, what is this place?"

"Oh, Roderick, it is the tent of their ruler, Saladin! His women have dressed me this way and brought me here. They say he intends to claim me as his bride!"

"Never!" I told her stoutly, although in truth my heart filled with horror at her words. "Be strong! We can foil their foul scheme if we but—"

There was a jangle and a clinking and the heavy tread of feet nearing the tent. The tell-tale clatter of armed men!

A harsh pagan voice rose above the commotion:

"Bring me the infidel boy!"

Marian thrust herself deeper into my arms.

"He is here!" she cried.

Pushing her aside, I rose unsteadily to my feet. If only I had my short-sword, or even a good honest staff! I balled my hands into fists—humble weapons, but the best I owned.

The fat nurse closed the book and held it on her lap. Her soft white hands move slowly over it. It seemed to take her a long time before she was able to speak.

"I was an only child," she said. Her voice was almost a whisper. "I never knew what it was like to feel a sister's love for a brother." She leaned forward. "And what better love could there be than for a boy to fight, against all the odds, to save his sister?"

The fat nurse stood up and put the book down on the chair.

"Always protect each other, children," she said. "You are all you have."

The kids got up from the floor one by one. They seemed dazed, as if they had been in a dream. The fat nurse shook the red boy gently and helped him up. She took him by the hand and walked him out of the room. We all followed her. As I left I looked over at the windows and saw that the snow was glowing as it tumbled through the dark. The radiators hissed at me.

That night when the curtains closed around my bed, I stayed awake. After a while I could see in the dark, and I saw soft shadows floating over the white sheets. I listened deep inside my head, and I thought I could hear the wind and snow blowing against the hospital, and feel the building shaking. For some reason, I remembered the pigeon I had seen floating in the strange shaft of air outside Dr. Benson's office. I thought of it out in the snowstorm, getting tossed by the snow, up and down. I thought of the pigeon being thrown against the hospital by the wind, its wings folded up and torn, and then of it falling, faster and faster.

By listening hard enough, I could hear the pigeon crying in a soft little voice as it fell. I burrowed down under the covers, but the crying didn't go away. It was a little whistling sound inside my ears. I tossed and turned. The sheets held me tight and finally I kicked them off. The soft crying was everywhere. The white curtains shook around my bed.

A little while later I said, "Where are you going?"

I was kneeling up on the bed putting my bathrobe on.

"What are you doing?" I said.

"I just *told* you."

I crawled over the side railing and let myself down onto the cold floor. I pushed through the swaying curtains into the dark room and heard the pigeon's soft cries very close. They were coming from the red boy's bed. His curtains were open a little bit, and I could see him. He had his pajamas off and he was sitting naked with his legs crossed underneath. I moved closer. The red boy took the backs of his fingernails and lightly stroked his legs. His eyes were squeezed shut, and he made his soft cries. He arched his neck and twisted his head.

He was rubbing his hands all over himself. It was like he was petting himself. His lips hardly moved as the cries came through them. His voice was like the little whistle of a pigeon.

I backed away. I was shivering.

"What a baby," I said. "He's just a baby."

I went out into the aisle and stood there. The long room was very dark. I could just make out the shapes of the beds and their white curtains. I heard the rustling sounds of tossing and turning and the dry, scraping sound of scratching. A little boy cried out "Mommy!" He sounded mad. I went to the door and peeked out into the hallway. Way down at the end, I could see the fat nurse sitting at a desk with a little white lamp on it. She was reading something. I started walking down the hallway, staying close to the wall. The fat nurse never moved. I got to the door of the play-room, looked inside, and froze. It seemed like the whole room was moving. The storm blowing outside the windows sent shadows flapping across the dark floor and walls. I took a step inside and then ran across the moving floor as fast as I could, feeling the shadows grabbing at my feet. I jumped up on the armchair and tucked my legs underneath and huddled there.

I picked up the big book the nurse had left behind and hugged it to me. It was smooth and heavy. I opened it and its wings fell against my knees. I looked down at its words, but I couldn't read what they said in the dark. I stroked them lightly with my fin-gernails and ran my fingers all across the book. I felt the thin smooth pages and the small black words.

All I wanted was for it to be quiet, but the radiators clanked and hissed in my ears, and it seemed like I could hear the moans of the kids in their beds and the soft cries of the red boy, and the sound of everyone scratching and scratching.

It seemed to me that no one ever let me do what I wanted to do. They yelled at me or beat me up or put me in the hospital. There was nothing I could do that I really wanted to do. The rash held me in, the people around me held me in, the stiff covers of the high white bed kept me in.

I got down from the chair and walked over to the window. I jumped up and stood on the windowsill. Standing that way, I could reach my hands almost to the top of the window. I pressed my whole body against the cold glass. The storm was blowing and shaking outside. My heart was pounding.

The window was like two tall glass doors next to each other. The handles were the doorknobs. I could open the door and walk through at any time. I laughed at the thought of it. I pushed one half of the window open and the wind took it and slammed it against the side of the building. Snow blasted into my eyes. I looked down and I couldn't even see the sidewalk. My slippers slipped on the cold sill.

"Stop!" I said.

The wind teetered me. I felt like I was starting to fly. I looked up and saw an airplane high up in the sky. Its lights were on. Men were riding in it. They smiled and waved at me. They all wore hats. The plane swooped very close. It was a toy plane flying through the sky. I reached up to grab it. There was nothing but empty air under my foot. I was going to fly.

A hand grabbed my ankle and I slipped and fell backwards and hit the floor hard and lay there. There was something under me that kept moving and squirming. I rolled away and saw that it was the red boy. He was completely naked, red and shiny. He lay there curled up. His eyes were so wide they looked like they were spinning. His mouth was open. He was making his soft, pigeon sound.

We stared at each other. I was shaking. My leg hurt from falling down. After a minute, the red boy sat up. He sneezed and then he sneezed again. The window was still wide open and snow was blowing into the room. I tried to get up, and at first I couldn't, but then I did and I limped over and pulled the window shut. I looked down at the red boy shivering and shaking on the floor, and then I grabbed his hand and pulled him up.

I could hardly talk. I didn't even know what I was doing.

"C'mon," I said. "Let's go!"

We walked across the floor's flying shadows and back out into the hallway. The fat nurse read at her desk. "Shhh!" I said to the red boy. He stopped making his whistling sound. We snuck back to the long room and walked softly down the aisle and got up onto the red boy's bed. His teeth were chattering.

"You're going to catch cold," I told him.

He looked at me, but he didn't seem to know who I was. He kept on running his fingernails over himself. I looked around on his bed and found his bathrobe and his pajamas.

"You're a big moron," I said. "You're going to freeze."

I knelt behind him and took his arms and put them in the sleeves of his pajamas. I was very careful in the way I touched him. His skin was hot and very, very smooth. While I buttoned up his buttons I looked at his face from up close. His tiny lashes blinked quietly. His eyes were smooth and clear. His teeth were little and round and shiny and white. They looked like baby aspirin. His hair was sticking up and I patted it down.

After I got his pajamas on, I closed his bed curtains tight so no one could see us. I sat facing him on the bed. I was still shaking. I said the first thing that came into my head.

"They're going to fix me up," I told him. "They're going to give me brand-new blood."

The red boy stroked his legs through his pajamas. I couldn't tell whether he was listening or not.

"There's a big red pool of it," I said. "It contains all the blood that anyone needs. They take my old blood and put it in garbage cans, and then they fill me up with new. The scabs all come off."

I raised up my pajama leg and showed him my skin. The scabs were all over like little black islands. Some of them were the size of half-dollars and some were the size of dimes. Sometimes longer pieces of scab ran between the big scabs, like bridges. More and more, the scabs were growing and reaching for each other.

I touched the scabs very lightly. They felt thick and smooth, like walnut shells. The red boy leaned close to my leg and reached out with his finger. I pulled my pajamas down.

"Don't be a moron," I said.

The red boy smiled and reached under his pillows for his tractor. He got up on his hands and knees and crawled, pushing it in front of him. He seemed excited. He was trying to make zoom noises, but it came out like a little bee buzzing, bzzz-bzzz-bzzz.

"Shhhh!" I said. "Calm down. You're all wound up. What are you doing up, anyway? You're supposed to be asleep."

The red boy stopped making noises but kept pushing the tractor. I took it away from him. It was a metal tractor with most of its red paint scraped off. It had thick black rubber wheels.

The red boy watched me holding the tractor.

"Get under the covers," I said to him. I pulled the covers

down, and he got inside. "You're not supposed to be up in the middle of the night. Go to sleep."

The red boy's eyes closed. His chest started going up and down. I stared at him until I was sure he was asleep, and then I put his tractor next to him and and went back over to my bed. I got under the covers and listened to the storm blowing outside. After a while, I heard the pigeon crying again, but this time I didn't open my eyes, even though my heart was pounding.

2.

The next morning the red boy and I were sitting in our baths in the bathroom. The very fat boy with the skin that looked like he had dried leaves stuck on him was in the other bathtub. He was whimpering and moving around in the tub, and the blonde nurse told him to stop.

"It hurts," he said.

It was quiet in the big bathroom. The air was thick and steamy. The boys standing alongside the wall shuffled their feet. The fat boy looked up with his eyes very big as the blonde nurse came up to him.

"What hurts?" she said.

"My wiener," said the fat boy.

I laughed. The red boy looked at me and laughed, too. He splashed up some water. He was so tiny and bright red in the big bathtub. I saw Billy and the sack-faced boy staring at us. I stared back at them. The blonde nurse came by and put her hands in my hair and started shampooing it hard and I closed my eyes and sank back into the water. Her fingers dug into my scalp like spikes, but I didn't care.

Instead of taking us to the playroom after the baths, the blonde nurse made us get back into our beds because the doctors were coming to see us. When she left the room, the red boy got down from his bed and climbed onto mine. I sat there watching him push his tractor. He had little traces of cream on his cheeks. It looked like he had been shaving.

Dawn came over and stood by the bed. "He likes you," she said. "He'll never come to me."

"What do you want?" I said.

Dawn stuck out her chin. "Can I come up?"

"I don't want everyone on my bed."

"He's on it." She put her Raggedy Ann on the bed and acted like she was going to climb up.

"Don't do it," I told her.

Dawn pulled her doll down and looked at me like she was going to cry. When I didn't say anything, she sighed. She watched the red boy.

"Does he ever talk?" she said. "He will laugh."

"He's retarded."

"What's that?"

I was about to say, "He's stupid," but I didn't really think the red boy was stupid. The red boy felt light to me, almost like he could float away.

"There's something empty inside him," I said to Dawn. "There's a big hole of air."

Dawn put her thumb in her mouth. "Here come the baddies," she said. She grabbed her doll and turned around and ran back to her bed.

Dr. Benson and some other doctors had just come into the room. They were talking to the blonde nurse, who was holding a tray with glass tubes and needles on it. The blonde nurse said something to Dr. Benson and he and the other doctors went to the bed of the fat boy with the dried leaf scabs all over his face. The blonde nurse drew the curtains around his bed.

The Snow Train

"They're going to check his wiener," I said to the red boy. I laughed out loud and picked at one of my scabs, trying to pull off a piece without making it bleed. The red boy stared at me with his mouth half open. For some reason, I felt very big and rough. I felt like I could hurt anyone I wanted to hurt. I was in a hurry for Dr. Benson to get to me. I wanted to tell him that I was ready for the new blood to come into me. I was sure that my rash would fall off right away. I wondered what it would be like to not have the rash. I thought of how I might look without it. I would probably look very white. There might be little scars, like small circles, where the scabs dropped off.

I thought of myself yawning and stretching. I thought how wonderful it would be to stretch like Gretl stretched, without a scab ripping.

I saw myself running as fast as I could over a field to where some boys were playing. The ground jiggled up in front of me. I was waving and yelling. The boys looked up and smiled.

Dr. Benson and the other doctors and the blonde nurse came down the aisle and stopped between my bed and the red boy's. I saw that some of the glass tubes the blonde nurse had on her tray were full of blood.

"Rob, you've got our next patient," Dr. Benson said. The blonde nurse came over and lifted the red boy off my bed. He seemed very stiff. He was hugging his tractor to his chest. He was scared.

"Hey," I said, but no one paid any attention. The blonde nurse carried the red boy to his bed and the doctors gathered around.

"Here with us again, pal?" Dr. Benson said to the red boy. "You must be fond of us." The blonde nurse pulled the curtains and I couldn't see anymore. I heard Dr. Benson's voice talking very low and then the low voices of the other doctors. I could see their shoes beneath the curtain, moving back and forth. Then I heard a strange cry. It was like the red boy's pigeon cry, except louder and sharper. It was almost like a loud squeak. A minute later, the blonde nurse swished the curtains open. She was putting a little tube of blood onto the tray. I could see the red boy. His mouth was open. He was holding his arm. His tractor lay on the bed next to him.

The doctors came over and crowded around me. Dr. Benson picked up the chart that hung at the foot of my bed, the one the fat nurse wrote on in the morning. He sat down next to me as if nothing had happened. I couldn't stop looking over at the red boy.

"What's the matter with him?" I said.

"Nothing," Dr. Benson said. "We just took a little blood, Rob. Nothing you haven't done."

"He doesn't like that," I told him.

"No, I'll bet he doesn't."

Dr. Benson kept staring at the chart. The blonde nurse shut the curtains and the air turned a soft milky color. The sounds from the room faded. The other doctors stood very close. They all wore glasses and were taller than Dr. Benson. Their eyes watched me. Their white shirts smelled like starch. My rash began to prickle.

Dr. Benson put the chart down and patted me on the knee. "How goes it?"

"Okay," I said.

"You've been doing a little scratching." He tapped the chart.

"A little bit."

"The night nurse, Nurse Kilmer, reports you're sleeping restlessly at night."

"Tossing and turning?" I said.

Dr. Benson nodded his head.

"I mean, was *she* saying I was tossing and turning?" I thought the fat nurse liked me.

Dr. Benson read the chart again. "It says restless here, Robbie."

"I might be," I said. "I didn't know that I was."

"Well, why don't we take a look." Dr. Benson leaned over and began unbuttoning my pajama top. The blonde nurse helped him. "Lift up," she said to me. She pulled my pants down and off. Then she turned on the lamp at the side of my bed. The light was bright and it made me squint.

"Kneel up, Rob," Dr. Benson said. "Just for a sec. That's it."

I knelt up on the bed in the bright, milky air with my arms hanging down. It got quiet for a while. The doctors' eyes stared at me. Their mouths got tight. They leaned forward and I could feel little puffs of their soft breath on me. Dr. Benson touched a scab on my chest. I shuddered. "Shh," he said. The other doctors moved closer, but they kept their hands behind their backs. Dr. Benson touched my bum, feeling the scabs there. "Some of these are open," he said. I didn't know who he was talking to. He kept saying things. I felt his fingers move lightly down my legs. They were like little moths landing on me and then flying away.

Finally, he stopped and all the doctors stood back a little bit. One of them was rubbing his glasses with a tissue. He smiled at me when he saw me looking at him, and then looked away. Dr. Benson rubbed my arm with alcohol. "We're just going to take a little blood. Just a sting."

He took a big needle with a tube attached to it and slid it into my arm between two big scabs. My skin felt full and tight, and then it ached. I watched my blood pouring into the tube, and I realized that I wasn't afraid. I liked to see it go out of me. I thought of all of it leaving me like that, just pouring out. I thought that I would feel so light. The blood I could see in the tube was very dark. It was the old blood. The new blood was going to be a light red, like a cherry gumdrop. It would flow through me with a whoosh and I would be clean.

Dr. Benson handed my blood to the blonde nurse and put a little bandage on my arm. He wrote something on my chart while the blonde nurse helped me get my pajamas back on. When I was under the covers again Dr. Benson put his hands on his knees and smiled at me.

"When are you going to change my blood?" I said to him.

"Rob, if it's okay with you I think we'll want to discuss that with your mom and dad. Of course—"

"Go ahead!" I said. "Change it. I want you to!"

"Well," said Dr. Benson. He laughed and looked at the other doctors. "That's an eager patient." He patted my leg. "I think we probably will go ahead, Rob. Three days at most, it looks like."

The doctor who had smiled at me said, "This is a first for Detroit, Rob. We should have the newspapers here."

"My mommy writes poems for the Detroit *Catholic*," I told him.

"Well, there you go!" the doctor replied. They all smiled at me again and then the blonde nurse opened the curtains and the doctors went over to Dawn's bed. She put her head under the covers and the nurse had to pull her out. She started to cry. I thought she was so silly to be afraid.

I looked over at the red boy. He staring straight ahead, holding his arm with one hand.

"It's not that bad," I told him. "You're all right."

A nurse I hadn't seen before came up to the foot of my bed and looked at the chart and then looked at me. "Robert O'Conor?" she said. "If that's you, you have a phone call."

The Snow Train

"A phone call?" I said. The young nurse had dark hair like Nurse Nelda, and the same kind of smile. "A phone call for me?"

I got down off the bed and followed her out of the room and into the hallway. It felt strange to be going with her by myself. I walked as close to her as I could. She smelled good, like some kind of flower. I wished she would take my hand in hers. I wondered if she would think I was brave if she knew what I was going to do.

"I'm getting my blood changed," I told her. "They're taking out the old blood and putting in the new blood. It's a first!"

"That's wonderful," she said. "I think we could probably all use a little of that."

"It might hurt, but I don't care."

"My," said the nurse.

We came to the desk in the hallway where the fat nurse had been sitting the night before. There were three other nurses standing around talking. The young nurse gave me the telephone and pushed a button. She watched me and smiled as I held the phone to my ear.

"Sweetie," I heard a voice say. "I'm sorry. We couldn't get there."

"Who's this?" I said. "Hello?"

There was a pause. "Sweetie, that's you, isn't it? It's Mommy."

"Oh," I said.

"The snow has got everything shut down. It's incredible. Your father couldn't even go into the lot."

I turned around and nearly bumped into the red boy. He was standing next to me, still holding onto his arm. I stared down at him.

"How did you get here?" I said.

"I said, we're not coming, Robbie," Mommy said. "Can't you hear me?"

"Yes," I said.

"What did Dr. Benson say? He was supposed to see you today. How does he think you're doing?"

"Okay."

"Sweetie, I can hardly hear you."

"It's okay," I said.

The red boy reached out and grabbed hold of my bathrobe and held on. He seemed to want something from me. I looked around. The young nurse in the striped dress was talking with the other nurses. They were walking down the hallway together.

Daddy's voice came on the phone. "Champ, what's going on there?"

"Nothing," I said. "The doctors came to see me."

"So, what's the verdict?"

I didn't know what he was talking about. I didn't say anything. I looked at all the stuff on the nurses' desk, papers and pencils and envelopes. It was boring. I sat down on the nurses' chair. The red boy kept hanging on to me.

"Robbie?" Daddy said.

"Yes?" I said.

There was a pause, and then Mommy came back on.

"Sweetie, we're going to come down first thing tomorrow morning," she said.

"That's okay." I said. "I'm fine."

Mommy made a little sound like a cough.

"I know that, honey. We know that."

"They're going to take my blood out," I told her.

"When?"

"Pretty soon. Then I can leave."

But as I said it, I looked at the red boy. He stared back up at me. His eyes were wet. He looked scared. If I left, I wouldn't ever see him again.

"Sweetie, that's wonderful," said Mommy. In the background, I could hear Daddy say something, but I couldn't make out the words. I saw both of them standing in the kitchen by the telephone. I couldn't make out their faces. It was dark in the house, and the white snow blew outside.

I hung up the phone and looked down at the red boy. He was wobbling a little bit as he hung on to me. The nurses were nearly out of sight down the hallway. The red boy and I were alone.

"Let's go," I said.

We walked down the hallway. No one stopped us. It was very crowded. Old ladies shuffled along in their bathrobes and slippers. Nurses pushed people in wheelchairs, or came running by with papers in their hands.

The fishbowl lamps hanging from the ceiling left soft round yellow glows in the shiny dark floor. They were like a trail.

"We can just follow these and we'll be all right," I told the red boy. "We have to be sure to step in each one."

I stepped in all of the soft glows. The red boy did, too. He kept looking left and right. His head was like a large chick's head. He seemed very curious. Sometimes he would stop and I would have to go back and get him. He stopped by the door to the bathroom where the blonde nurse had taken us for baths.

"We already did that today," I told him. "Let's go."

The red boy reached out and took my hand. His fingers were tiny and hot. I held onto them carefully. I had to walk very slowly so he wouldn't stumble and fall. We came down to the end of the hallway and turned a corner and kept going. In this part, things seemed emptier. There were big windows along the wall. The red boy and I stopped at one of them and watched the snow falling. From here I could look down at the neighborhood around the hospital, at the streets with the big houses and wide lawns. The houses looked dark and empty, and the snow poured right up the steps to the front doors. A few cars with yellow headlights moved slowly through the streets.

The red boy stood on tiptoe to look out.

"Those houses are all empty," I told him. "No one lives there but ghosts. They come out at night and play in the snow, but if you're walking down the street in the day they'll send the wind out to freeze your face and make you fall down."

The red boy stared up at me. I could tell he was listening to my voice.

"Can you say something?" I said. He blinked and cocked his head. "Talk!"

The red boy opened his mouth and smiled. Then he turned and walked away. I followed him. We came to a large room that was just like the one we stayed in, with two long rows of beds. Instead of kids, the room was full of men. They wore bathrobes and white t-shirts and pajamas. They paced up and down, or talked together standing at the foot of their beds.

It was very noisy. Some of the men had a cardtable set up in a corner and they were playing cards. They yelled at each other. A radio was playing very loud next to them. Cigarette smoke filled the air.

The red boy walked right into the room like he'd been there before, but I stopped at the door. All the men had rashes. Their faces were red and scabby. They walked in the same stiff way we did.

The Snow Train

"Stop," I said to the red boy. I cleared my throat. "Hey!"

The red boy didn't pay any attention. He went halfway into the room and stood by a bed. He stared at a man lying there.

On the bed closest to me, a man lay groaning and tossing and turning. He made his hands into claws and held them above his chest, frozen.

"Shitfire, boys!" he yelled. "Stop me!"

Some of the other men laughed. The man's face looked like he had stuck it in a prickly bush. He pushed his hands down on his chest and began scratching himself hard through his t-shirt. He twisted and arched on the bed as his fingers tore at himself. He ripped open his pajamas bottoms and curled his legs up to his chest and started scratching them behind the knees.

I turned around and left. Before I knew it, I was walking very fast back the way we had come. When I came to the window, I stopped and looked out over the dark neighborhood below me, but I didn't really see it. I was seeing the men walking around in that smoky room in their pajamas. How did that happen? I wondered if they had had their rashes when they were my age. Did they just grow up that way? Didn't the rashes ever go away?

I thought of the red boy standing there in the aisle. I saw how tiny he was, so tiny that the men walking around might bump him over, or maybe burn him with a cigarette, or just hurt him with their loud voices. I turned around and went back to the room and walked up to where the red boy was standing. I pulled at his sleeve.

"You have to watch out here," I said. "It's time to go."

The red boy wouldn't move. The man he was staring at was lying on his back reading a magazine. He was very skinny and unlike the other men in their bathrobes and pajamas he wore a pair of black pants and a regular white shirt. He had hair that was strawcolored. His skin was deep red, as red as bricks.

The man said something under his breath and swung his feet over the side of the bed.

"What did I tell you about comin' round here?" he said to the red boy. He threw his magazine on the floor. His voice was loud and hard. "Don't you be lookin' at me!"

I felt other the men in the room watching us. The red boy's mouth was wide open. He kept staring at the man.

"Little creep!" the man said. He started to get up.

I grabbed the red boy by the collar and started to pull him away. As I turned around I bumped into somebody standing right behind us. It felt like I had walked into a tree. I looked up to see the man in the black dragon bathrobe standing there with his hands on his hips.

"This is a signal honor," he said, looking down at me. He had a strange, mumbly voice that seemed to grow from deep inside of him. He held out his hand. "It's not often I have visitors. I'm Mr. Topping."

"My name is Robbie O'Conor," I told him. I looked at his hand. It was very big. The fingers looked like he had stuck them in mud that had frozen on them. They were swollen and cracked and grey. But when I put my hand in his palm it felt very warm and smooth. I shivered a little bit. I didn't mean to.

The man let go and smiled down at me. He had on black glasses that were about to fall off his nose. His face was swollen with his strange grey rash. I thought his head looked as big as a pumpkin.

His eyes were like little black balls. They moved from side to side very fast, almost like he was looking for someone who might be sneaking up on him. Yet he stood very quietly.

The red boy was holding my bathrobe with one hand. He put his thumb in his mouth and stared at the red man with his eyes wide. The man looked at Mr. Topping and then looked away. He sat back down on his bed and picked up a cigarette and lit it. His lips moved as he smoked, and he seemed to be talking to himself. He didn't look at us again.

Mr. Topping's eyes darted. He smiled at me. "Why don't you and my old friend Frederick come over to my domicile for some cookies?"

I looked at the red boy. "Do you know him?"

"Of course, of course. We're chums. We're old pals, you see."

Mr. Topping put his hand on top of the red boy's head and walked him down the aisle. I followed them. We came to the very end of the room, where there was a bed set against the wall near a window. There was a rocking chair with a soft grey blanket thrown over its back, and a tall standing lamp that had fringes hanging from its lampshade. Next to the lamp was a small table that held a pile of books and an ashtray and a round metal can decorated with pictures of flowers.

Mr. Topping sat down in the rocking chair, and the red boy crawled up on the bed and turned around to look back at the red man. Mr. Topping opened the metal can and handed it to me. It was full of square yellow cookies. I took two and climbed up next to the red boy and put one near his hand. He didn't pay any attention to it.

"All the comforts of home," Mr. Topping said. I nodded my head, but I couldn't think of anything to say. I watched him rock back and forth in his shiny robe. He wore a pair of soft purple slippers that could hardly hold his thick grey feet. His ankles looked like they had towels stuffed inside of them. His toenails were like potato chips.

He picked his pipe up from the table and started to put tobacco in it. The lamp shined down on his eyes as they jumped back and forth. His eyes moved much faster than the rest of him. They seemed like they belonged to somebody else who lived inside of him.

I thought that his rash was the worst that anyone could ever have. It was like he really was a rhinoceros or an elephant. It was like his skin had had an earthquake and cracked open. High up on his cheeks the plates of his skin were a grey-purple color.

Mr. Topping lit his pipe and puffed on it. The rash around his mouth broke into wrinkles that spread up his face like spider-webs. Out the window behind him, I could see snow falling on the dark neighborhood, but the wind had stopped. The snow was coming down in big, soft flakes. Next to me the red boy was asleep on his stomach. He was sleeping so hard it looked like he had fallen from the ceiling onto the bed. He lay there in a crumple. His arms and legs were sprawled out.

"He always goes to sleep," I said.

"Best thing for him," Mr. Topping said. "It's natural. His body tells him to escape. The last time the poor lad was here, we nearly lost him. He gets these fevers, you see."

"His skin is so hot," I said.

Mr. Topping nodded his head. "It's like a fire within."

"Has he been here a lot?"

"Probably three or four times, since he was just a tiny tyke. He's like me, son: a repeater. A good, sturdy repeater."

"What does a repeater do?"

The Snow Train

"A repeater is a regular here, Robbie. They don't know what to do with us poor souls, so we keep coming back so they can try out the latest thing on us."

I looked around the room. The men were all reading or playing cards, or wandering around in their bathrobes. They seemed very lonely to me. The red man was lying on his bed with his magazine on his chest, as sound asleep as the red boy.

"Why does he keep staring at that man?"

"All animals seek their own," Mr. Topping said. "The two of them probably have quite a lot in common, if only they could communicate. It's the story with so many of us."

I looked around to see if anyone in the room looked like me. There was one man who was sitting on his bed reading who seemed to have a trail of black scabs down his arms. I looked away.

"They're changing my blood," I told Mr. Topping.

His eyes moved quickly. "That's a new one on me, son."

"I'll have new immunities. It's like Superman. They'll kill the rash. The scabs will probably all fall off."

Mr. Topping seemed to be frowning.

"It probably won't happen right away," I said. "But it might happen in a week or something."

I looked around at the men pacing up and down. My rash began to tingle. I reached down my little finger and began lightly rubbing a scab on my ankle.

"I won't be here when I grow up," I told Mr. Topping. "Do these men stay here all the time? Have you been here since you were little?"

I felt like I was going to cry. Mr. Topping leaned forward in his rocking chair. Blue smoke floated around him like a cloud.

"Robbie, you're not a repeater, if that's what you're worried about. Your rash lies very loosely on you. I can see it, son! It's ready to go. It just needs a good shove, so to speak. A reason to leave."

I thought of my rash lying loosely on me, ready to fall off. I thought of the scabs dropping off with just a touch. It made me feel light. Mr. Topping passed me the cookies and I ate another one. I looked down at the red boy.

"He could be my brother," I said. "I'm thinking of taking him home with me. We could adopt him."

Mr. Topping laughed. "He has a home, I believe."

"It's not really a home," I said. "It's where he lives with retarded kids. It's not much."

"How do you know? Have you been there?"

"No," I said.

Mr. Topping sucked on his pipe. He looked out the window at the dark sky and the soft snow.

"You never know whether someone's home is good, do you? Look at my case, Robbie. I live across the river over there and I had a cozy little place with my beloved wife. Nothing fancy, mind you. But then this stuff took a turn for the worse, and she tossed me out head over heels."

"You lived in Canada?" I didn't know anyone who lived there. He nodded his head. He took another cookie and ate it in little nibbles. When he was finished, he carefully brushed the crumbs off his robe.

"She didn't like you because of your rash?"

Mr. Topping smiled sadly. "Who's to blame her? I'm like some monster out of a nightmare. You're a child. Haven't you seen me in your fairy stories?"

"You're not that bad," I told him. Mr. Topping's big head

The Snow Train

shook. I kept on talking so he wouldn't cry. "My rash hurts all the time, although it didn't used to." I lifted up my pajamas and showed him my scabs. He leaned down slowly and looked at them, and then grunted. "You're a brave young boy, Robbie."

"I was all right when I was born," I told him. "But when I was eight months old it came."

Mr. Topping nodded his head.

"You're pure before you enter here," he said. There was a strange sound to his voice. His black eyes jumped. "But in this vale of tears—something goes awry."

He twisted his face and sucked on his pipe. His slabs moved up and down. The wrinkles spread everywhere.

"What caused my own situation, you might ask?" He waved his hand in the air. "What led me to this pass?"

I didn't really know what he was talking about. The soft snowflakes falling through the dark sky were making me sleepy. I yawned. Mr. Topping was still talking. I laid my head down on my arms and watched the red boy's back go up and down as he breathed.

"Burma," Mr. Topping said, suddenly.

"Is that your wife?"

Mr. Topping laughed so hard he began coughing and had to take his pipe out of his mouth and and hold his hand to his chest. When he was done, the skin around his eyes was a dark purple.

"No, son, Burma's got a much deeper hold on me than that. No, Burma's where I made my stand with Mad Mike Calvert and his boys. We fought the Japs there, fought 'em hard! Haven't you ever heard of Burma?"

"Yes," I said, although I hadn't. "Daddy fought the Germans. When my Mommy met him, he was in the Air Force."

Mr. Topping sighed. He squeezed his eyes shut. "Burma was a place in a dream. A land of jungles and waterfalls and beautiful clouds so low you could wash your face in them. It was so hot you sweated out your insides and then started all over again. And yet you could see these towering, snowy mountains...."

The red boy shifted beside me and stretched. His legs poked into mine. He opened his eyes. Mr. Topping smiled at him.

"It's a funny thing," he said, "but you make your family where you can find them. In Burma, I was attached to those rough men in a way that I never was before or since. We were brothers."

He lifted his big grey hands, and then put them down again on the arms of the rocker. The slabs of his face shifted, and his eyes looked out the window, and then back again. He smiled at me and the red boy. He didn't seem to know what to say. Behind us there was a clattering noise. I sat up and turned around to see the white-coated men setting up cardtables.

"It's time for our daily slopping," Mr. Topping said. He seemed very quiet. "You two had probably better be on your way. Come again, son."

Right after lunch, the blonde nurse set herself up in a chair near the door and began writing in a pile of charts she held on her lap. Most of the kids were reading or sleeping. I lay on my bed and stared up at the ceiling until I began to have a dream that I was hearing a loud voice.

"Champ," the voice said. "Hey, sport!"

It felt like someone was tickling my nose with a feather. There was giggling, and then a very soft kiss landed on my forehead.

I opened my eyes. Aunt Cecilia and Sam Sullivan were standing over me, smiling.

The Snow Train

"Hi, sweetie," Aunt Cecilia said. "Surprise!"

"Hello," I told her.

They both had their thick coats on, and they were covered with snow.

"How did you get here?" I said.

"By dogsled," Sam said.

"We caught a fast caribou," Aunt Cecilia laughed. "How are you, pal? You're looking awful good."

"Thank you," I said.

I looked around the room. I had been asleep for a little while. There were a few mommies and daddies visiting, but not as many as usual, because of the snow. Most of the kids were still sleeping. I felt tired. Aunt Cecilia and Sam sat down on the bed on either side of me and the bed sagged so much I had to push myself up with my hands to keep from sliding down.

Aunt Cecilia's perfume came into my nose with its sweet, bright smell. Her red hair was wet and soft. Sam took off his big hat and flopped it against his knee to shake the snow out. He was wearing a brown suit with a red tie. He crossed his legs, pulled a cigarette out of his pocket, and lit it. He looked for someplace to put the match.

"Here," said Aunt Cecilia. She reached into her purse and took out a little metal ashtray with a lid that flipped open. She put it on the bed between her and Sam. "Voilà!"

"Her own ashtray," Sam said.

"Comes in handy." Aunt Cecilia smiled at me. "Rob, you wouldn't believe what we went through to get here. The streets are stunning. It's a winter wonderland."

"Here you go, Rob," Sam said.

He was holding out a small paper bag.

"What is it?"

"So suspicious!" Aunt Cecilia said.

Sam turned the bag over and dumped it out. A shower of candy fell onto my lap, jelly beans and gum drops and candy corn and tiny chocolate bars and a big lollipop and some bubble gum and sour balls. The candy spilled over the bed in bright colors. The jelly beans rolled down the white sheets, red and yellow and green and black.

"It's all for you," Sam said. "Your special supply."

He picked up a jelly bean and ate it.

"Hey," said Aunt Cecilia. "Leave this boy's candy alone." But she took a gumdrop and popped it into her mouth.

They both seemed to be in a very good mood. Aunt Cecilia eyes sparkled, and she hugged herself when she smiled at me. Sam's face was blustery and red and he smelled warm and sweet, like he did after cocktail hour at our house. He winked at me and stole another jelly bean.

"You comfortable in here, champ?"

Before I could answer, the blonde nurse came running up. She seemed out of breath.

"I'm sorry, but there really is no smoking allowed in this ward," she said.

"There aren't any signs," Sam said. He took a puff on his cigarette and looked at her.

"There don't need to be any signs," the blonde nurse said. "This is a hospital ward full of sick children. That ought to be enough."

"That's fine, nurse," said Aunt Cecilia. She took Sam's cigarette out of his hand and put it out in her little ashtray, then put the ashtray back in her purse. "We were just having a quick smoke. We had quite a time getting over here to see Robbie."

The Snow Train

"It's cold out there," Sam said, looking right at the blonde nurse. "Frigid."

"Okay, Sam," Aunt Cecilia said.

"Do you know what I'm talking about?" Sam smiled at the blonde nurse.

"Who do you think you are?" the blonde nurse said. Her face was turning red and the red was rising up into her hair. "Did you sign in downstairs?"

"We signed in and we'll sign out," Sam Sullivan told her. The blonde nurse folded her arms over her chest, and shifted her feet from side to side, staring at Sam. Then she turned around and left, walking very fast. We could hear her heels clicking.

"You shouldn't have provoked her," Aunt Cecilia told Sam.

Sam coughed. "I didn't provoke her in the slightest."

Dawn walked up holding her Raggedy Ann. I could tell she had come over for some candy. She was staring at it on my bedspread.

"She can have some jelly beans," I said.

"What about that big lollipop?" Dawn said.

"All right."

Dawn picked it up and unwrapped it. "He's not usually this nice to me," she told Aunt Cecilia.

"I can imagine," Aunt Cecilia said.

I pushed the covers away and got out of bed. I picked up two pieces of chocolate and took them over and put them on the red boy's bed. He stuck them in his mouth.

"One at a time," I said. I thought he might choke on both. I jumped up next to him. He took one out and sucked on the other slowly, looking up at me.

"They're special friends," I heard Dawn say.

Aunt Cecilia came over and sat on the red boy's bed. "My, you're all lit up."

The red boy stared up at her like he was looking at a cloud high in the sky. Sam Sullivan came over and stood jingling the change in his pockets. For some reason, I didn't want either one of them too close to the red boy.

"How old are you?" Aunt Cecilia said.

The red boy put the other piece of chocolate in his mouth. He didn't look at her. His eyes seemed a little blank. She was making him nervous.

"He's all right," I said.

Dawn came over and got on the bed with me and the red boy.

"He doesn't talk," she told Aunt Cecilia.

The red boy moved a little closer to me. His hand came out and held onto my pajamas.

"Aww," said Aunt Cecilia.

Sam Sullivan smiled. He patted his shirt for another cigarette. I looked at Dawn's soft curly brown hair. I felt like I had known her for a long time. The jigsaw puzzle pieces of her face seemed very bright to me. The red boy suddenly shifted and burped. His eyes opened wide. He seemed surprised. Dawn started smiling as she sucked on her lollipop, and for some reason, I smiled, too.

At dinner that night, I sat at a table with Dawn and the red boy. We were having hamburgers and potato chips and pickles. Every time I opened my mouth wide enough to take a bite of the hamburger, the rash around my mouth cracked and I started to bleed. So I took off the bun and cut up the hamburger and ate it that way. The red boy pushed his plate over at me, and I cut up his hamburger, too.

The Snow Train

Dawn just looked at us.

"You act like you're his big brother," she said.

"I am his big brother," I said. "And you're my little sister."

"I'm not your little sister," Dawn said. "God made me different from you. My mommy and me have brown skin."

"You are my little sister," I repeated.

"For a while after I was born, I could remember God," Dawn said. "I could remember His voice."

"What did it sound like?" I said.

"Like an old man's grumbles."

"Was He talking to you?"

"He was talking to His friends." Dawn reached over to the red boy's plate and took one of his pickles. "Besides, if I were your little sister, I'd live in the same house with you, and I don't."

"You can live in the same house without knowing it," I told her. "You just have to be invisible."

"What's that?"

"You live inside the air," I said.

The fat nurse came over and sat down at our table. Her skin looked very white and smooth. She was so fat she had to push the chair back from the table so that she could fit.

"This looks like a good group," she said. She took one of the red boy's potato chips.

"Stop taking his stuff," I said.

"He thinks I'm his little sister," Dawn told her.

"He's just being friendly," the fat nurse said.

The red boy was watching me with his head cocked, but I couldn't tell what he was thinking about. His eyes were small and clear. He looked back at me with a sweet smile, like he was about to laugh.

"Robbie," the fat nurse said, "aren't you proud of being chosen to have your blood changed? Do you know what that might mean? If it works for you, it might work for a lot of other children here. It might mean a new start for them."

"What is he doing?" Dawn said.

"He's changing all his blood," the fat nurse told her. "It's the work of a hero. He's giving up his old blood for new, and you never know what will happen then."

"Nothing will happen," I said.

"I'll do that, too," Dawn said. "I'll change my blood."

"I don't think it would do you any good," the fat nurse said sadly. "You don't have that kind of problem."

The pieces on Dawn's face twisted. Her face looked like a quilt wrinkling up. She stared down at her plate.

"I'm so ugly," she said in a little whisper.

"Why sweetie," the fat nurse told her, "you're the most beautiful one here. Don't you know that?"

Tears streamed down Dawn's face, even though she didn't make any sound. Looking at Dawn, I thought the fat nurse was right. She was pretty. All of the pieces of her face fit together in the different colors to make her as pretty as a pony.

That night in the playroom I sat on the floor with Dawn and the red boy on either side of me. The fat nurse sat on the armchair with the big book on her lap.

"Many of you might not know it," she told us, "but you are the luckiest children on earth."

I looked around at the kids sitting in their white bathrobes, on the floor and at the little school desks. Two girls who had rashes around their mouths like clown smiles lay on the floor together with their hands on their chins. Another girl softly scratched herself under her arms. Billy and the sack-faced boy sat together in the shadows against the wall. Billy seemed to be staring at me.

"I don't think that we're lucky," Dawn said.

The fat nurse leaned forward. "Oh, yes, you are, sweetie." She put her hand to her chest and seemed to push at it, like she was pushing air into herself. "You are chosen. All of you are chosen. God has chosen you to be happy. To be as happy as you can be—for only those who suffer can know the true meaning of happiness. That is the moral of the story we have been hearing."

The fat nurse cleared her throat and put her black glasses on her nose. She opened the book, smoothed its thick wings, and began to read: "Chapter Eight: 'The Falcon.'"

> Blinding desert light shattered the gloom of the tent as two Saracens burst inside, hands clutching the bejeweled grips of the curving daggers at their waists. They wore strange high helmets, and gleaming metal breastplates upon which were engraved a dark falcon's head.
>
> When they saw me standing with clenched fists, the taller of the two laughed a wild laugh.
>
> "Saxon boy, you die!" he roared.
>
> He lunged for me, dagger drawn, but to my dumbfoundment, Marian leapt on his back like a hellcat, banging with her small fists at his helmet, causing him to stagger blindly into a pile of cushions and fall to the floor with Marian still riding him.

The fat nurse shivered. "Oh, dear," she said.

"Oh, dear," I heard Billy whisper to the sack boy. I didn't pay any attention to them. I saw Marian as Dawn and me as Roderick. I was grinding my teeth. The fat nurse continued and I listened as hard as I could.

A slap rang out and Marian cried shrilly. I raced at her tormentor, only to be rewarded with a cuff on the head from his partner that set my ears ringing.

Suddenly the harsh pagan voice rang out:

"Buffoons!"

The voice issued forth from a white robed figure who stood in the open entranceway of the tent. The blinding desert sunset behind him wreathed him in a yellow glow, as though he were a God. A hooded falcon clutched his wrist.

The foul Saracens immediately ceased their molestation and stood at desperate attention, heads bowed. Despite my injury, I raced to Marian's side. She lay as if dazed, a red blotch across the pure skin of her cheek.

Now, our positions were reversed, and it was she who was senseless on the floor of the tent, in need of my succor.

As the fat nurse read on, Dawn slowly shifted herself down and put her head on my shoulder. The red boy lay on the other side of me, fast asleep.

Before I could attempt to rouse her, swift footsteps sounded and the awesome figure from the doorway was standing in front of me, looking at me curiously. He was, in sooth, a man, not a God, although finely proportioned, with smooth dark features, and none of the simian cast of his countrymen. His curving nose hooked boldly from his handsome face, and his skin shone like burnished hardwood. His glittering black eyes gave off the sharp intelligence of a predatory animal. It was no coincidence that the falcon that rode his wrist was both his familiar and mimic, twisting its blind head with every move of its master's, uncannily cocking it in the same sharp fashion, restlessly shifting its perch on its jeweled leather wristlet.

Saladin's voice was like the sound of chain mail dragging on rock.

"I told you to bring them to me," he said to his quivering minions. "I did not tell you to cripple him or his woman."

The tall wretch fell to the floor and began sobbing uncontrollably.

His ruler ignored him, stepping even closer and looking at me appraisingly.

"You are a brave lad," he said, "and I daresay intelligent. Would that I had a thousand like you!"

"King Richard has a thousand like me," I told the frightening stranger stoutly. "Nay, 50 times a thousand!"

Saladin smiled thinly.

"Is that why you came here, roustabout boy?" he inquired in his hoarse English. "To spy on me for your King?"

I raised myself to my full height.

"I spy for no man, king or commoner," I declared. "If your wretched skells had not fallen upon a defenseless baggage train and kidnapped my sister, you and yours would feel the taste of cold steel in man to man combat!"

"Your sister?" Saladin said. He glanced at Marian's supine figure and gave a short laugh. His eyebrows rose. "This dainty morsel is your sister?"

The fat nurse stopped. I wished her voice would go on forever. I felt like I was shaking inside. I wanted to leap on Saladin and kill him.

The fat nurse closed the book and stood up and stretched. She put her hands above her head and held them high. Her body twisted and shivered in her white dress. She looked at us and smiled. Her eyes were bright. She clapped her hands: "Up! Up!"

Slowly the kids began to move. Dawn took her head off my shoulder and shook the red boy, who rubbed his eyes and sat up. She helped him stand. I watched the fat nurse put the book down on the chair. As we walked out of the room, I looked at the windows and saw that the snow had stopped. I caught my breath and ran over to the window. There were lights shining all over the city. They were very bright. My mouth fell open. The lights sparkled at me. The whole city seemed to be awake. The red light of the tower that blinked on the horizon seemed seemed beautiful to me.

In the middle of the night the curtains shuddered and Dawn came up on my bed. I didn't know whether I was awake or asleep when she did. All of a sudden she seemed to be sitting on the sheets, staring at me. In the dark, I couldn't see her eyes, just the twisty colors of her face.

"Hi," she whispered.

"Hi," I said.

"I like that story," Dawn said.

"Are they going to be saved?" I said. "Who will rescue them?"

It was quiet. Dawn looked down at the sheets.

"He will," she said, finally.

"I know," I said.

"You don't have any more of that candy, do you?"

"I have a little bit." I took the bag out from under my pillow and gave it to her. She reached in and took some jelly beans and sat there eating them. I had a piece of chocolate.

Dawn shivered. "I have a hard time sleeping at night here. It's so cold." She lay down next to me on the bed. Her thin twisty face was very close to mine. Her breath smelled like sugar.

"Why did you say the red boy was your brother?" Dawn said.

I stared at her face in the dark. I tried to see her eyes.

"He could be in our family," I said.

"It would be nice to have a family and never have to go home again," Dawn said. "It would be nice to have a family that would be just us."

"We could take care of the red boy," I said.

"Maybe he would talk to me."

"I don't know if he would."

Dawn was quiet for a second. "When they change your blood, what happens to you?"

The Snow Train

"It whooshes through," I told her. I didn't know how to say it. Just thinking about it made my heart pound fast. "The scabs fall off."

"I wish it could happen to me," Dawn said.

"Maybe it could."

"No, it couldn't," Dawn said.

"You don't have scabs," I told her. "You just have those colors. They even look pretty."

Dawn ducked her head down. There was a noise from the red boy's bed.

"He might be awake," I said. "Let's go take a look at him."

We jumped down and went over to the red boy's bed and climbed up through the curtains. He was lying there with the covers up to his chin. All we could see was his red face and his white hair. Even his arms were under the covers.

"He must be hot," Dawn said.

The red boy was breathing hard. His mouth was open and it seemed to be grabbing at air. His skin was shiny and wet.

"Maybe we should untuck him," Dawn said. She pulled down the covers. The red boy didn't move at all. His pajamas were soaked in sweat. I touched his hand and it twitched.

"If we're going to adopt him he'll have to sleep in the same room as us," I said. "We'll have to take care of him. He can't sweat like this. He has too many covers on."

Dawn began humming. She pulled the red boy's covers halfway off his chest. "There," she said. "Now he won't be so hot."

We sat there for a while watching the red boy. Once, his eyes started moving. He half opened them, and then moaned.

"He's dreaming," Dawn said. She lay down next to the red boy and put both her hands underneath her head and curled her legs up. I noticed that the skin on her legs was very brown and shiny. It didn't have her patches on it.

I lay down beside her. "Let's sleep for a while," I said.

I closed my eyes and listened to them breathing. Dawn's breaths were so soft I could hardly hear them. The red boy was breathing like he was running in his sleep. Dawn's hair tickled my face. It smelled like the green shampoo.

3.

The next morning I sat with the red boy in the playroom, which had big squares of sunlight on the floor from the bright sky that came through the windows. There were toy soldiers tossed in a box in the corner of the room, and I pulled a bunch of them out. They were tiny old-fashioned World War I soldiers, only as big as matchsticks, and made out of metal. The English had flat hats and the Germans had tiny spiky helmets. There were two Germans sitting behind a machine gun, and there was one British wearing a gas mask. The rest had their guns over their shoulders and were in a marching position.

"These aren't as good as my soldiers at home," I told the red boy as I set them up. "Most of these aren't even pointing their rifles at each other, so you have to pretend too much. And they don't hide very well."

I gave him the British soldiers and I took the Germans so I could have the machine gun nest. The red boy didn't seem to care. I set my army up behind the legs of a chair and behind a book and a sports car that I put on its side. I took the machine gun nest and set it up on the windowsill, so that the British would have to climb the mountain to get it.

When I turned around the red boy hadn't done anything with his soldiers. He was just staring at them with his eyes slowly closing. He seemed especially sleepy to me. He kept putting his head down.

"Hey!" I said.

The red boy smiled at me, but I thought he looked sad.

"What's the matter with you?" I said. "You're supposed to be setting these up."

I put his soldiers in a long line in front of him, coming at my soldiers.

"They can be attacking," I said. "They have to capture that machine gun!"

I started making explosion sounds and moved his soldiers forward, but he didn't seem to really care that much. I watched his eyes. They seemed very bright. My machine gun fired and killed some of his soldiers. A bunch of them fell down, and the rest had to go and hide in a plastic castle on the floor. They started shooting at my soldiers. One of the soldiers guarding the machine gun nest got hit, and fell off the windowsill.

"Ahhhh," I said. "Crash! He's dead."

The red boy moved his head at the loud noises. He shook it twice, very hard, like he was trying to shake water out of his ear. Dawn came over to us from where she had been sitting, writing things on a slate.

"He looks like he's sick," she said.

I took the red boy and sat him up in my lap. I had to hold him very carefully, because his skin was so hot. It seemed hotter than usual. I put my hand on his forehead. "You're burning up," I told him.

Dawn picked up his wrist and held it to her ear. "I'm checking his pulse," she said. "Oops, he's sick. There isn't any!"

Holding the red boy in my lap with my arms around him I

felt how light he was. He didn't make any noise. I held him and rocked him. Dawn watched us. I thought that just rocking him would make him better. I leaned down and smelled his skull. He smelled like a boiled egg.

Suddenly, a rubber ball came flying over and hit me on the side of the head. It didn't really hurt, but it surprised me so much I fell over with the red boy in my arms. I put him on the floor and stood up. Across the room from us, Billy and the sack-faced boy were laughing. I went over and found the rubber ball lying against the wall. Without even aiming I turned around and threw it as hard as I could. It nearly hit the sack boy in the face. He ducked and took a step back and stood there with his sacks wobbling. The room got quiet. All the kids stopped playing.

Billy walked over to me and stood very close. "Go get that ball."

"You have a face like a red bum," Dawn told him.

"What?" said Billy. His face seemed to bunch up like a monkey's. I started to laugh. Billy reached out and grabbed my bathrobe and I punched him in the chest as hard as I could. He pushed me hard and I fell over a school desk. I got up as fast as I could and started throwing some of the soldiers on the floor at him. He ducked. I heaved a book and a slate at him, and Dawn took a handful of her jacks and threw them hard. They were like tiny little stars flying through the air and they bounced off his puffy red face. All of a sudden, he slammed his hand to his eye. "Ow," he said. "Ow! No fair in the eye!"

I ran at him and shoved him hard and he fell back on the floor. I jumped on top of him and began hitting him with my fists on his head and on his shoulders. He was kicking and yelling. He pushed me off him and got up, still holding his eye. He was crying and walking in circles.

I got up and went back to the red boy and Dawn.

"I think he's really sick," said Dawn. She had her arm around the red boy. His head was down on his chest, and he was drooling. I began to feel afraid. I stuck my face down into his face.

"Hey," I said. "Hey, moron. How's your wiener?"

The red boy looked at me. I thought that he was going to smile. His mouth opened, then closed. His eyes moved away from me.

"He's sick," I said.

The blonde nurse came into the room with the sack boy walking behind her. She looked around with her hands on her hips.

"What's going on?" she said.

"He threw something at me and hit me in the eye," Billy said.

"Who did?"

"The scabby one."

The blonde nurse walked over to us. Her heels clicked across the sunny room. As she came, I looked out the window into the bright blue sky. A puffy white cloud flew by the roof of the hospital. It was flying so fast it was like a bird. It zipped away.

The blonde nurse came and stood in front of me with her hands on her hips.

"What's happened here?" she said.

"This boy's sick," said Dawn.

She knelt down and took the red boy from Dawn and held him. He was loose in her arms. His head hung upside down.

"Hey," I said.

The blonde nurse picked up the red boy and began to run. She ran out of the room, dodging around the toys that were on the floor. The red boy bobbled in her arms.

"Where is she going?" Dawn said.

The Snow Train

I ran out into the hallway. The blond nurse was shouting something as she ran with the red boy. Other nurses stopped what they were doing and ran after her. The old people in pajamas sitting on the benches threw their heads up and stared. They began whispering to each other.

Dawn came up and stood next to me in the hallway. She looked like she was going to cry. "He was so hot," she said.

"He's sick," I said. "He's got a fever."

"In bed last night he was hot," Dawn said.

We walked down the hallway to the long room and went inside. No one was there. All the beds stood white and clean, with their covers neatly tucked in and their curtains open. The card tables were put away and the floor was shiny and white.

Dawn and I got up on my bed. We didn't know what to say. She kept turning her head and looking around.

"Where is he?" she said. "Where is he?"

I thought of the cloud that had raced past the window just as the blonde nurse reached down for the red boy in the playroom.

"He flew away," I said.

Dawn started crying. "He's sick! What are you talking about?"

The other kids started to come back into the room. They stared at me and Dawn sitting on the bed. Billy and the sack-faced boy walked by us with their heads down. The two little girls who had rashes around their mouths were holding hands. They got up into a bed and lay down and hugged each other. Dawn sat on my bed with her legs dangling. Her bathrobe was pulled tight around her, and her curly hair fell over her face. She picked at her Raggedy Ann's dress. Then, without saying anything, she got down off the bed and went over to her own and got up on it and went to sleep.

Mommy and Daddy both came in a little while later. They didn't notice the red boy's bed was empty. They had big smiles on their faces as they sat down.

"I'll bet you're glad to see us, huh?" Daddy said. He was sitting on the bed holding his overcoat on his lap. He jiggled his foot and smiled at me.

"I think he's sick," I said to Mommy.

"Who?" she said.

"Him." I nodded my head to the red boy's bed. "He got sick in the playroom and he didn't come back."

"Do you mean Frederick?"

"The red boy," I said. "Can you go and see?"

She got up and put her coat down on the bed.

"Let me find out," she said. "I'll talk to the nurse."

She got up and left the room. Daddy and I sat there for a few minutes, neither of us saying anything.

"Is this guy a friend of yours?" Daddy asked, finally.

"Yes," I said. "He's in my family."

"Your family?" Daddy said. "I didn't see him around the house."

"No," I said. "We were going to adopt him."

Daddy laughed. "It's nice you're making arrangements, Rob."

I stared at Daddy. He sometimes looked like a little doll, with little white hands and little ears and very neat little black hairs.

My skin was throbbing. It wanted me to scratch it, but I was holding off. I was waiting for a time when I would be by myself, so that I could rake my hands over it. I kept thinking about it, about how the scabs would come off in my hands.

For some reason, Daddy was talking about the weather.

"No one's seen anything like this winter, Rob. We've had

more feet of snow than in 100 years. And now it's all melting and it's fifty-five degrees out there in February. The weather is a funny thing. No one can figure it out." Daddy laughed. "Weather means *whether or not*. That's an old weatherman's joke. No one knows what it's going to do."

"Whether or not," I said.

Mommy came back and sat down on the bed and put her hand on my knee. "Robbie, I can't seem to find anybody that knows anything. But I wouldn't worry. Nurse Kilmer told us he gets these fevers sometimes. It's part of his condition." She leaned over and put a hand on my head. "He'll be fine, sweetheart. Remember, you've got your big day coming up. Day after tomorrow. Concentrate on that."

"He's my baby!" I said. "I want him to be here."

Mommy and Daddy stared at me. They were making me mad.

"Robbie, he's not your—baby," Mommy said. "What are you talking about?"

"He needs to come back."

"He'll come back," Daddy said. He scratched the back of his neck and twisted up his chin and tugged at his tie. "Maybe you can go visit him."

I looked up and saw the fat nurse come in the room. I didn't know what she was doing here. It was too early and she wasn't in her nurse clothes. She had her coat and her hat on and she was hurrying as fast as she could.

When she got to us, I thought that she looked like a saint. Her cheeks were all rosy and red and she had her hands together in front of her and she was shaking them.

"Oh, oh, oh," she said. "Oh, Robbie! Your friend has gone to heaven."

"Heaven?" I said.

"No," said Mommy.

The fat nurse started to cry.

"Did he boil over?" I said.

"No, sweetie," the fat nurse said. "It was just too much for him. I think his little soul just flew away."

"I knew that he could fly," I said.

"Nurse," Mommy said.

The fat nurse was holding herself and sobbing.

I looked over at the red boy's bed, but he wasn't there. He wasn't anywhere.

"He was very light inside," I said.

The fat nurse was making so much noise that the kids started to get upset. They got down from their beds and began walking back and forth, but they didn't seem to be going anywhere. They were just kids walking in their bathrobes in a big room with white beds.

The fat boy with the dried leaf scabs started whimpering. He stood up and then sat back down again. Some of the kids started scratching themselves.

The fat nurse stood in the aisle shaking and crying.

"Tom, get her," Mommy said.

Daddy got up and tried to put his arms around her, but they would hardly reach, and the fat nurse was shaking so hard he couldn't hang on to her. He let go and came back.

"Do you think we should call someone?" he asked Mommy. His face was all red. "I don't know if she should be going on this way."

"Oh Lord," said Mommy. "Damn it all!"

She put her hand on my shoulder and looked at me. "I'm

sorry, sweetie. He was your pal. You're not having the best of luck, are you?"

"He was our baby," I said. "I was going to adopt him."

Mommy leaned down and kissed me. "I think that would have been a great idea."

Dawn came up to the bed. She had her thumb in her mouth, but she didn't have her Raggedy Ann. She stood there, twisting back and forth on her feet. Mommy looked at her.

"I'm sorry for what happened," she said.

"I didn't know him," Dawn said.

"It was the red boy," I told her.

"I didn't know him," Dawn repeated. "You were his friend. What happened to him?"

"He flew away," I said.

"Robbie—" Mommy began, but then stopped. She pressed her hands to her face. When she took them away there were tears rolling down her cheeks. Out in the aisle, the fat nurse began crying in a way that sounded like moaning. She bent over and held her stomach. Daddy went over to her again, but she pushed him away and ran out of the room. Daddy went running after her. I could hear him yelling in the hallway.

"He burnt up," said Dawn.

More and more of the kids were crying. They huddled in their beds and cried to themselves. Even Billy was crying, sitting by himself in his bathrobe with a model airplane on his lap. Across the aisle from me, the two little girls with rashes around their mouths were taking turns scratching each other's backs. I could see pieces of scabs flying in the air with drops of blood. The sack-faced boy walked up and down in the aisle with his sacks bouncing. His face was completely blank.

It seemed like all the noise made a wind that was going to cause an explosion. It was like a roaring. It was building up to something. I put my hand over my ears. I wanted to jump up and down.

All of a sudden, nurses came running in through the door. They stood there in all the noise and stared. They looked like they were seeing ghosts, ghosts who were crying and scratching and screaming. They started grabbing kids and putting them back into bed. They made the fat boy stop whimpering, and tore the two scratching little girls apart. They picked up the sack boy by his arms and dragged him back to his bed. They kept making shushing noises at everyone.

I watched everything. I wasn't crying.

That night, all night long when I was lying in my bed in the dark, I remembered the red boy.

There was a big hollow space inside of me. I thought it must be just like how the red boy had felt all the time. I was afraid of the space. I was afraid of how empty it was.

I tried to cry, but I couldn't. I kept thinking of the red boy rolling his head and drooling. I wondered where he had gone. I wondered if he was around somewhere and I just couldn't see him. I was worried about him.

If the red boy was gone, what would I do? I sat up on my bed. What was left for me to do?

I got up out of bed and went out into the aisle. I listened carefully. Instead of all the cries and the scratching sounds, I heard nothing. I wondered if everyone had left but me. Maybe I was the only one who hadn't flown away? I went over to Dawn's bed and pushed through the curtains. She was lying with her knees curled up to her face and her arms wrapped around them. Her Raggedy Ann was tucked under the covers with her.

I watched her. I saw her back going up and down.

"Hey!" I said.

She didn't move.

"Hey, moron!"

Dawn stirred and shifted. I touched her leg. She jumped.

"Shhh!" she said. She raised her head and looked around. Her eyes were still closed.

"It's me," I said. "Let's go out in the hallway."

She finally looked at me. Then she closed her eyes again.

"Leave me alone," she said.

"It's me," I said.

"Stop it!" Dawn said. She put her head under the covers. I stood there for a second, and then I walked away. I went down the dark aisle and out the door. I walked down the hallway to the bathroom and pushed open the door and went inside. It was very dim there, but the room was so white it seemed to light itself, just from the gleam of the toilets and sinks. I went to the urinals and opened up my pajamas and took out my thing and peed. It just kept coming and coming. "Oh," I said. The burning went out of my thing and it felt all soft and warm. I felt very light and sweet.

I went over to the sinks and turned on a faucet, and watched water splashing in the bowl for a while. I turned it off. I looked into the mirror above the sink. Immediately, I stepped back. The ugly boy's face had more black little zippers on it. It was red and crusty around his nose and eyes. There was a streak of blood on his cheek. I tried to find his eyes, but I couldn't. They seemed to run away from me when I looked at them. His head seemed big and swollen.

I ran out of the bathroom and down the hallway, and went back to the long room and got into bed. The minute the sheets touched me my rash began whispering. It told me stories. It told me that my skin was like a map of the world, and that there was time to roam all over it. The rash whispered and talked, and the curtains around the bed breezed in and out. The rash told me good things, and it told me bad things, and it showed me that it was part of me, and the only thing I had. I was inside of it, and it was me. When it was done, there were black scabs all over the bed like bugs and I was breathing very hard.

4.

In the morning the fat nurse was there. Her eyes looked like someone had hit them. She walked very slowly, almost in a little shuffle, and she kept sniffing. Her big white dress looked stained. Her hair was lying flat on her head.

Her breath went in when she peeled off my pajamas.

"Oh, Robbie," she said. "Oh, my God."

"It doesn't matter," I told her. "When my blood changes, it's all going to get better. I can scratch as much as I want now. As much until tomorrow."

"No, sweetie, no," the fat nurse said. "That's not right."

My skin looked like it was covered with raspberry jam. It burned so bad that it was like someone was holding a match to it. The fat nurse put her gloves on and started putting cream on me, but it didn't really matter. The cream just soaked right in, and the rash ate it up.

The fat nurse's white cheeks were red as she put the medicine on. Her lips were moving, but they weren't saying anything. When she was done she helped me get my robe on and I went over and sat down next to Dawn.

"You've got a very bad face this morning," Dawn said.

My face felt all tight and glowing. It might have been like what the red boy's face felt like all the time.

"I heard God last night," Dawn said. "He was talking to the red boy."

"What was He saying?"

"I don't remember," Dawn said. "But the red boy was talking back."

She took her banana and threw it down on the floor. The fat nurse came back and picked it up and put it on the table and walked away. Dawn looked at it. She picked up her Raggedy Ann and hugged her. I didn't recognize her face anymore. I thought that her skin was taking her over, too. All her colors turned into a Halloween mask.

"The red boy was saying, You should stop now and pay attention to me," Dawn said. "But God didn't! He was too busy."

"He's up there in the sky," I said.

"I'm going home," Dawn said.

"When?" I said.

"Just as soon as I hear more of those grumbles."

Just then I saw the blonde nurse come in with the brown-skinned woman who took care of the red boy. They went over to the red boy's bed, where the fat nurse came up to them. The three of them stood there talking, and then the brown-skinned woman bent down and reached underneath the bed and took a suitcase out.

I got up and walked over. The woman opened up the suitcase. Inside of it were the red boy's clothes. The woman had something in her hand. As I got closer, I saw that it was his tractor. She put it in the suitcase and started shutting it, but then she saw me coming.

She smiled at me and held out the tractor.

"Frederick was always trying to give this to you," she said. "You can have it if you want."

"I don't want it," I said.

The brown-skinned woman nodded. She put the tractor in the suitcase and closed the suitcase. I told her that the red boy was going to be in my family.

"I might have adopted him," I said.

"That's good," she said. "I think he would've like that better than where he was."

"Did he have a room of his own?"

"No," the woman said. "It's a big room, sort of like this. He had to share it with a lot of boys."

"But he liked me," I said.

She looked at me. Her eyes were black and they watched me. Then she smiled.

"Yes, he liked you."

I went and got up on my bed and watched the fat nurse and the blonde nurse walk the woman out. The fat nurse came back in a few minutes with her coat and her hat on. She sat down next to me and took my hand in hers.

"Please don't be too sad," she said. "He's in a much better place. You heard her. That wasn't a good place."

"He liked me," I said.

"Yes, he did," said the fat nurse.

I looked at her in her coat and hat. She was so fat she looked piled up and round, like a snowman. She was breathing, watching me. I watched her back. There didn't seem to be anything that we could say to each other. It didn't seem like we knew each other anymore.

The blonde nurse led us down the hallway for our baths. All the people were out, the people sitting on the benches and the nurses moving fast in their white shoes, walking with a clicking sound. The old lady with the bandages on her ears was there, leaning forward and bobbing, but I didn't see Mr. Topping.

My rash was wet and soft on me as I walked. It talked to me. It said, don't get your blood changed. Stay with your old blood.

"Hah!" I said.

I thought of the new blood, a big pool of it in a room somewhere, waiting for me. If I could get to it and dive in, I would be all right, I would come out of the pool without any scabs at all, and I would be as smooth and red as the red boy.

The blonde nurse took us into the bathroom and the white light shined down on us. I couldn't believe it. It was like the glow that had come into our bathroom on the morning of my birthday party. We lined up and I had to put my hands up to my eyes to keep the light out. My elbow nearly hit the sack boy, who was standing next to me.

"Stop it," he said.

"It's too bright," I said.

He didn't say anything. I finally took my hands down but I had to squint to see anything. The glow was rolling through the room like a cloud. It covered the first boys who got into their baths and it covered the blonde nurse and then it covered all of us, until I couldn't see anything at all. Inside the cloud there was a brighter glow, and I saw that it was me. Inside my pajamas, I was glowing red, bright red, like a fire that was flaring. I took off all my clothes, and I could see that I was as red as the sun. My whole rash was glowing, and it didn't even hurt anymore, it had just become smooth and red. The blonde nurse came out of a cloud and stood there looking at me. Her eyes were very large. I was so bright she had to take a step back.

The Snow Train

"Why don't you—" she said, but then she stopped. She knew that she couldn't talk to me. I walked past her in the mist and got to my tub and and sat down into it and I was so hot the water started hissing. I held up my arm and looked at it, and it was blazing hot, and smoke was coming from it. The red was glowing so much that my arm glowed from the inside, and I was amazed to see it.

The glow slowly blew away and I could see everyone staring at me, but I didn't care. I just sat there and didn't say a word and made my eyes very light, and I smiled with my little teeth.

In the playroom I sat up on the windowsill and looked out. The sun was very bright and the snow was melting. Long drips of white-blue water fell from the roof of the hospital, and the ambulances that came up to the curb splashed the people walking by on the sidewalk.

I opened the handle of the window a little, and the air that blew in smelled muddy, like spring. I thought of the green lawns on our street coming out from under all the snow, and of the water that came rushing down the gutters in the spring. I thought of things that I liked to sail on the water, twigs and leaves and pieces of Daddy's shirt cardboards.

Spring was when things broke up and the air felt fresh and cold and when the clouds raced by in the blue sky, and when there was a cold wind inside of the breeze. It made me want to get up and go downstairs and run down all of the streets as fast as I could.

I suddenly felt like I could do anything I wanted to. I laughed out loud. It was a strange feeling. I felt it in my chest, it was like a cold wind rushing through me. I wanted to jump up and down. I looked at all the kids and they made me want to laugh. They seemed like little mice playing with their toys in this little room. I was going to get out and walk and run and go anywhere I wanted to, and no one could stop me.

I got down from the windowsill and wrapped my bathrobe tight around me, and started walking through the room. All around me the kids played. The fat boy with the dried leaves on his face had some Lincoln logs he was building into a log cabin. He was putting on the roof, which was made out of green boards. I stopped and looked down at him. He stopped what he was doing and looked back up. When I didn't go away, he started building his roof again, but he kept looking back at me, as if I was going to knock it over. I watched his fat fingers, and then I kept on walking. Dawn was playing jacks with two other little girls. Dawn kept bouncing her ball and taking their jacks. One of the little girls was thin and yellow-looking and her skin had strange wrinkles on it. Her head was very large and swollen and there were stitches on the top of it.

The little girl pushed her pigtails back over her ears and looked up at me. Her eyes were black and sore.

"Help me," she said.

She was crying. Tears flowed down her cheeks. I walked out the door and down the hallway without even thinking about her. I was going to Mr. Topping's room and I felt so free. I knew that I could walk free forever, and that no one could stop me, there was nothing that anyone could do but let me do what I wanted. When I got to the emptier part of the hallway where the red boy and I had stopped, I slowed down. Already I could smell cigarette smoke and hear the radio and men's voices from way down the hall.

I thought of the red boy walking right into that room. He wasn't afraid of anybody, anybody at all, and neither was I. I went right inside the room and stopped and stood there staring around.

The Snow Train

None of the men noticed me. The air was thick and smoky, and the room was very messy, with clothes and magazines and coffee cups lying around. I walked over to the bed of the red man. He was lying flat on his back, reading a magazine that he held up to the ceiling with his arms straight up in the air. I stood by the foot of his bed until he looked at me. He slowly put the magazine down.

"He's dead," I said. "From a high fever. He burnt up."

The man stared at me. "What are you talkin' about? I don't know you. Get out of here! Go away."

"You could burn up," I told him.

The red man looked to the right and to the left. "What do you want? Do you want a quarter? Is that it?" He opened his table drawer and reached into it and took out a quarter and flipped it at me. It hit the bed rail and bounced up high in the air right in front of my eyes. I let it fall on the bed. I thought that the red man would be very sad when he heard about the red boy. Who would be his shadow then? Who would come and look at him?

I walked all the way down to the end of the room. Mr. Topping was sitting on his rocking chair with his blanket over his lap. He watched me come. His eyes were rolling very fast in his head and he was twisting his thick hands in his lap. His big mouth opened and closed.

He held out his arms as I got closer.

"Come here, boy, come here."

I went to him and he wrapped his arms around me and hugged me. I felt like I was getting hugged by a bear. As he held me against him I could hear his heart beating. It sounded like a drum thumping inside my ear. Finally he let go of me. I sat up on his bed and looked at him. His slabs were a deep grey. Tears were running down the cracks between them.

"I'm so sorry, Robbie," he said. "I'm terribly sorry. He was an angel from heaven."

"A boiled angel," I said.

"An angel," Mr. Topping said. "He came here for a reason and now he's left. His job is done."

"What's his job?" I said.

"Who knows?" Mr. Topping said. "Is that for us to say?"

Mr. Topping stood up and began to pace back and forth in his bathrobe. The yellow dragon on the back rippled and blew red fire.

"Lord, it's a difficult thing to make sense of," he said. "We must be sure of His will."

"He's in heaven," I said.

"That he is, that he is."

Mr. Topping kept on pacing. He stopped at the window and stared out. I could see that he was looking very far away, to Canada or maybe even Burma.

"That man doesn't know," I said. I pointed down the ward at the red man, who was lying on his bed, watching us.

"He knows," Mr. Topping said. "He knows, son. He just won't face it, like the rest of us. Anytime a child dies, it becomes a true sorrow to go on living. So you try to deny it. You pretend it never happened. Sometimes, you pretend the child never was alive."

I stared at him.

"The red boy was alive," I said. I felt myself shaking inside. I felt hot and cold all over.

"He certainly was," said Mr. Topping. "You and I know that."

"I took care of him," I said.

Mr. Topping looked at me.

"I know that, son, I know. But there are some people who

try to change the nature of things. Not you, my lad. You're far too sensible. But there are some who try to change what is. It's what leads to hauntings. Troubled men from Macbeth on down have been plagued by ectoplasmic apparitions because they have refused to face the dread nature of the reality of death." He sighed and shook his big head. "I too am haunted," he said. His eyes darted. He filled up his pipe and lit it. He puffed hard. Smoke rose up into the sunlight, the sunlight that the red boy could never go out in.

Mr. Topping lowered his voice to a hoarse whisper. He leaned forward in his chair and stared at me. "Have you ever struggled hand-to-hand with a person who is actually bent and determined on physically killing you? A housebreaker or a common thug, perhaps?"

"No," I said.

"Few have," said Mr. Topping. "But those who have will never forget it. You and your would-be murderer are thrown into an unnatural closeness, skin to skin, hand to hand, breath to breath. The feeling of his skin on yours—it's the most hateful, revolting thing in the world. You feel you'll never be cleansed of it."

He shuddered.

"I was in Burma, just poking along through the bush on the banks of the steamy Sittang, when up jumped this skinny Jap fella, bayonet pointed. He charged me at a run. He was a skeleton, but he looked mean and determined. I should've shot him, but I was too surprised. I parried his thrust with my rifle, but I tripped. He fell upon me and tried to strangle me.

"I killed that strange creature, all right—threw him off me, leapt upon him and throttled the life out of him! But even as I did, his hands clung to me, and it was that slimy foul yellow skin that became my undoing. The doctors here tell me it can't be so, but that dead Jap gave me what I have today, this rot, this fungus, this living death!"

Mr. Topping stopped. He was breathing hard. I stared at him open-mouthed. His eyes were very far away. Finally he looked at me. He seemed to be seeing me for the first time.

"I'm terribly sorry, Robbie, old son. I get carried away at times with my memories. I'm an old man."

"They're changing my blood tomorrow," I told him.

Mr. Topping seemed to sigh. "That's good news," he said. "That's wonderful, Rob."

"Yes," I said. "I'm going to get better. I'm not going to die."

"No one says you're going to die, son," Mr. Topping said.

"But I might, though," I said. "It could happen. Then I might be a ghost."

"You're not going to die, Robbie," Mr. Topping said in a firm voice. "You've got the breath of life on you. I can feel it."

"Didn't the red boy have the breath of life?" I said.

"He was just a breath," Mr. Topping said. "He was breath itself."

I thought of the red boy as a breath. Maybe that was why he was so light. Maybe he didn't die. Maybe he just floated away, like a ghost. I thought of the Jap that Mr. Topping had talked about. I thought of him floating out of the shining jungle. Mr. Topping had tried to forget about him, but he came back, and hurt him. I wasn't going to forget about the red boy.

Mr. Topping didn't move and I saw that he was asleep. His chest moved up and down and his glasses slid down on his nose. The light from the window made him look like a peaceful monster sitting in his den. I looked back around the room, and saw that it had turned very quiet. The men were sleeping like some fairy had come in and put sleep dust on them. I could see their chests going up and down, and I could hear them snoring. It sounded like someone very softly beating pillows.

I stood up and walked down the aisle. When I got to the bed of the burnt man, I stopped. He was sound asleep on his face with his mouth open. As he breathed he made little squeaky noises, little soft whistles, that sounded like the red boy's pigeon cries. I wondered if he knew that the red boy might sometime come up and take him for a walk way down to the end of a long street, past all the big houses and their lawns, to water that was bright and shiny, like the river.

Before dinner, Mommy and Daddy both came to see me. I looked at their hair. They both had such nice black hair, and it shined so bright in the light.

Mommy had her lipstick and makeup on. She said they were going to a play with Aunt Cecilia and Sam Sullivan.

"It's about a queen who grants everybody just one wish," she told me. "And they can do anything they want with that one wish, but they can't have it back, or ask for another one."

"Be careful what you wish for is the moral," Daddy said.

"I wish I could go with you," I said.

"I wish you could too," Mommy said. "In fact, I'm going to wish for you when I get to the play tonight."

"We'll both wish, champ," Daddy said.

The fat nurse came up while we were talking.

"Tomorrow's the big day," she said. "Tonight is the last time you can have food, Robbie, until the procedure is over, so eat good!"

"Listen to what she tells you, Robbie," Daddy said.

The men in the dirty white coats were setting up the tables and the young nurses in their striped dresses were coming out with the trays of food. The air smelled like steamy vegetables. The kids walked out slowly and sat down at the tables. Mommy and Daddy got up and put their coats on. I looked over at the red boy's bed. The sheets were stretched so tight. They looked as cold as ice and snow.

Daddy smiled at me. He patted my shoulder.

"We'll be here bright and early, Rob," he said.

"I'm not afraid," I said.

"We know you're not," Daddy said. "You've got a lot of people rooting for you."

"And," Mommy said, "we may have a surprise guest. A mystery visitor."

"Who?" I said.

Mommy just smiled. "You'll find out." She leaned down and kissed me. Daddy ruffled my hair. They both said goodbye and before I knew it they were waving at me from the door of the long room. I waved back and then jumped down from my bed. I brushed my hand over the red boy's bed, and then went out to the tables and sat down next to Dawn.

I tried to eat some chicken, but I wasn't very hungry. Dawn stared at me when I put down my knife and fork.

"You're not eating your dinner," she said.

"I don't like it."

"I don't like it, either," said Dawn. She pushed her plate away.

"You already ate most of it," I told her.

"No, I didn't. I hardly ate any."

"That's okay," I said. I sat there. I felt like I was empty inside, and that it didn't matter if I ate or not. Nothing could fill me up. My stomach began to twist up for no reason. I began to get very afraid.

The Snow Train

I looked around the room at the other little kids. They were all eating or talking. The two little girls with the clown mouth rashes were sitting at the same table as Billy and the sack-faced boy, and they were laughing together.

No one but me and Dawn remembered the red boy, it seemed to me. I thought it was strange that the kids could laugh and talk and eat and walk around and play with their toys when the red boy was gone. It didn't seem like it was the right thing to do. It seemed to me that we should all be standing by his bed, looking at it and waiting for him to come back.

I thought of what Goodie said to me, how death ran in families. I thought of myself dying like the red boy. I thought of myself dying in a red pool of blood that was like a lake. I saw myself coming out of it, and standing on the beach with no one there. I tried to look into the dark woods, but there was no one there at all. I couldn't see anything.

Then I saw myself walk into our house. I was going to try to wake up Mommy and Daddy and tell them to get up and help me. But they didn't wake up no matter how I shook them, they were like stones. Then I saw myself in my room staring at my empty bed. No one was there but the two little dolls on the other bed. The room was glowing white from the snow falling outside. And I was standing there.

I started crying right at the table. I knew that no one and nothing could stop me from dying if that was what was going to happen. The tears were rolling down my face.

"Stop that," Dawn said. "Why are you crying? Don't cry."

I couldn't say anything. I tried to stop, but I couldn't. The tears were stinging my rash. They were falling on my plate.

Dawn started crying, too. She hugged her Raggedy Ann and put her chin down on its head and cried as hard as me. The other kids looked at us, but I didn't care. They would cry if they were us, too.

After dinner, the fat nurse came and took us all down the dark hallway to the playroom for our story. The playroom was very quiet. The air felt cool and thin. None of the radiators were banging or hissing. Outside, I could see the lights of all the houses and buildings in the city. I thought of Mommy and Daddy walking through those lights, all bright and glittery.

Dawn and I sat down together in two school desks that were side by side. Dawn put her head down on her arms. I looked up at the fat nurse, who was sitting very quietly in her chair. Her face was very pale. She held the book closed on her lap and stared straight ahead of her. She wasn't looking at us.

All the kids waited. The fat nurse gave a long sigh. Her chest moved, and I could her the little whistle of her breath.

"We lost one of our own," she said in a low voice. "We lost someone we loved very much. He used to lie right here."

She pointed to the floor at her feet. I heard Dawn start to sniffle.

"He was a poor lost soul, but now he's happy," the fat nurse said. "We're the ones who need to account for ourselves. We're the ones left behind. But there's a reason. There is a reason!"

The fat nurse wiped her eyes. She flopped the book open on her lap. Her fingers flew through the pages. I closed my eyes as she began to read.

"Chapter Nine," she said. "'Escape!'"

When Saladin had strode out of the tent and rode away with his minions, I knelt beside Marian and gently bathed her brow with cool

The Snow Train

water. Her cheeks were in a high flush, her breath was shallow, and her eyelids fluttered like the wings of the swift swallows that darted low over the summer fields at Evensong.

"Marian," I whispered. "Dear Marian."

My heart beat wildly. Here my sweet sister lay, her hair spilled around her like black wine, her breast heaving in unnatural rhythms, while I knelt helpless and unmanned in the midst of the enemy camp.

"Marian," I whispered into her ear. "Marian, please return to me."

The fat nurse paused and looked at each of us in turn, as if she was counting us. The kids around the room were so still I thought they were statues. When the fat nurse went back to her reading, the sound of her voice, with its light little sighs and whistles, was like a bird.

Such was the depth of my sorrow that when the first soft cry came to my ears I thought it was but an echo of my own harsh sobbing. But then another cry, and another, entered my grief-besotted mind, and I raised my head with a start.

Marian had pulled herself up on one elbow.

"Water," she murmured in a voice so soft it might have been but the whisper of a breeze, "Water, please!"

I flew to her side, helped her sit up, and with my own cupped hands, poured water down her poor, parched throat. Her eyes slowly opened and regarded me with wonder and fear.

"Oh, Roderick, I had such a dream...."

Tears of joy trickled down my face.

"There is no time for dreams, now, dear sister, for we must make plans to escape these foul creatures." I kissed her poor hands. "Can you stand?"

The fat nurse paused for breath. I saw that her cheeks were red. She didn't look at us, but down at the book, as if it might run away from her.

Dawn's head was up, and she stared at the fat nurse. In the dark room, the colors of her face were shining.

With my help, Marian rose shakily to her feet, the bells on her out-landish costume tinkling in a merry way that reminded me I needed a disguise. I threw a hooded robe over my shoulders and crept to the door of the tent and peered out. The desert night had fallen swiftly, and the camp was alive with the sounds of evening—dogs barking, women singing. Marian pulled her veil around her mouth and togeth-er we stepped outside. We bowed our heads and hurried along, she a few steps behind me, as befits a Saracen maid. At the outskirts of camp, a small group of ponies were tethered. A young boy guarded them with a stick. He bowed at us as I came up—and one smight of my fist left him senseless on the ground, as poor reward for his courtesy. I separated a pure black pony from the tethering rope, mounted, and pulled Marian up behind me. Just then, there was an explosion of guttural shouting and and then the screeching of their infernal pagan horns.

"We are discovered!" I cried. Digging my heels desperately into my steed, I urged him away. Marian and I flew like the wind. Soon, the sound of the horns faded, and all we could hear was the hard clatter of the pony's hoofsteps. The desert sands rose in dunes around us like sleeping giants, and still we rode on, up and down, up and down. Finally, alone on the vast sea of sand, we paused to let the frothing pony rest.

Marian and I sank thankfully to the ground. Marian rested her head on my shoulder, and smiled at me. Lying in the cool embrace of the sands, we looked up into the black sky, where there were thou-sands and thousands of stars. Despite my exhaustion, I felt a wild exhilaration. We had escaped! The night sky was beckoning us, and I thought that our next adventure might be among the very stars themselves!

The fat nurse's voice stopped, but I kept my eyes closed, squeez-ing them as tight as I could. Inside my eyelids, I was seeing the same stars that Roderick saw. They were bursting and shooting and falling. The black sky was so alive and so wide, and I wanted to climb up into it and hide there forever. Walking through the stars, jumping from one to another, I saw the red boy.

Late that night, I woke up. My stomach was burning and my throat was dry. I heard voices. It was the two girls with the mouth rashes talking back and forth from their beds. I couldn't make out what they were saying. I thought their voices were two little birds flying back and forth through the night air.

My rash was throbbing. I got out from under the covers and put my feet over the side of the bed and sat there. I pulled up my pajama legs. On each leg, the scabs had become one complete black scab, from my knees down to my ankles. The scab was black with red around the edges. It had a flaky crust. I pushed my finger inside and broke the crust, and my leg tingled like an electric shock.

I reached down with both hands and scratched the huge scabs. I grabbed handfuls of them. Broken pieces of scabs fell all over the sheets and the floor. Blood spurted out onto my hands. The scabs crumbled away and left raw red slick spots on my legs, like a slick puddles on the street. They looked clean. They gleamed.

I was shaking. I got down from the bed and went through the curtains and got up onto the red boy's bed. I was like a ghost, a ghost creeping through the dark. I pulled the curtains tight and got under the covers. I thought that this must have been what it was like to be the red boy. This is what he saw, and this is how his covers felt.

I lay back and watched the ceiling. I could barely see it in the dark. I thought of Roderick saying to Marian, our next adventure will be up there in the stars. I thought of the red boy and me running through the stars, jumping around in the sky. I pulled the

Once There Was a Village by Yuri Kapralov
163 pages, trade paperback
ISBN: 1-888451-05-X
Price: $12.00

"If there were a God, then *Once There Was a Village*, Yuri Kapralov's chronicle of life as an exiled Russian artist on the Lower East Side, would have gone to Broadway instead of *Rent*. Only the staging of this book, set amid the riots of the late '60s and the crime-infested turmoil of the early '70s, might look like a cross between *Les Miserables* and *No Exit*." —*Village Voice*

Manhattan Loverboy by Arthur Nersesian (author of *The Fuck-Up*)
203 pages, paperback
ISBN: 1-888451-09-2
Price: $13.95

"Nersesian's newest novel is a paranoid fantasy and fantastic comedy in the service of social realism, using methods of L. Frank Baum's *Wizard of Oz* or Kafka's *The Trial* to update the picaresque urban chronicles of Augie March, with a far darker edge . . ." —*Downtown Magazine*

Heart of the Old Country by Tim McLoughlin
224 pages, paperback
ISBN: 1-888451-15-7
Price: $14.95

"Tim McLoughlin writes about South Brooklyn with a fidelity to people and place reminiscent of James T. Farrell's *Studs Lonigan* and George Orwell's *Down and Out in Paris and London*. Among the achievements of his swiftly paced narrative is a cast of authentic and frequently complex characters whose voices reflect dreams and love as well as desperation to survive. No voice in this symphony of a novel is more impressive than that of Mr. McLoughlin's, a young writer with a rare gift for realism and empathy." —Sidney Offit, author of *Memoir of the Bookie's Son*

These books are available at local bookstores. They can also be purchased with a credit card online through www.akashicbooks.com. To order by mail, or to order out-of-print titles, send a check or money order to:

Akashic Books
PO Box 1456
New York, NY 10009
www.akashicbooks.com
Akashic7@aol.com

(Prices include shipping. Outside the U.S., add $3 to each book ordered.)

photo by Diane Kinerk

Joseph Cummins was born
in Detroit and now lives in
Maplewood, New Jersey,
with his wife and daughter.
The Snow Train is his first
novel.

covers tight up to my chin. The rash was beginning to hurt on my legs. Mommy said that was because new scabs grew after I scratched it, and they hurt coming in. I thought of the new scabs coming in, little baby scabs growing over and over again. No matter how hard I scratched, I could never make them disappear.

I closed my eyes, I began to think about the pool of blood that was waiting for me. I thought of it like the lake that was lying there with the waves breaking black. I could see the stars shining in it, and when I thought about it flowing into me, I shook.

My rash began hurting all over, not just on my legs. It pierced and hurt me and attacked me. It knew that in the morning the doctors would take big buckets of blood from the lake and put them inside of me, and then the rash would fall off and be gone forever. That was why it was attacking me now. It bit and nipped and grabbed at me. It tore itself. It bled all over me. I was leaking.

"Don't be afraid," I said.

The air felt freezing on my skin, and I began to shudder, over and over again. My body was shaking. It had nothing to do with me.

"I'm not afraid," I said.

I knelt up on the bed. I took off my pajamas. I closed my eyes. I took my fingers and rubbed them lightly all over the rash, I rubbed the backs of my fingernails on it. My body began to tingle when my fingernails touched the sore skin. I gasped and jumped. I heard myself making little squeaky noises. After a while, I heard a noise.

"Who's there?" I said.

"Who?" I said. "I didn't hear you."

I opened my eyes. The curtains were moving around the bed.

The Snow Train

A breeze blew over my body. It was the breeze that smelled like spring, so fresh and wet and cool. It blew all over the rash like soft hands stroking it.

I got down from the bed and went out and stood in the aisle. I could see the bed curtains blowing up and down in the long dark quiet room.

It felt very good to be standing there completely naked. I didn't care who saw my rash, and I felt that my rash was very smooth and clean right now. The breeze blew into my face, and I nearly laughed out loud. It blew into my hair and into my eyes.

It was coming from the doorway. I walked down the aisle past the rows of beds with their curtains flying like sails, and I walked right into the breeze, and it swirled all around me with such a soft, soft touch.

I followed it down the dark hallway and didn't even bother to hide from the fat nurse reading at her little desk. I just kept walking as the breeze blew so cool on my hot skin. I held my arms out straight from my sides and felt the breeze run all over them and I wondered if it would lift me up so that I could fly.

When I got to the playroom the breeze was coming from the open windows, and I ran to them and looked out. The lights of the city looked so bright and happy, and I could see half a moon shining high in the sky, and underneath it a star that seemed to be hanging from it by a string. I breathed the breeze very deep. It smelled like our backyard, and like the puddles in the alleyway, and like the grass beginning to grow.

I turned around and saw the little girl sitting on the big armchair where the nurse read us our story. She had the book in her lap and she was stroking it. I went over to her and sat down next to her.

"The story of this family," the little girl read, "is the story of a happy family. A Mommy, a Daddy, a sister, and her little brother. They lived together happily after all."

The little girl's finger followed the words.

"I remember that," I said.

"Of course you do," said the little girl. "How can you forget your sister?"

I started to cry.

"C'mon!" said the little girl. "Don't be a baby."

The little girl was smaller than me. It was strange that she was so small. I got down on the floor and put my head in her lap and looked up into her face. She had a big white face, a face as wide as the moon. Her black eyes watched me. Her pigtails hung down over her shoulder.

"Where did you go?" I said.

"I don't know," she said.

"I love you," I said.

The little girl smiled. She blushed. She twisted her pigtails with her hands. She looked so pretty. She began to read again. I couldn't understand everything she was saying, but I listened very hard anyway. She was mumbling.

I stood up. I stared down at her while she read. She seemed to have forgotten I was there. Her words were about finding a place to put herself in and stay there. While I was staring at her, the red boy came up to me. He held onto my hand. I sat down and put him on my lap. He was finally talking. Arbo said the names of things to me and I said them back. He was sitting on my lap so white in his pajamas. He was smiling with his white, white teeth. The little girl looked up from her mumbling. She smiled at us. She reached her hand to pat me. His soft head fell on my shoulder. I nodded and fell asleep.

5.

The next morning the doctors made me get into a wheelchair and wheeled me down the aisle of the long room with all the kids watching. Dawn sat on the bed with her Raggedy Ann and waved and waved at me. Billy and the sack-faced boy stared at me, and I knew they were jealous because I got to ride in the wheelchair.

Mommy and Daddy were with me. They had come very early in the morning and sat with me on the bed while all the kids ate breakfast.

"I'll bet you're hungry, champ," Daddy had said. "Don't worry. We'll order you a cheeseburger with all the trimmings later."

"And ice cream," Mommy said. She reached out and brushed my hair with her hand. She had her bright red coat in her lap. Her face looked so sad. She seemed to be looking at me very closely. I saw her green eyes blink. She seemed so different from me, but then I suddenly recognized her. I remembered where I met her. I almost laughed. My skin was hurting so much that I could hardly move, but I looked at Mommy and said, "You used to walk in your room and say poems out loud."

"What?" Mommy said. She felt my brow. She was so fresh and clean. I could smell how clean her skin was. "When was this?"

The fat nurse came up. She had a pill and a paper cup of water.

"This will make you feel a little quieter," she said. "It might even make you feel sleepy."

"That's all right," I said.

Now Mommy was walking next to me as I rode in the wheelchair. Her hand was on my shoulder. She said something to Daddy that I couldn't hear, and he left and walked back the way we had come. The man pushing the chair went out the door and turned down the hallway. All the people walking by and all the people sitting on the benches looked at me and then looked away. The fishbowl lights hung above us in the hallway. We followed the trail of their yellow glows in the floor past the bathroom and way down the hall.

We came to the window the red boy and I had looked out of and I saw sunlight shining bright, so blue and white, on the melting snow. Cars flew far below us, sending out big splashes on the street.

We kept on going, past the men's ward, with all its smoke and noise. I tried to look in and see if Mr. Topping was there, but we moved past too fast.

Finally, we came to a door and the man pushed me inside. It was a little room with a bed with curtains in it. Dr. Benson and the blonde nurse and the doctors in glasses were all there.

When he saw me, Dr. Benson rubbed his hands together.

"Hello!" he said. "Hello!"

He seemed to be very happy.

The man who was pushing me wheeled me up right next to the bed and Dr. Benson and the blonde nurse helped me up on it. When they put me on the bed, I thought that I landed with a thud, but then I realized that the pill was making me sleepy. Time was slowing down. I thought that it was funny. I remembered Mommy saying, wouldn't it be funny if time would disappear, just like that?

"Laugh," I said.

"That's right," said Mommy. Her hand was on my head again. I didn't know how it got there. People seemed to be crowding into the little room. Doctors and nurses were doing things, walking with quick steps. A nurse put white metal stands on either side of the bed. They looked like lamp stands, except they were on wheels and they had empty bottles with long white tubes hanging down.

"Where's the blood?" I said to Mommy.

"Shhh," she said. She leaned down and kissed me. "You know that I love you best of anything in the world, don't you? Tell me that you do."

"I do," I said. I looked up at her. Her thick black hair was so beautiful. I reached up to touch it, and she smiled. I smiled, too. I knew her. I remembered her. I knew her from when we used to sail the world together.

Dr. Benson came up and said something to Mommy, and she got up. He sat down next to me.

"Are you all ready, Clark Kent?" he said.

"Yes," I said.

Dr. Benson nodded his head and got up and left and Mommy came back and sat down. There were a lot of people around, and I looked up at the ceiling. I tried to smell the spring breeze, but I couldn't anymore. I wanted to more than anything.

"Is the window open?" I said to Mommy, but she didn't seem to hear me. She was looking back at the door to the room. Daddy was standing there with a little girl. The little girl was wearing a flat pink hat like a pancake. Her face was all red and she looked out of breath. Her hair was long and straight.

"This was my surprise," Mommy said.

I looked at the little girl. She smiled at me, and waved her hand.

"Rosie," I said.

Mommy looked at me and blinked. "No, no, sweetie, it's Deanna. From school."

The blonde nurse came up to her. "Mrs. O'Conor, we need to start now. You'll have to take her outside."

The little girl looked at Mommy, and then waved at me again. She smiled. Her eyes were bright.

"Sweetie?" Mommy said to me. Her hand was to her mouth, but the blonde nurse was already pulling the curtains around the bed. Mommy and the little girl disappeared. As the doctors and nurses moved around me, I stared hard through the curtains, hoping that I could make them out, but I couldn't. I laid my head back down. I was feeling very sleepy. A nurse came up and rubbed alcohol on my left arm and attached me to the bottle on the stand. There was some time that seemed to go by, and then I saw the dark blood pouring out of me and into the bottle. It rose very slowly. The nurse stood there, watching carefully, with an empty bottle in her hand.

The blonde nurse rubbed my right leg down by my ankle with alcohol, and put a needle into me. It hurt, but the hurt seemed far away by now. The needle was attached to the tube leading to a bottle on the stand. The bottle flowed the new, fresh blood into me.

The flowing had begun. The blood was pouring through me. I looked up at the ceiling. I could hear voices, and it took me a second to realize that it was Mommy and Daddy and the little girl talking outside the curtains. It felt strange to hear them. I closed my eyes. The new blood was cool and clean inside of me. It made my heart beat faster and faster, and jump and flutter, like that pigeon beating its wings.

Also from Akashic Books

Adios Muchachos by Daniel Chavarría
245 pages, paperback
ISBN: 1-888451-16-5
Price: $13.95

"Daniel Chavarría has long been recognized as one of Latin America's finest writers. Now he again proves why with *Adios Muchachos*, a comic mystery peopled by a delightfully mad band of miscreants, all of them led by a woman you will not soon forget: Alicia, the loveliest bicycle whore in all Havana."
—Edgar Award-winning author William Heffernan

The Big Mango by Norman Kelley
270 pages, paperback
ISBN: 1-888451-10-8
Price: $14.95

She's Back! Nina Halligan, Private Investigator.

"Want a scathing social and political satire? Look no further than Kelley's second effort featuring 'bad girl' African-American PI and part-time intellectual Nina Halligan—it's X-rated, but a romp of a read . . . Nina's acid takes on recognizable public figures and institutions both amuse and offend . . . Kelley spares no one, blacks and whites alike, and this provocative novel is sure to attract attention . . . " —*Publisher's Weekly*

Michael by Henry Flesh (1999 Lambda Literary Award Winner)
with illustrations by John H. Greer
120 pages, paperback
ISBN: 1-888451-12-2
Price: $12.95

"Henry's the king. He writes with incessant crispness. Sex is reluctantly juicy, life is reluctant and winning—even when his characters lose. What's it all about, Henry? I think you know."
—Eileen Myles, author of *Cool For You*

Outcast by José Latour
217 pages, trade paperback
ISBN: 1-888451-07-6
Out of print. Available only through direct mail order.
Price: $20.00

"José Latour is a master of Cuban Noir, a combination of '50s unsentimentality and the harsh realities of life in a Socialist paradise. Better, he brings his tough survivor to the States to give us a picture of ourselves through Cuban eyes. Welcome to America, Sr. Latour."
—Martin Cruz Smith, author of *Havana Bay*

Kamikaze Lust by Lauren Sanders
287 pages, trade paperback
ISBN: 1-888451-08-4
Price: $14.95

"Like an official conducting an all-out strip search, first-time novelist Lauren Sanders plucks and probes her characters' minds and bodies to reveal their hidden lusts, and when all is said and done, nary a body cavity is spared." —*Time Out New York*